REDEMPTION OF THE DESERT WOLF

JADE

RED ROCK PACK
BOOK 3

JD WOLFE

Redemption Of The Desert Wolf

Paperback: ISBN: 979-8-9919512-4-1

Ebook: ISBN: 979-8-9919512-5-8

Note from Author: This is a work of fiction. Unless otherwise indicated, all the names, characters, businesses, places, events, and incidents in this book are either the product of the author's imagination or used in a fictitious manner. Any resemblance to actual persons, living or dead, or actual events is purely coincidental.

Edited by: JD Wolfe

Cover Design by JD Wolfe

jdwolfebooks@gmail.com

Another Note From the Author Because She Likes Words. This book contains; violence, abuse, blood, gore, murder, and a mention of the devil. It also describes in detail sexual acts and nudity. As well as every known cuss word with some new made-up ones.

To the wolves who kept going when the path was lonely and the night felt endless—may you find your pack, claim your place, and never doubt your worth.

To Hubs—my Griz—thank you for letting me choose you, holding the line, and loving me through every version of who I am.

Now, go get your shirt off the counter.

CONTENTS

Red Rock Pack

CONFIDENTIAL

Council of the Animal Society

Threat Level
1 2 3 ④ 5

File Number	#45695622-66
Shifter ID Code	#W122581-F

Intended for Official Use Only.

CONFIDENTIAL

Name: Devereaux, Jade

Pack: Red Rock Pack

Pack Position: Enforcer

DOB: M 12 | D 25 | Y 81 **AGE:** 41

Registered Animal: Wolf

US Citizen: Yes **Language:** English

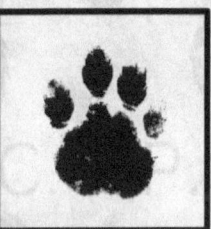

Height	5'9"
Weight	130
Hair Color	Black
Eye Color	Hazel
Build	Athletic

Pack Information

Registered Address:
117 Stanley Dr
Lake Las Vegas, NV

Mate: N/A

Alpha: Randolph, Charlotte

Beta: Sheridan, Harper

Pack #'s: Unknown

Psychological Profile:

- Reserved and vigilant, maintains a controlled demeanor, always assessing her environment for potential threat
- Trained in hand-to-hand combat, extremely dangerous in animal form
- Possesses sharp analytical skills, excelling in tactical planning and real-time problem-solving
- Deep-seated fear of vulnerability and betrayal

Sidney Pack

Council of the Paranormal Society

Threat Level

1 2 3 ④ 5

CONFIDENTIAL

Name: Sheridan, Ryder

Pack: Sidney Pack

Pack Position: Enforcer

DOB: M 06 | D 18 | Y 78 **AGE:** 43

Registered Animal: Wolf

US Citizen: Yes **Language:** English

Height	6'0"
Weight	223
Hair Color	Brown
Eye Color	Hazel
Build	Solid

Pack Information

Registered Address: Unknown

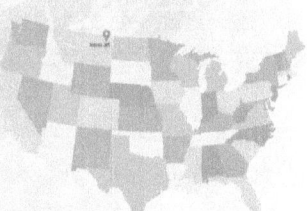

Mate: Unknown

Alpha: Jones, Dezmond

Beta: Warren, Emily

Enforcer:

Psychological Profile:

- Exhibits strong protective instincts toward vulnerable individuals
- Avoidant of personal conflict but extremely capable when provoked
- Uses logic and routine as stabilizers
- Shows minimal ego; prioritizes group safety over personal status

READ AT 3:14 PM

What the fuck, Jade?

??

You've barely texted. You ghost me all week, then drop one-word answers like you're possessed.

You ARE possessed, aren't you?

Just tired.

Nope. Try again. You don't do tired. You do caffeine, bitch about dogs in clothes, and calling people out when their eyeliner sucks. But not tired.

Clothes DON'T belong on dogs!!!

Rough day, Gotta go.

You're lying.

Luna looks down...
Delivered. Read 3:14 PM.
"She's lying," she mutters, just to hear it out loud.

Sitting criss-crossed in her ridiculous overstuffed pink computer chair, Luna looks like she's being swallowed by a cotton-candy throne. The armrests practically eat her tiny frame alive, but she barely notices.

Dropping her phone into her lap, she glares at the neon rope light tacked perfectly—*too* perfectly—down the corner of the wall, its rainbow glow bleeding into everything. Like it's mocking her.

It doesn't have answers. Staring anyway, forcing her vision back into focus until each tiny bulb claims its own place again.

Her fingers twitch before her brain even decides. She grabs the phone again and flips to her messages with Harper.

Her last text still sits there.

I miss you bitch.

Delivered. But not read. No response. That was three days ago.

Luna knows Harper misses her too. She's just wrapped up in trying to piece together a broken, feral pack—one that Lucas Williams, her mate, took by Right of Kill.

He killed the Cascade Pack's alpha. And now? According to Brock—the little piss-ant that didn't run—they expect Lucas to lead them into something better.

Luna's sure Harper's over there making the best of it— probably teaching savages how to cook some ridiculous gourmet meal with nothing but spaghetti noodles, green beans and a stick of butter. *Typical.*

It's been annoyingly quiet without them in the ten-room mansion. The mansion now feels like it's twice as big. Empty. The bustling voices of the Humboldt Pack, the Red Rock allies, and even little Henry with Mama Ivy, help, but the space has an echo of absence that won't fade.

Luna feels it. The pull to the pack is thinning, fibers loosening one by one. Harper's strand has been slipping since that morning hug, since the door closed behind her.

This feeling is all to familiar. She leans back in her chair, her fingers twitch, hovering over the screen of her phone. All she wants right now is to talk to Jade.

Fucking bitch won't talk to me.

Jade doesn't know it but, she's the wall Luna leans against when the rest of the world starts spinning.

Growing up, it was just her and her twin brother Jon. Their bond, forged in pain and survival, was the only thing that ever came close to filling the emptiness inside her. But even that had its cracks, the raw edges that always bled. The hell they'd been through together had left scars that, no matter how much time passed, would never fade.

She keeps staring at her phone, but nothing sharpens. Not the screen. Not the ache. It feels like she's the only one still bleeding from it—sisters lost, bonds torn apart, grief buried instead of named. No one talks about it. Maybe they already learned how to move on. Or maybe she's the only one who broke beyond repair.

Luna closes her eyes for a second, breathing in the silence that fills the room. *It's so fucking loud!*

She must've brushed the screen, because suddenly her phone lights up again—and there they are.

Charlotte, Harper, and Jade. Frozen mid-laugh in the

wallpaper photo like they're still there. Like nothing's changed.

Before she can second-guess it, her thumb taps Harper's name again...

Bitch! Answer me!

> Hey! Sorry I didn't write back the other day. It's just so busy here.

Yeah whatever. I have bigger concerns. Something is off with Jade. Have you talked to her?

> No. Why do you think something is off? She said she had a bad client. Maybe it's just that?

Nope. I looked. I can't find anything in Ghost Orchid's scheduler about Jade on an assignment.

> Maybe you're just being paranoid?

Fuck you Harp. I'm worried.

> Fine. I'll text her and see if I can get anything from her. You said her scheduler doesn't have any information on who this client is?

> And does Charlotte know you hacked into Jade's company?

Yes. She told me not to do it again but the bond told me she's worried too.

> I'll let you know if I get anything back from her.

...

The three little dots are there for only a moment then disappear.

Staring at the cheap green walls of the hotel she extended for a few more nights, Jade feels nothing.

No fire. No fight.

Just that gnawing, familiar emptiness.

Drained of all give-a-shits, as Luna would say.

She flexes her right hand in her lap, fingers curling slow. The skin across her knuckles is raw and cracked, a deep purple bloom spreading beneath the surface like rot.

She tells herself it's just bruising. *Just surface-level damage.*

But it's been three days since the last fight, and the ache still pulses beneath her skin.

Her shifter healing should've handled it by now. But her wolf is quiet.

Too quiet.

Sometimes Jade wonders if she's even still there—until the moment she steps into the ring.

Then she comes alive. It's like the wolf is only awake when blood is in the air.

No threat? No adrenaline? She sleeps. *Fucking bitch.*

She should've stopped. Should've walked away after the

second match. But the rush was too sweet. The crowd too loud. The pain too quiet.

Jade presses her thumb into the worst of it until her hand trembles. Not enough to break it. Just enough to feel something.

She exhales slowly, jaw clenched. The guilt creeps in, low and unwanted.

She should go home. Should walk through that front door, tell Luna the truth, face whatever fallout is waiting.

But she doesn't move. Because going home means *stopping*. And she's not ready for that.

Her phone buzzes against the nightstand. Once. Twice. She doesn't look at it right away. The third chime pulls her out of the spiral.

Glancing over... Harper.

> Why are you driving Luna crazy?

> You know she's going to hack into your shit and send a barbershop quartet to sing some stupid song just to get your attention.

Jade snorts. Somehow, Luna's chaos is still the thing that steadies her.

Of course Harper would check in like that—disguised concern, wrapped in sarcasm. She stares at the screen.

Her thumb hovers. A reply? A lie?

> I'm fine. Working.

> Miss you, too.

Nothing feels right. So she locks the phone and tosses it back onto the bed as she stands. The room feels colder the second she moves.

Maybe a shower will thaw my soul.

LONE WOLF STATUS

The black '68 Camaro hums quietly beneath him, engine idling like it's got a temper just waiting to be unleashed.

Resting one arm on the wheel, the other dragging through his thick, dark hair, pushing it back from his face like the weight of the past week is woven through the strands.

He hasn't slept. Not really.

The hotel across the street is lit up in tired green neon. Cheap. Discreet. The kind of place Jade would pick when she doesn't want to be found.

But he found her. *He always does.*

The phone buzzes in the console beside him. He doesn't need to look. He already knows the name.

Dez—from the Sidney Pack.

He lets it ring once. Twice. Then swipes to answer, putting it on speaker without a word.

"Still ignoring protocol, huh?" Dez's voice is dry. Familiar.

"Didn't realize I had to follow rules I no longer answer to," He replies, voice low.

"Right. The lone wolf thing. Forgot you love the drama."

Ryder doesn't answer. Doesn't need to explain why he left the pack—why he walked away from all of it four weeks ago. The pack bond has been fading ever since. A constant hum, now just a whisper at the back of his mind. Duller by the day.

That ache? He ignores it. Like everything else.

Charlotte doesn't know. Harper sure as hell doesn't. And Jade...

Jade would kill him if she found out.

But the day she had him pinned to the floor—knees on either side of his hips, breath hot with fury, knife pressed against his dick like she was seriously considering taking it off—he knew. Not because she was angry. Because of her eyes. There was no heat in those amber eyes. No thrill. Just something hollow.

She'd looked at him like she wanted to carve the world out of herself and leave nothing behind. And that's when he knew. She was going to spiral. *Again.*

Knowing her, feeling her, his wolf told him it was time to follow her off the edge. So he did. She just doesn't know it. Call it loyalty. Call it obsession. He doesn't care.

The phone call ends. Dez says something about "checking in" and "not dragging the rest of them into it," but Ryder's already tuned him out.

His eyes are locked on the second-floor window of that hotel. Curtains drawn. Light still on. Movement—maybe.

He leans back in the seat and mutters to himself, "What the fuck are you doing, Jade..."

ROUTINE. CONTROL.
CAUSE AND EFFECT.

Her fingers slide through her goddess braids, the thick ropes heavy with water, clinging to her back like armor. Her scalp's tender near the roots—new growth soft and stubborn, fuzzing out around the parts like it's trying to rebel.

She exhales hard through her nose. *I need to get home. Tasha's gonna kill me for letting these go this long.*

She can almost hear her stylist's voice now—sharp, familiar, wrapped in love and judgment all at once. *Girl, you better not be out there letting your hair tell on you.*

Something tugs at the corner of her mouth before she can stop it. A smile. Small. *Uninvited.* Her emotions betray her, just for a second.

Then it's gone.

She used to love the weight of the braids. The ritual of them. The feel of fingers moving with purpose through her hair, tugging her thoughts into place.

Now? They just remind her of how long she's been avoiding everything that matters.

She presses her palms against the cool tile and forces

herself to breathe. *Where the hell are you wolf?* The silence isn't just quiet—it's hollow.

Like she's screaming into a void that should answer back. Like something inside her shut a door and it won't open until there is the promise of blood. Jade used to feel the hum of her instincts. The low growl under her skin when something was off. Now?

The water beats down harder, scalding her shoulders, and she doesn't move. Her mind flashes—unexpected—to the mansion.

To *him*. Ryder.

She knew the second she saw that Camaro parked in the mansion's driveway—she should've turned her bike around and left. Her gut told her it was him. She just didn't recognize the car.

She still can't believe it. He risked himself. *For a stranger. For a kid.* That's not him. Not the Ryder she knows. Not the asshole who always acted like the world was one big inconvenience. Why would he do that? What was he really up to?

Her jaw tightens. *Ryder's acting like some kind of protector? Please.*

Dragging the soap across her umber skin, slow and methodical, she maps the damage. Every pass over a bruise draws a sharp breath. The worst ones—along her ribs, her lower back—send tiny flashes of heat through her limbs.

She tells herself it's just pain. Just the aftermath. But some twisted part of her catalogs the ache like it matters. Like it's proof of something. The split on her shoulder stings under the spray, and her hand hovers there for a second too long. She presses into it anyway. She can't tell if she's cleaning the wounds or *feeding* them. There's comfort in it— *Routine. Control. Cause and effect.*

She says it like a prayer. Like if she repeats it enough, her bones will remember what it feels like to hold everything together.

But still... she's not healing. *They should be gone by now.*

She's had worse. Much worse. And by now, the bruises should've faded, the cuts should've knitted back together.

What the hell is wrong with me? She doesn't say it out loud. Doesn't need to.

Her wolf sits quiet. Just like *always* lately—silent, distant, buried so deep inside her chest she's not even sure she's still there. And maybe that's the real reason nothing's healing.

I'm breaking... and she doesn't want to stick around to watch it happen. She clenches her jaw, swipes at a bead of water like it offended her, and drags the soap back over her shoulder.

Routine. Control. Cause and effect. She just has to keep moving. Keep fighting. Because if she stops... she might have to admit she's not okay.

Fighting gives her the one thing nothing else can, certainty. Its the only thing that gets her wolf to be with her. Even though she can't shift, her wolf fights with her. She becomes one with her again. A hit always delivers. The pain is predictable. The bruises make sense. Unlike everything else.

Like him.

He's not a savior. He never was. He's selfish. Unapologetic. Arrogant. And worse—he's unpredictable. And she doesn't trust unpredictable. Not from anyone. Especially not him.

And Ivy... sweet, quiet Ivy. Too quiet. Too perfect. No pack history. No family name. And fuck, they don't even know what her animal is.

Just *showed up,* scared and bruised with a baby in her

arms and a shadow behind her. It should make her want to protect Ivy more.

Instead, it makes something cold settle in her gut.

She rinses off. Turning off the water, she stands there letting the cool air hit her smooth glistening skin.

The moment her wolf should stir—should *respond* to all this unease—nothing. Just silence. And suddenly, the bruises don't feel like the worst part of her anymore.

ASSHOLES

The neon sign buzzes overhead like it's holding in a scream. EAT HERE flickers, missing the "E" half the time, casting a soft strobe against the rain-slicked pavement.

Jade pulls into the lot, headlights sweeping across the front windows and blinding the fucks inside.

She kills the engine but doesn't move. Just sits there, a beat too long. She tells herself it's because of the rain.

It's not.

Move Devereaux.

Inside the diner smells like burnt coffee and reheated bacon—a scent that somehow always lands just shy of disgusting.

The hostess gives her a half-smile, jerking her chin toward the back booth. Third from the window. Same one every time. She likes that. Predictable. Honest.

Jade shrugs out of her jacket and slides onto the cracked vinyl. Her ribs protest the movement, but she bites it back.

The server doesn't come by. Doesn't need to. Within two

minutes, her coffee hits the table, black and steaming. No sugar. No cream. Nothing that softens it.

Good. Too much softness lately.

Her phone buzzes once against the cheap laminate table, face-down. She doesn't look right away.

Outside, a truck rumbles past, kicking up puddles. The glow from the flickering streetlamp casts a jittery halo on the window, lighting up the raindrops still clinging to her braids.

Through the streaked glass, she can just make out the Strat rising in the distance—blurred by weather, but unmistakable. Vegas, trying to be beautiful in spite of itself. Some days, it feels like the only thing that hasn't left her.

Another buzz.

She flips the phone over lazily.

> Picked up a gig. Some playboy from Dubai.
>
> Wants guards while he tramps around the Strip like he owns it. Want the file?

She stares at the message like it belongs to someone else. Like the version of herself who would've jumped on that job is *dead and buried.* Her thumb hovers. Then taps.

> Yeah. Forward it. I'll pretend to care.

A pause. Then another message.

> Also… the team thinks you're in Santa Fe.
>
> You're not. Which means I'm lying for you. Again.

Jade sips her coffee, lets the bitter coat her tongue.

I didn't ask you to lie, Sam

And just a quick reminder, I'm the boss.

🙂 Yeah. Copy that. Boss.

She locks the screen and tosses the phone face-down again, watching the rain collect in the corners of the window.

Fuck.

Ghost Orchid Protection. The company Jade built from scratch—broke bones, burned bridges, and bled for. High-end, high-risk clients with too much money and too many enemies. Playboy types that their sole purpose in life is to be seen.

Half of them didn't even *need* security. But this was Vegas. And in Vegas? Image is everything. So they hired "protection" to make themselves look important. Security guards with earpieces and black shirts made great accessories.

Ghost Orchid makes them look good. Tight protocols. Clean intel.

Her team is sharp—both female and male, shifter and full blooded humans, hired from across the globe, trained to neutralize threats and babysit egos at the same time. It was her everything. Her legacy. Her empire.

And now?

I ghosted my own damn company. Thank the fuck for Sam.

That woman could run ops in her sleep and still find time to bitch about Jade skipping protocol. *Protocol's that I wrote.*

The server drops her burger off with a nod. No words. Just staring at it.

You should eat. Routine. Control. Cause and effect.

Finally picking up the burger with bruised fingers, the first bite tastes like cardboard and something close to normal.

And for one breath—just one—she lets herself pretend that everything isn't falling apart.

A voice already too loud for the space pulls Jade from her pity-party.

"I said bacon, sweetheart. Not whatever *that* is."

Jade doesn't look up right away. Just listens. Knife still in hand, pushing half a pickle around her plate.

The voice again—condescending, aggressive.

"Hey. You deaf, or just slow?"

The server—a girl barely in her twenties, hair pulled back in a frizzy ponytail, circles under her eyes like she hasn't slept since Tuesday—murmurs, "Listen, Mister. I'll get you another order, but please stop yelling. I can't get fired."

"Jesus. You *should* get fired," the man snaps, loud enough for half the diner to hear. "Can't even get a simple order right."

His buddies snicker around the booth like it's the funniest thing they've heard all day.

The server turns to leave, holding it together with one thread.

He slaps her ass. "Don't worry, sweetheart," he says, loud and smug, "if you *do* get fired, I know a few ways you can still make money. No skills required."

The laughter that follows turns Jade's stomach.

She doesn't stand right away. Not yet. First, she sets her coffee down. Neat. Calm. Wipes her mouth, like she's thinking it over.

You really picked the wrong fucking night, dude.

Then she slides out of the booth and walks toward him

like she's got nowhere else to be. By the time she's standing beside his table, the guy's still mid-smirk.

"Hey," she says, her voice calm. Too calm. "Did your mother drop you on your head or just forget to love you entirely?"

He looks up, confused. Then amused. "Relax, lady. It was just a joke."

"No. That wasn't a joke. That was you letting everyone in here know you're a walking pile of shit."

His mouth opens to argue— Jade slaps him.

Whomp.

The sound cracks through the diner like a dropped plate. All eyes turn.

"Now I've slapped *you* on the ass," she says, voice like steel."What's your next move?"

He lurches halfway to his feet, red-faced and puffed up.

"I'm calling the cops. That's assault, lady!"

Jade steps in close—so close he stumbles back.

"Oh, you *fucking* idiot. You really think grabbing her ass doesn't count?" She tilts her head, a slow smile curling like smoke. "Or do you just assume the rules don't apply to you? Let me guess—mommy told you you were special, right?"

He opens his mouth—she cuts him off.

"Call the cops. Please. I'd *love* to explain how I slapped you after you sexually assaulted someone half your size." Jade pauses, slow and deliberate, letting her gaze cut across the whole table—one by one. "Hell, maybe I'll even frame the police report and hang it over your hospital bed."

His buddies are dead silent now. One of them slides his phone off the table like he's not part of this anymore.

Jade's gaze doesn't waver.

"Touch another woman like that, and I won't stop at a

slap next time." She leans in just enough to make sure he feels the heat behind her words. "I *dare* you to test me."

The entire diner goes quiet. The kind of quiet that hums in your teeth.

"Now, say sorry."

He stammers, sputters. Tries to act tough—but no one's buying it now.

"S-Sorry," he mutters, eyes fixed on the floor, not even looking at the server—the blonde girl still standing there, ever-so-slightly shaking, like her body hasn't caught up to the fact that it's over.

Jade steps back, breathing steady.

"Louder."

"I'm sorry!"

Nodding once, Jade steps away from the pig in a black t-shirt.

Her *no-talky* server follows Jade back to her booth. "Dinners on me tonight sweetheart."

"Thanks. Can I get a to-go cup." Pointing at the probably now cold coffee.

"You got it."

Lifting the plate holding a half-eaten burger and a few fries, Jade slides the hundred-dollar bill she had planned to pay for dinner with under it.

The waitress steps up with a to-go cup in one hand, lid in the other. Her red hair is pulled into a loose twist, fading at the roots but still defiant.

Faint crow's feet frame her sharp green eyes—wrinkles not from age, but from years of watching this city chew people up and spit them out.

Fake nails glint in the diner light—long, red, a little chipped at the tips. Probably the only indulgence she's still clinging to.

"Here you go," she says, handing Jade the cup and lid. Her voice raspy, like it's filtered through decades of cigarette smoke and bad tips.

"I know we don't exchange a lot of words, but I gotta tell you—that was some beautiful shit right there. Thank you for takin' care of our Jessica. Men like that?" She snorts. "Should be shot."

Jade takes the cup without a word, but there's something in the way she nods—sharp, respectful.

From one dangerous woman to another.

Turning to leave, she walks past the booth she nearly flipped. The man is still trying to pretend he's invisible.

Just for fun, she flips her butterfly knife with shifter speed—barely a flick of her wrist—and makes sure he sees it tucked against her thigh as she moves. Glancing over her shoulder, she catches the slight shiver that runs through him.

Good.

The bell above the door gives a soft, almost apologetic chime as she pushes into the night.

Outside, the rain has stopped—but not before turning the Vegas dust into a streaky, mud-colored mess. Her pickup looks like someone dumped a double espresso over it and called it art.

Desert rain. All bark, no cleanup.

Yanking the door open, hinges groaning in protest, Jade climbs in. The seat's still damp from where her hoodie soaked through. She doesn't care. The engine of her old beater truck rumbles to life with a cough, headlights slicing through the wet dark like they're tired of trying.

She left the black Raptor at home. Too flashy.

The places she goes now? That kind of truck gets windows smashed, tires stripped.

Ol' Red, though? She can get beat to hell and Jade wouldn't lose a wink. The Ford F-150 doesn't scream money or status—it screams *keep walking, I've got nothing worth stealing.* And that's exactly the vibe Jade wants to carry tonight.

The city smells like ozone and asphalt—Vegas trying to pretend it's something it's not. She pulls out of the lot, heading toward the edge of town where the real fights are held. No lights. No rules. No reason to go but one:

Routine. Control. Cause and effect.

And maybe... maybe tonight she'll finally take enough hits to feel something.

Jade turns into the lot, tires crunching over loose gravel and broken glass.

She pulls into a spot near the edge, where the shadows stay thick.

A torn black tarp snaps against the chain-link fence, the kind meant to keep tourists out—or maybe just keep them from seeing the entrance to hell.

Whatever.

She kills the engine and scans the lot, eyes cutting through the dark with that sharp shifter edge.

No cops. Not her kind of cops—the human ones.

Stepping around the corner of the fence, Jade stays low, boots hitting packed dirt and cracked concrete. The alley stinks of wet cardboard, piss, and old oil. Classic Vegas flavor.

Tucked behind a stack of broken pallets and a half-dead cactus, there it is... a metal door, painted black, peeling at the edges, forgotten by the city.

Just as she opens the door, Jade is introduced to a wall of muscle. Big. Broad. And too damn pretty to be working a door in a place like this. His T-shirt stretches across a chest that should be illegal. Thick arms, tan skin, jaw sharp enough to cut through excuses.

Well, hello, trouble.

"What are you doing here?" His voice is low, even. Professional. But there's something in the way he looks at her—just a flicker—that says *he knows exactly what she's here for.*

Jade doesn't blink. "Looking for the restroom. Figured I'd crawl through the trash and take my chances."

His brow cocks up. Just one. The left one just how it has every time she has these exchanges with him. And damn if she isn't half-convinced she pokes at him just to earn that lift —like it's her own private win in a game she shouldn't be playing.

She sighs and leans in slightly, just enough to make sure he hears it.

"Violet. Center bloom. No thorns."

A beat. Then a small nod. "You're late," he says, stepping aside.

"I'm never late," she mutters, brushing past him, shoulder to chest—and not by accident.

The door creaks open, heavy and loud. And just like that, it hits her. Blood. Sweat. Desperation. And beneath it all, the sharp tang of *human.* Not just the scent, but the *energy*—fear, hunger, adrenaline.

For an underground event, the lights are *offensively* bright. Overhead fluorescents buzz like they're auditioning for a horror film.

Fuck! Why does it feel like I just walked into a butcher shop sponsored by Home Depot?

The door slams shut behind her with a metallic clang. Voices echo off the concrete—too loud, too close. The crowd hasn't gathered yet, but the energy is already rising. Jade pushes through a narrow corridor, past crates, busted folding chairs, and a guy passed out next to a tipped-over cooler. The stink of beer, old sweat, and blood only thickens the deeper she goes.

At the far end, a crooked sign—spray-painted on a cracked piece of plywood—reads: "**Locker Room**"

That's generous.

Stepping inside, she finds the familiar four walls. No door. A warped mirror and two busted benches. No privacy. No noise dampening. No comfort. Just the way she likes it.

She drops her bag beside the bench and pulls out her wraps, fingers already moving through the familiar ritual.

Routine. Control. Cause and effect.

She's halfway through wrapping the first hand when a shadow falls across the doorway.

"Jade. We gotta talk."

She doesn't need to look. The nasal, smug tone gives it away.

Great. Ratface is here.

The bookie—real name's Tony, but nobody calls him that—steps into the room like he owns it.

Thin, wiry, always sweating. Expensive shoes, cheap cologne, and a gold chain that looks faker than his smile.

"Listen," he says, eyes darting around even though they're alone, "tonight, you're going down in the second fight, third round. Clean. Dramatic. But not too quick. I want sweat, not blood."

Jade knots the last strip of tape, flexing her fingers until the joints pop. "You want me to throw the fight?"

"I want you to make us both a shit-ton of money." Sweat drips from his potmarked face. "Odds are stacked on you. Crowd's cocky. Let 'em get sloppy. We shark the pot, everyone walks away happy."

Except me.

She stands, slowly, towering over him just enough to make his confidence crack.

"What if I don't like playing puppet for greasy little men who couldn't survive five minutes in the ring?"

He chuckles—nervous. But he doesn't back down. "Then maybe your name comes off the card for next month. And the month after that." He gives a shrug, but she can smell the nervousness waft off him. "Plenty of girls who'll fight for half your cut and follow directions."

Jade steps in close, wraps dangling from her fists like warnings. "And none of them will bring the crowd to their feet like I do."

His smirk twitches. "Third round. Make it look good."

He turns and walks out fast, like he's proud of himself for not getting hit.

She watches him go, flexing her hands.

Third round, huh?

She tightens and ties off the wraps, jaw locked.

We'll see.

Outside the locker room, the underground hums to life. Fighters like her, chasing an escape. Locals, desperate for a bloodlust fix. And clueless tourists, about to pay for front-row seats to something they don't understand.

Jade's senses spike. The damp stench of old concrete and dried blood turns her stomach, but it's too late—her wolf is awake. A low growl thrums under her skin, hungry for what's coming. The fight. The blows she'll take. Even the restraint it'll take not to kill the fragile humans trying to prove themselves. It's all a rush.

"Jade. Back so soon? You must be a glutton for punishment."

She doesn't bother looking back. She knows that voice—

smooth as whiskey, sharp as a blade. The man who's become her most persistent mistake. He always shows up when she's bleeding or broken, like a bad habit that tastes good going down but burns like hell later.

"Mason."

He leans against the splintered doorjamb, paint barely clinging to the wood, like he owns the place—arms crossed, smirk loaded, eyes scanning her like he's counting bruises.

"I heard you were here last night too. You know this shit's gonna catch up to you, right?"

She snorts, tugging at the wraps that are already tight enough, but she needs something to do with her hands.

"Don't start caring for me, Mason. It might get you a broken heart."

He chuckles, low and rough, moving his hand and placing it over his heart. "I've already got the bruises."

She turns then, gaze sharp enough to cut—and there he is. Tall, broad, all hard muscle wrapped in a worn T-shirt that clings to his biceps like it's been glued there. His face is carved from stone, every angle sharp, every line earned keeping the streets of Las Vegas safe. *Oh, the irony.* Bald head catching the low light, jaw dark with a five o'clock shadow he wears like armor. All human. No beast inside—just the kind that bleeds and breaks the old-fashioned way.

"And just because we fuck doesn't mean you get to play boyfriend. You want to watch me bleed? Fine. But don't pretend you're here for anything more than the show."

"You got it." Mason turns to leave but stops. "So, how about that fuck after the show then?"

"Nah." Jade doesn't budge. Feet planted, body ready—not for Mason, but for whatever the night throws next. "I've already got a date with the guy at the door."

"Suit yourself. But be careful. His rap sheets is a mile long. You wouldn't want to hurt your little business."

"Jealousy's ugly, Mason. And it reeks of feelings. Don't start messing with the terms of our twisted little arrangement."

The echo of boots on concrete cuts through the tension like a blade. One by one, the other fighters drift in—some silent, some loud, all carrying the same hungry look Jade knows too well.

A stringy kid with taped knuckles sizes her up, eyes lingering too long. Her wolf twitches, a low growl rumbling beneath her ribs. He looks away. *Smart.*

Two women pass, one with a busted lip already, laughing like this is just a Friday night poker game. But Jade catches the flash in the taller one's eyes—recognition, maybe respect. Maybe not.

The air thickens—sweat, metal, blood. It crawls into her nose, her lungs. Her wolf stirs again, pacing just under her skin. Eager.

She breathes deep, slow. Not yet.

A sharp voice cracks through the room—someone barking names from a clipboard. One of the new handlers. Green. Shaky. Jade's name gets called and half the room shifts. Some glance. Others avoid looking altogether.

She doesn't move. *Fucking humans.*

She grabs the straps of her gym bag and slings it over her shoulder, never breaking her stare. Slow. Steady. She heads for the makeshift bleachers circling the cage.

Rusted. Busted. *Familiar.*

The chain-link walls bow inward in places, warped from too many bodies hitting too hard. Blood stains on the mat.

Her wolf perks up. This is the part she likes—the stillness before the storm. *Finally, you bitch.*

She slouches on the edge of the bleacher, elbows on knees, phone in hand but not looking at it. Just a prop. Her eyes stay locked on the cage.

The first fight's a mess. Two humans—all rage, no skill. One's gassed out in less than a minute, breathing heavy like a wounded animal.

Another match starts—better this time. Cleaner strikes. The woman in yellow wraps lands her hits sharp and fast. She's quick. Too quick.

Jade tilts her head, watching her move. Something's off. The way she pivots, the speed of her recovery. It's too fluid. Too balanced.

Not human. Not fully.

Her wolf stirs, ears up. Not quite growling, but alert. That itch behind her ribs. Instinct saying you know what she is.

But the scent... muted. Not full shift. And the strength? It flares and fades like a flickering flame.

She's holding back, Jade thinks. *Or something's holding her back.*

Jade watches from the bleachers as the bitch finishes the match with disgusting ease—a roundhouse to the ribs, followed by a clean uppercut that drops her opponent like a sack of bones.

No celebration. No cocky flair. Just a curt nod to the ref and a walk-off like she's done this a thousand times.

She has strength, and it seems something else. *Note to self.*

Her wolf growls low. Suspicious.

"I'll see you in a few weeks," Jade whispers. Semi-finals. The idea curls like smoke in her gut. *We'll see what you're really hiding.*

Her name cuts through the noise. Jade stands and drops

to the floor. The crowd shifts, sound blurring as she moves through it like a blade—clean, sharp, cutting straight to the cage.

Her bag hits the ground with a dull *clang*, smacking the bent metal pole where the cage floats just off the concrete. She paces behind the cage wall, rolling her neck, fists loose. This third-round bullshit still clings to her mind like wet smoke. Throw the match—keep the peace. Stay welcome. Keep fighting.

Or win. Because she *can*. Because no one here—human or otherwise—stands a real chance once she lets the wolf off its leash.

She smirks, stepping into the ring. *Let's see what bitch they throw at me tonight.*

A fresh ripple of energy rolls through the crowd as the next fighter is announced.

She steps into the cage like she owns it—tall, lean, wrapped tight in shiny black tape and ego. Blonde ponytail bouncing, chin lifted just enough to scream *look at me.*

Oh great, Jade thinks, *a showboat.*

The woman throws a few warm-up punches in the air. Fancy footwork. Flashy spins. The kind of shit that impresses tourists and YouTube viewers.

Jade doesn't move. Doesn't blink.

Her wolf, however, perks up—ears twitching at something off. Not threat. Not scent. Just... *off.*

The woman grins across the cage, like this is some kind of game.

"You ready, sweetheart?" she calls, voice cocky, nasal.

Jade's eyes narrow.

She doesn't answer. Just steps into the center of the ring and shrugs one shoulder.

The ref gives a half-hearted speech about clean hits and no claws—irony dripping off every word. The bell rings.

Time to play.

SECRETS

Jade doesn't bother looking back as the announcer calls it—TKO, another opponent down. The hairs on her neck snap to attention, and her wolf claws at her insides. Not like the usual post-fight buzz. This is different.

Her eyes flick up, against every instinct screaming *don't*.

For a split second, the crowd thins, and she catches him in the shadows—broad shoulders, that unmistakable posture, the quiet certainty that the world should bend around him. He doesn't move. Doesn't have to. Then the bodies close again, erasing him like a trick of the light.

Jade blinks once. Twice. A third time, hard enough to sting. *No. No fucking way.*

Her heart rockets, the traitor drum pounding against her ribs. Her wolf claws at her insides, tail-wagging like this is the best day of her life.

She scans the room again. Nothing but sweat-slick bodies, neon shadows, and the stink of blood and stale beer. No him.

Did I really just see...? The thought shreds itself before it's whole.

Another blink, slower this time. Just the crowd—rowdy, shifting, faceless. Whoever she thought she saw is gone.

Ghosts. That's all it is. Ghosts.

Her pulse is sprinting, her wolf is acting like this is a reunion party, and Jade wants to scream. *We hate that bastard. Wolf, what the fuck are you doing?*

She drops her gaze, grabs her bag, and bolts before she starts hallucinating Luna next.

Plopping onto the splintered bench, Jade yanks at the tape, each strip peeling off in stubborn jerks. She shakes her hands like maybe she can fling off the night itself—

Then a voice slices in, sharp enough to stop the motion cold."New girl," a voice says, low, amused. A guy in a gray hoodie leans against a pillar. Stringy hair pokes out under the hood, eyes too bright, a smudge of chocolate at the corner of his mouth. He's built wiry, twitchy. Raccoon energy in human bones.

"Not new," she says.

He grins like he's found a shiny coin. "Well, I haven't seen you in *this* hole. Special shipments. Lots of... tourists." He says the last word like it tastes bad.

"Thanks for the weather report," she says. "Who are you?"

"Hm." He pulls a little brown nugget from his pocket, chews with his mouth open, words slipping out between sticky bites."Sometimes I'm nobody. Sometimes I'm a rumor. Tonight I'm hungry." He offers the bag. "Chocolate?"

She doesn't take one. "Do rumors have names?"

"Sometimes," he says around a mouthful. "Call me Jim."

"Okay, Jim. Why are you talking to me?"

His gaze flicks past her, over the crowd. The chain-link

shivers as someone tests the tension. "Watch the corners. Watch the men in nice boots. They don't look at the fights— they look at the exits. Means they're not here for the show."

Her ears perk. "And what are they here for... Jim?"

He licks chocolate from his fingers. "Moving night. I only steal snacks, not people. But some folks... they move what doesn't want to be moved." His eyes land on her wristband, then on her ribs, reading the paint of pain there. "Keep your head down, girl."

Before she can press for more, the mic screams. "Main card in ten! On deck, Ortega versus 'Sweet Mercy.'" The crowd laughs. They want blood as proof they're not small.

Jade digs into her bag, yanking out another roll of tape. Fingers stiff, ribs barking, she starts again—strip by strip, winding her knuckles, her palms, pulling tight enough to sting. Fresh armor over split skin.

"I guess I'll take my chances with the fancy shoes."

Jade pushes toward the ring, weaving through the bodies, skirting a knot of men in matching black jackets. Their boots shine—too clean for this floor, not a scuff among them. One has a braided red cord coiled around his wrist, a loose end dangling, brushing against his fingers like it's waiting to be put to use. Not fashion. A signal. Or worse.

She keeps moving. But she clocks it.

A server squeezes by with a tray of beers that looks heavier than she is. Some slob in a tank top smacks her ass hard enough to slosh foam. The tray wobbles. The girl flinches but keeps going.

Jade stops. "Fuck. Not again?" Her wolf doesn't move, but the quiet sharpens.

"Keep walking," Tank Top says without looking at Jade, already lifting his next drink. "We're celebrating."

"Yeah?" Jade slowly turns to face the pig. "Celebrate with your hands to yourself."

Returning the gesture, now facing her, his smile oozes. "What are you gonna do, sweetheart? Fight me?"

"I don't want to break the rules of the ring," she says, tilting her head. "But if you touch her again, I'll break every finger you've ever used to touch anyone in here."

She holds out her pinky. "Pinky promise."

He snorts, a wet sound. His fingers flex like he might test it. He doesn't. The server meets Jade's eyes, gratitude quick and fragile. Jade nods once and steps away. Her fingertips buzz with restraint. Good. *Control.*

"Ortega!" The ledger woman points with her pen. "You're up after this. Opponent listed as Clarissa aka Sweet Mercy."

"Oh, Sweet Mercy." Jim echoes, suddenly at her side again.

This guy moves like dropped glitter—everywhere at once.

"She's strong, but stupid. Thinks power means wind-milling until something lands. Right shoulder's taped. She favors the left like it owes her money. You'll see."

"Oooookay, thanks. Are you some type of sports commentator or something?"

Jim blinks. "Nah. Let's just say, you scare the right people."

Then he's gone—swallowed by the crowd.

The fight before hers ends ugly. The fighter named Plain Jane totally lives up to her name. Blood freckles the chalk. The crowd roars.

Jade climbs into the ring as Plain Jane is dragged out, toes leaving red streaks. The chain-link scrapes rust onto her knuckles when she test-taps it.

Sweet Mercy steps through the opening opposite her, and the room seems to shrink to fit her shoulders. She's taller by a head and a half. Tattoos creep up her neck like poison vines, curling toward a black brand scar at her collarbone—a horseshoe snapped in half, words circling it in jagged ink, Luck Is Bullshit.

Her stomach knots. She knows that ink—seen it in photos slid across her desk. Clients with money, power, and enemies too sharp for the police.

"Ready?" the referee asks. He's a scarecrow in a hoodie.

The bell clangs. It reverbs through her sternum like a tuning fork.

The amazon comes in heavy, just like Jim said—no footwork, head first, arms wide. Telegraphed.

Jade pivots. The bitch eats chalk and spits curses. The crowd eats it up, loving the big woman swinging at air. Mercy—my ass—resets, barrel-chested, pissed—and drives a right. Jade ducks, air whipping her locs. On the rise, Jade buries a left into her ribs. Solid. A grunt breaks loose.

"Faster," she whispers to herself. Measured. Control.

The fighter charges again, but Jade back steps, chainlink biting her shoulders. She springs off it, riding the recoil into a jab-cross that snaps her head back. Eyes flash wide. Good. Surprise means openings.

She drops low, shoulder slamming Jade's hip, and the floor cracks into Jade's spine. Air blasts out of her lungs.

In a blink, she's on top, weight crashing down like collapsed scaffolding.

Her wolf watches.

She frames her neck with her forearms, shoves a knee between their bodies, and turns with her whole torso. Mercy rolls, her elbow snagging on the fence. Jade finds her taped right shoulder and drills two, three short punches into the joint. Her roar is a real animal thing. Jade can see her gritting through the pain when attempting to bring her arm back and tries to pin her again.

She gives her what she wants—her ribs open—for a heartbeat. She bites at it, greedy. Jade tucks, grabbing her wrist with both hands, and uses her own weight to send her face-first into the chalk, head bouncing. The crowd goes feral.

Sweet Mercy—or whatever the fuck her name is—staggers up, blinking hard. Blood strings from her lips. She swings wild.

Jade slips under, slides inside her guard, and drives a palm heel through the hinge of her jaw. Teeth clack. For a split second, Mercy's legs forget their job. Jade steps through, sweeps, and drops her flat. The mat makes the decision Ratface wanted her to throw. Jade makes her own.

"Finish it!" someone howls. Money changes hands around the fence, paper fluttering like birds.

Jade plants a knee on Mercy's sternum. Breath knifes out. One strike could crush her windpipe clean. Easy.

But Jade doesn't. She leans down until Mercy can smell the peppermint on her skin. "Don't come back," she says, voice low enough for only Mercy and the fence to hear. "I know who you are and next time I won't be polite."

The ref scrambles in, waving his arms. "That's it! That's it!" He snatches Jade's wrist and lifts it, sealing the win.

The crowd roars—loud enough to make anyone bigger or smaller, depending on what they already are.

Jade steps back, chest heaving, fire sparking along her ribs. The wolf stays silent. No praise. No reprimand. Just a mirror. And that unsettles her more than any bruise.

At the edge of the ring a man in a leather jacket that cost more than the building, raises a hand. He wears the same braided red cord she noticed before. The cord glints with something woven in—metal? He smiles, but it's not happiness.

"Nice work," he says when she's close enough. His cologne is expensive and mean. "We like fighters who know when not to kill. Shows... restraint."

"Well, her name is mercy," Jade wipes some blood from her perfectly shaped brow.

"Mercy's a luxury," he says. "I'm a practical man." He slips a folded envelope into her palm with fingers that don't touch her skin. "If you want to make real money, we have private nights. Smaller audience. Bigger stakes."

Jim was right. They aren't here for the show. There's a lot more going on here.

"Not interested," she says, handing the envelope back. "I prefer crowds. Witnesses."

Leather Jacket smiles again, edges sharp. "Witnesses can be bought."

"Not all of them," she says. She lets him see she's memorizing his face. The cord. The boots. The raven shaped tie clip. She files it alphabetically in her bones.

He laughs like he's bored and steps away, leaving toward the side hallway where two more men stand with the same cords. They guard a door painted the exact color of the wall. If you aren't looking, it's not there.

Jade is watching when Jim steps into her space, blocking her view.

"What?" she snaps. "You're like a piece of shit stuck to a dog's ass."

He smiles, unfazed. "Oh, if only I could be a wolf."

Her wolf goes still.

Not startled. Calculating.

Does he know?

It's in the way he says it. Too casual to be random. Too close to the truth to be harmless.

"Or maybe," he continues lightly, eyes never leaving hers, "I'm just good at spotting the difference between teeth and wool."

Her pulse stays even, but something shifts behind her ribs. She's been the lamb before. Soft voice. Lowered eyes. Taking the hits and pretending they didn't hurt.

That version of her died a long time ago.

"Do I look like a lamb?" she asks.

His gaze drops. Her ribs. Her hands. Her eyes. He smiles like he's already done the math.

"You look like bait that bites back," he says. "They love that."

Jade swallows the ache in her chest and nods toward the side door. "What's through there?"

"Storage," he says lightly, but his pupils shrink. "And sometimes things that don't want to be stored." His jaw works. "Trucks come late. Leave earlier."

"What do you want from me?" Jade's wolfy senses are on overdrive. Her wolf doesn't seem to notice.

"I'm not sure yet. As soon as I figure it out I'll let you know."

She can't quite pin whether she likes this Jim or not. Jade wants to tell him to quit stalking her and just go about his business but she's piecing together that he's telling her humans are in trouble and maybe she can help.

"Ok, fine. How late?"

He chews, thinking. "When the crowd is loudest. They move under noise." He flicks the pretzel stick away like he's rejecting something larger. "If you're going to play hero, don't do it alone."

"I'm no hero," she says.

"No," he agrees. "You're a problem. That's more useful."

Suddenly Rat-face shoves through the crowd pressing in around the octagon, grin wide enough to sell it. "That's my girl!" he calls, palms clapping slow, greasy. Then lower, meant for her alone, "You just cost me a stack, sweetheart. Funny thing—slots filled up real fast. No more fighties for you," tilting his head to confirm the scumbag in him, "until I *find* a slot for you."

"Yeah? I'll see you Friday then." Pushing past the stench of his rat breath.

The next bout kicks off, the roar of cheers swallowing the sound of her boots on concrete. Jade slips along the chain-link, eyes forward, but her ears snag the faintest code: a tap-tap-pause-tap against the wall. It vanishes under the noise, but she knows the rhythm. From deeper inside, an answer knocks back. The painted door cracks open just enough to leak a sliver of shadow and a sterile sweetness— citrus and hospital wipes, the stench of sedatives. She doesn't linger. Not her door. Her money waits two turns down.

Jade hears the slight click behind her. Her jaw locks until it hurts. *Wednesdays are my day for being wrong,* she thinks. *But tonight I'm right. This isn't just fights. It's a funnel.*

The ledger woman appears with a cash box and a crooked smile. "Payout's light tonight," she warns. "House took a hit on a favorite. Sorry."

"I'm not here for the money," Jade says, and that's the truth. The envelope is heavy in her pocket anyway. "What's the cut on private nights?"

"Twenty percent," the woman says automatically. Then, more carefully, "Don't recommend it." Her eyes flick to the leather jacket, to the cords, back to Jade. "People go in with tons of confidence. They leave... quieter."

Jade signs where the greasy blonde gal leaves a small dirt fingerprint and says nothing more. Ribs complaining as she raises. Broken bonds, equal slow healing. Her soul misses her sisters through blood and bonds.

As she heads for the stairs, Jim—whoever-the-hell he is —drifts into her path, then vanishes back into the drunk tide of spectators. Jade files him under *don't trust that one.*

The server from earlier staggers under a heavy tray, unloading cans of beer and who knows what else. Jade pauses.

"You good?"

She turns, tray empty. "Yeah. Thanks for..." Her hand flutters midair, words gone. She lingers, as if her body hasn't caught up with her exit. "I should—" A breath trembles. "I'm fine."

Without looking, Jade slides the envelope into the girl's apron, lacing it with as much confidence as she can push through her hand. "Tip," she says. "From a generous donor."

The girl blinks, shakes her head. "I can't—"

"You didn't," Jade cuts her off, already moving. "Go home. Don't come back. There's enough there to buy you time to find a day job or be a stripper—I don't care—just don't come back here."

The warehouse exhales her into the night, the door clanging shut at her back. The desert air is cooler now, the sky a black bowl punched with only a few stars. The lights of Vegas always keep them veiled. The bass from inside turns to a dull heart under her feet.

The Adonis from earlier leans against the wall, cigarette ember pulsing. He watches her like he's been waiting.

"You collect?" His voice is rough, a stone rolling in his throat.

"Got everything I came for." She steps into his space. "Well, almost everything."

He looks down at her, smoke curling from his lips. "Could come back Friday. Less crowd. More privacy."

Jade almost laughs. "I have no intention of waiting until Friday." She should walk. Every nerve says keep moving. Instead, she slides deeper into the shadow beside him. Heat. Smoke. The scrape of his calloused thumb over her hip as he spins her against the wall. She lets him. Lets herself burn off the fight in the simplest way there is.

"Unzip your pants."

His eyes flick, surprised, but Jade's stare pins him in place. He obeys. Her hand is on him before he can speak, grip hard, no softness, no invitation. She shoves him back, only long enough to peel down her black yoga pants. The alley reeks of grease, piss, and smoke, but none of it matters. She'll take what she needs right here, right now.

"Lift me," she orders, voice low and sharp. "Give me what I need against this wall, and maybe—if it's good enough—I'll reward you Friday."

He grabs her thighs, rough hands locking under muscle, and she clamps him where she wants him. Concrete bites her shoulder blades, the world narrowing to motion, breath, control. No kisses. No whispers. Just the rasp of lungs, the grind of heat, the slap of skin against skin. His thrusts find their rhythm with her breaths. *Good boy.*

Her wolf should be there—hungry, restless, clawing for release. Instead, nothing. Silence, as if the animal part of her refuses to take part.

And then Ryder is there. Not in the alley, but in her head —smirk curling, voice dripping contempt, the only man who ever made her feel off-balance. She digs her nails into the door guy's shoulders, harder, trying to claw Ryder out. It doesn't work. Every thrust, every gasp drags Ryder closer until the release slips away, leaving her raw and empty.

When it's over, she pushes free, jerking her pants back up, jaw tight. "So why is there more privacy on Friday?"

"Friday's are by invite only."

The man's still catching his breath, thinking he gave her what she came for. He didn't. Ryder ruined it. And what burns worst is the truth clawing up her throat.

Jade hear's the deep voice behind her, "so do I at least get dinner first on Friday?"

"Let's see what Friday brings." Now she's hoping she can get that invite back.

As she turns the corner—as if molecules can just suddenly reform—Jim materializes like a shadow peeling off another shadow. *Fuck is he related to Isabell?* He holds out a paper cup with a lid. "Water. Not poisoned. Promise."

"Cheers." She takes it, drinks, knowing if there was anything in it she'd smell it. Her wolf wouldn't let her die by poison. Or would she? Her ribs throb a steady beat.

"Why are you in my face again?"

He shrugs, mouth twitching.

"I like watching the people who think they're hunters realize they've wandered into someone else's jaws." He tilts his head. "Also, you didn't break that fighter when you could have. Not many would've chosen that."

Mercy is a luxury, Leather Jacket had said.

"Mercy is leverage," Jade says instead.

Jim's grin flashes. "Careful. You'll make me believe in you."

"Don't," she says, and starts walking.

He falls into step anyway, a half pace behind, rustling like wrappers. "You coming back?"

Her wolf finally stirs. The quiet shifts—like a curtain moving when you're not looking.

"Yeah," Jade says, eyes on the alley mouth and the dark street beyond. "I'm coming back. And next time, I'm not just watching a door."

Jim's laugh is soft—and a little worried. "Then I guess I'll bring more snacks."

Just then, an envelope. The same kind she was denied earlier—now staring her in the face.

Adjusting the strip of cloth around her locs, she squares her shoulders against the ache and grabs the red envelope.

Her invite.

Jim just took every reason she thought she was here and flipped it on its side. She's been trying to figure out why she keeps coming back—fight after fight, bruise after bruise.

This must be it.

Somewhere beyond that painted door, the real fight is waiting.

And she's ready to make noise.

SHE HAS LOST CONTROL

"Fucking hell, Jade."

The words scrape low in his throat, too quiet for anyone but the shadows to hear. Ryder doesn't blink. Just watches. From the far end of the alley, tucked behind a dumpster half the size of a shipping container, he's nothing more than another dark shape in the night.

But his pulse is a war drum.

The guy has her back against the wall, her grip iron at his jaw. There's heat in it, sure, but nothing else. This isn't seduction. This is scratching an itch.

The toothpick bobs at the corner of his mouth, held tight between grinding molars. It's the only thing keeping his hands from splitting open and shifting. His nails burn beneath the skin. The beast in his chest wants blood. Wants her out of this damn alley. Wants *him* dead.

"What the fuck are you doing?" he mutters again, to no one.

She lets the guy think he's in control—lets him touch her. That fucking hand sliding around her waist, bold like he's earned it. Ryder shifts his weight, the joint in his jaw ticking. One more inch and he'll snap the bastard's spine like a twig.

His boots don't move, but it's close.

She pulls away, and for a second, he sees her face. Hard. Cold.

And yet...

And yet she's still the one his gaze tracks across every room. Still the one who shows up in his head when he least wants her to. Still the one who doesn't see him—*really see him*—but somehow still ruins him without even trying.

Ryder crushes the toothpick between his teeth.

The guy fumbles with his zipper, a cocky grin pasted on like he's the one in charge.

Dumbass.

Ryder's hand twitches.

If she wasn't already walking away, he'd end it right now.

He hears her toss over her shoulder, "Let's see what Friday brings," before she disappears into the dark, her long legs carrying her off like nothing happened.

Ryder doesn't move for three full seconds.

Then he spits the splintered toothpick onto the ground and steps into the alley.

The guy fumbles with his zipper, grinning like he just scored the winning ticket. Ryder's boot grinds down on a shard of glass, the crack sharp and deliberate.

That grin falters. *Good. At least he's smart enough to flinch.*

Does he really think squaring his shoulders makes him a threat? Ryder's not the biggest man in the room—never had to be. He closes the distance slow, stopping five feet out. Close enough to end it. Far enough to let the idiot sweat.

"You know who she is?" Ryder's voice is low, calm. Too calm. The kind of calm that promises blood.

The guy straightens, puffing his chest like a rooster. "Who the hell are you?"

Wrong answer. Ryder almost smiles.

Almost.

Taking one step closer, the air shifts. "I asked you a question."

The guy falters. "She didn't give a name—"

"That's not what I asked."

He blinks. Swallows. "No. I don't *know* her."

Ryder tilts his head, just enough to crack the bones in his neck. "Then let me give you some advice."

A pause.

"Keep it that way. You don't know her. You don't talk about her. You don't *look* at her." He leans in, quiet enough that the words feel like teeth brushing skin. "And when Friday rolls around, you don't talk to her."

The guy stutters something that isn't quite a word.

Ryder's done.

He turns and walks away without another glance. The guy doesn't move. Doesn't breathe. Just stands there with his back against the wall, trying to remember how knees work.

Back at the mouth of the alley, Ryder pauses. He looks down at the busted toothpick still lying on the wet pavement.

Then keeps walking.

WTF

The door handle slips under her grip, slick with rain. The storm's passed, but the lot still glitters, puddles catching the neon glow like broken glass.

Her wolf howls—sudden, raw—rattling straight through her ribs. It's not warning. Not hunger. Sadness.

WTF?

She freezes, scanning. Nothing moves. Cars sleep heavy under the orange lamps. Shadows don't twitch. The only thing alive is a white grocery bag tumbling across asphalt, caught in a phantom breeze. It skips, sways, almost like it's dancing to music only it can hear.

The hairs on the back of her neck lift, static crawling over her skin. Instincts scream *alert*, but even that feels...off. Wrong frequency. Too heavy, too personal.

Ryder.

Her wolf pushes his name into her skull, and the breath she drags tastes like iron.

"Where the fuck did that come from?" she mutters, furious at herself for saying it in her head.

The confusion is a weight she can't shake. Ever since he

walked into the mansion like he belonged there, nothing has been right. Her pulse skips when it should steady. Her head chants *enemy,* but her chest? That fucking thing feels like it betraying her from the inside out.

She hates him. She's supposed to hate him. After what he did when they were kids—unforgivable. Yet her chest still stirs like it didn't get the damn memo.

Anger surges, sharp enough to burn. She shoves it down, but it leaks anyway, bleeding into her veins until even the rain-damp air tastes bitter.

Slamming the door, Jade gives the stearing wheel a good slam. "Get your shit together Jade. Control is your strength. Now find it."

The sudden light from her phone pulls away from the anger. It's Luna. *AGAIN!*

> JADE!

> I'm serious. WTF is going on?

Head spinning, Jade picks up the phone she'd tossed on the seat.

> Hi Luna. What's up?

> WHAT'S UP?!!!!! That's all you got?

> Jade. Where are you? I am worried into sadness and we all know what happens when I catch the sadness.

> Yeah. You make everyone around you miserable and you eat too much.

> Keep in mind your room is unlocked.

Stay the fuck out of my room Luna.

I'll be home soon.

How soon? Kai is driving me crazy and
Charlotte and Liam are always kissy face. I
hate it here.

No you don't. You're bored. Do you need
me to send you more paint by numbers?

I'm not bored. I'm worried about you.

Luna. Why are you worried about me? I'm
doing my job, just like I've done my job a
thousand times. Why is this one different?

Don't be mad.

Why would I be mad Luna?

I tried to track your location and I know you
are using the blocking program I created for
you. You've never used it when you're not
on a job before.

So, now I have two questions. How would
you know that I've never used it when I'm
on a job? And, what makes you think I'm
not on a job now?

Don't be mad.

LUNA!

Promise you won't be mad.

> I'm already very pissed Luna so no promises.

> Then I'm not answering that.

Jade decides this texting shit is too much and hits dial. She doesn't even wait for a greeting.

"Luna, I get that you're a hacker. It's your instinct, but you said you wouldn't use it on me."

"Nooo, what I said was I wouldn't use it on you when you were on a job."

Jade takes a deep breath. "But I am on a job."

"NO YOU'RE NOT!"

The certainty in Luna's voice slams through the speaker. Jade lowers her tone, dread creeping in. "Luna. Why do you think I'm not on a job?"

Silence. Dead, heavy. For a second Jade wonders if Luna hung up.

"Luna? Why do you think I'm not on a job?"

"Because..." Luna drags it out like chewing broken glass. "...I hacked into your job board and you aren't assigned anything right now."

"LUNA! What the fuck?"

"Don't be mad."

"Don't be mad? You hacked my company?" Jade takes a deep breath. "Didn't you build the programs for me so that couldn't happen?"

"Oh my god, Jade. If I built it, I can hack it." Her tone is flat, indifferent. "Besides, it's barely hacking. More like... peeking. Just a quick peeky-peek. And guess what? Zero jobs assigned to you. Nada. Which means you're lying to me."

"Or maybe I don't list everything on the damn board!"

Jade can feel the teeniest bit of control she had slipping, voice sharper than she intended. Only Luna can drag her here, this messy place where rage tangles with affection, where she wants to shake her and hug her in the same breath.

"Eh-hhhh, wrong answer." The mocking buzzer noise is followed by Luna's smugness. "Even if you didn't add it, Sam would've. And yes, I called Sam. She lied for you too."

Jade's grip tightens on the wheel. "Listen, I just needed a break from Vegas, alright? Maybe a break from all the noise."

"Bullshit," Luna says, her voice flat. "You don't run from anything, Jade. Usually, anyway. So what the hell are you running from now? Because my WTF meter is in the red."

Jade drops her head, letting the fight drain out. Just a little. "I don't know, my friend. I don't know what's got my head so twisted. I just...need more time to figure it out, okay?"

"Jade. I flove you. You're my wolfy-person. I don't like it when I can't touch you."

A sigh slips past Jade's lips. "Fine. Give me a few more days. I'll be home Saturday. One more thing I need to take care of, then I'll come home. Okay?"

"What time Saturday?"

"Fuck'n A Luna."

"What time, Jade?"

"Before lunch. Is that good enough?"

"Yes. I'll have Isabell make you something tasty for lunch." Relief colors Luna's voice, obvious even through the static.

"And Luna."

Jade takes the breath. Maybe this decision is giving her some relief too.

"Yeah?"

"I love you big."

The screen goes dark. Again, Jade flings the phone onto the seat like it burned her fingers.

Thoughts churn, clashing loud enough to drown the engine. She should go back—back to the den, back to the only place that's ever felt like safety. Back to Charlotte. But the idea knots her stomach.

Her wolf hides from her, silent as stone... except when fists fly. Except when blood hits the floor. Down there, in the pits of Las Vegas, the wolf claws through just enough to remind her she still exists.

Leaving that behind? That feels harder than staying lost.

RISE AND SHINE PRINCESS

The sun knifes across her face. Luna groans and peels one eye open. Blinds—wide open.

"Fucking witch," she mutters, rolling over and yanking the blanket over her head.

She tries to disappear, staying buried, eyes shut, pretending the world doesn't exist. But the scent finds her anyway—warm bacon, melted butter, something sticky-sweet. It creeps through the fabric like betrayal, curling into her nose and dragging her back to the waking world.

"Shit. Fuck. Damn."

Suspicion sets in—knowing even with her wolfy senses the smell is too strong—she peeks out from her cocoon. There, in the doorway, stands a Liam and the steady humming of a fan, pushing the smells of breakfast straight into her room like a weapon.

"Oh, you've got to be kidding me."

From the hall, Liam's laugh carries. "Rise and shine, princess. Isabell made pancakes."

Her stomach answers before she does, and she buries her face again with a muffled curse.

"Damn," Kai drawls, "that almost smells better than you, not-girlfriend." His voice is scratchy—morning-rough and still sexy as hell. Luna rolls her eyes, but deep down... she kinda wants to climb on top and ride that smug grin clean off his face.

"Well, if your breath didn't smell like you've been chewing on a shit mound covered in flies..."

"Hey now." The wounded note in Kai's voice catches her off guard. It's faint, but real.

"We agreed—you can be savage outside this room. But in here?"

He glances at her, softer now. "You're my queen. And my queen doesn't talk to me like that."

Her stomach flips, the guilt sharp and sudden.

Last night's call with Jade took the edge off, but the churning in her gut hasn't quit. *What is Jade's fucking problem?*

Luna crawls over him, slow and predatory, her palms flattening against his annoyingly perfect bare chest. She feels the rise of his breath—smug and waiting.

"You're right," she murmurs, lips ghosting over his. "I'm sorry."

Then she kisses him—slow, deep, just enough tongue to make him forget the insult entirely.

By the time she pulls back, he's dazed.

"I forgive you," he whispers, blinking. "Mostly... because that was hot."

She smirks, sliding off him and tossing a pillow at his face. Finally succumbing to the promise of syrup sponges, she tiptoes out of bed and into the bathroom. Hair twisted into something resembling a white mop head, she gives her reflection a half-nod and pads down the stairs, chasing the scent of bacon.

The sound of her Alphas' voices—Charlotte's laugh, Liam's easy rumble—drifts up to meet her, and for the first time since yesterday, her chest feels a little lighter.

Just before turning the corner into the dining room, Luna catches the pack in their usual spots, voices bouncing back and forth.

"Did you put the fan in her doorway?" Ryan's all business tone carries.

"Yeah. She didn't look too happy to see me."

Stepping into view, arm crossed. "No, Liam, I was not excited to see you. But I'll forgive you—because Isabell's pancakes are involved."

Kai circles around, close enough to remind her that food —*always*—wins over everything else.

"Isabell's pancakes are my favorite. Except her burritos. Or those omelets…"

A spoon clinks hard against the side of the mug as he dumps in way too much sugar. "Oh—shit—what about the chilaquiles? Fuck, those things—"

"Señor Kai,"

As usual Isabell manifests out of nowhere with a giant plate loaded with pancakes balancing on one hand and the carafe of steaming syrup in the other.

"Language. No need for extras when speaking about my food."

"You're right," Kai says, grinning like she didn't just scold him. "I don't *need* them, but they prove how passionate I am." He turns, looks her dead in the eye. "You make the best—"

Nothing. Not a single word lands. Luna watches him fish for something worthy, something grand. Something smartassy.

"…the best breakfasts I've ever had."

The smile that follows could start a religion.

"Much better Señor Kai. Gracias."

"Okay, now that we've finally sorted all that out..." Charlotte sets her mug down with a soft clink. "Can we talk about why you're not as bitchy as usual, Luna?"

No shift in tone. No smirk. Just classic Charlotte — all business, no patience for shenanigans.

"Well, Jade finally answered me last night."

That stopped the room. All eyes made their way to Luna.

"And, she's fine. Right? You are all worked up for no reason." Charlotte's question hangs in the air a moment before the sounds of breakfast begin again.

"No! She's not fine. She's a mess. I can hear it. But, I did get her to agree to come home."

"You made her tell you when right?" Maddy's voice gets more and more confident every day.

"Yes. She said Saturday. Something she needs to finish before coming home."

Cutting into the food on her plate, she keeps going. "She did admit she's struggling with something..."

Luna shoves a bite of pancake into her face hole—easily twice the size it should be. Syrup drips with zero hesitation from Luna.

"...Sh' d'no wha' it ishh tho," comes out thick, sweet, and completely unintelligible.

Charlotte blinks slowly. "Did... did you just say words?"

"I got 'what it' The rest? No idea." Kai mumbles around his own mouth full of pancakes.

"Thanks for being the Luna Whisperer." Liam chuckles. "We're going to need you to just join the Red Rocks and keep you around."

"Nooo!" Luna overreacts.

SOME SECRETS
SHOULD STAY A SECRET

F *uck you Friday.*

Too fast and not fast enough, Friday is here.

Tomorrow, she'd have to walk back into the mansion, into those stares. The pack would want answers—where she'd been, what she'd been doing, why her knuckles still carried shadows of bruises that haven't quite healed, even though they should have.

She didn't have answers. Not the kind they'd accept anyway.

The truth was simple and messy, she wasn't fighting for her wolf tonight. Not for rage, pride, or the thrill of it. She was fighting because Jim had hinted that people were going missing. He was a strange little man. Not to be trusted. But she couldn't shake the thought—what if he was right? What if she ignored it and later found out she could've stopped it?

It sounded like humans. But she knows there are other shifters here so maybe shifters too. And the whispers pointed straight to that painted door.

If she could pull someone out—just one—maybe all the blood and lies would finally mean something.

She pulled her hoodie tighter, the scent of sweat and concrete already in her nose. The air tasted like the calm before a storm.

She stays low, watching. The blink of the hazard lights makes the scene flicker—light, dark, light, dark—until she catches the faint glow of a cigarette inside the cab.

Odd. Why bring attention to anything around here?

Staying low, eyes track the dull pulse of the hazard lights —light, dark, light, dark—each blink gives her a fraction of a second to read the scene—shapes, movement, timing. Inside the cab, a cigarette flares. She notes it. Counts the drag, the pause, the angle of the wrist. Left-handed. Nervous tick in the shoulder. Probably security—not her target.

Routine. Control. Cause and effect.

When the ember dies, she moves.

Keeping to the shadows, she circles the dock until she reaches the familiar door at the far side of the building—the one that leads into the den of vipers. She also knows he's here. The one from Wednesday. The one she told—half teasing, half not—that if he turned out to be a good fuck, she'd buy him dinner first on Friday.

It's Friday.

The door opens, and immediately Jade regrets her indiscretions from Wednesday.

He's hot as fuck, but now, not only does she have Mason to deal with, she's got this Greek god as well. *The Greek god that right now, looks anything but divine?*

Shoulders tense, eyes darting like a kid caught stealing candy.

"Oh. Uh—hey," he stammers, stepping aside quickly. "Wasn't sure you were... uh... going to make it."

Jade arches a brow. "You sound disappointed." Jade

pauses with the realization she never asked his name. *Fuck Jade.* "Uh, what's your name?"

"No! I mean—no, not disappointed. Just... surprised." He scratches the back of his neck, avoiding her gaze. "And it's, uh, *George*."

"George," she repeats flatly, stepping forward as she holds up the red envelope. "That's what you're going with?"

He swallows hard, eyes flicking to the envelope like it's on fire. Then he snatches it from her hand and shoves it under the podium.

"What? It's a good name."

"Sure," she says, voice dropping to a dangerous purr. "If you're an accountant."

His laugh is forced, breaking halfway through. "I like to think I've got range."

"Uh-huh."

His adam's apple bobs. "You're cleared. Go ahead." George steps aside to reveal the hallway that Jade knows leads to her fix for the night, but something about this exchanged feels off. This is not the "George" she *had* the other night.

She tilts her head, studying him. "You look like a man who is worried."

He forces a weak smile. "Let's just say... I got reminded to mind my business."

Her eyes narrow. "By who?"

He hesitates. "Doesn't matter. Just—let's forget about Wednesday, okay?"

"Wow," she mutters, brushing past him. "That's usually my line. Feels weird hearing it from someone else."

Jade slides past him but turns back, gaze sharp. "Still curious who gave you this reminder, though. I don't have anyone who decides my business."

He shifts uncomfortably, glancing down the hall over her shoulder, like someone might appear any second. "Let's just leave it, okay. I shouldn't have said that."

"You're afraid of someone?"

"Just helping myself to stay breathing."

Her brow furrows, but he's already turning away—pretending to check something on the tablet by the door, the conversation clearly over.

Turning, over her shoulder, "I got you, George." Let him hide behind half-truths. "Just so you know, you did earn yourself dinner."

His mouth opens like he wants to respond—but doesn't. So he's not all brawn after all.

As she walks away, the words start to itch. *Who the hell would warn him off?*

Jim? Maybe. He's sus as fuck. That walking, talking pop-up ad for car insurance—legal extortion dressed like a favor.

Mason? *Nah.* Too proud for that kind of whisper game. He'd rather throw a punch than a warning.

Her jaw tightens. *Luna?* The woman's got enough tech tucked under her skin to track a shadow and she's now revealed that she has used her trickery even when she said she wouldn't.

A chill hums up her spine, threading through the edges of her control. Someone's paying attention. Jade thought her little rompa rompa was far enough into the shadows that only her and *George* knew.

Good. Let them.

She rolls her shoulders back, steps into the low light of the arena, and lets the noise swallow her thoughts.

She pushes through the next door, the heavy scent of oil and sweat wrapping around her like armor. Whatever game they're playing—she'll finish it on her own terms,

But the thought sticks, whoever's watching, whatever game they're playing—it won't matter once the bell rings.

THE FIGHT AREA is too damn bright. Ryder found the one shadow in the place and claimed it. Hasn't moved or taken his eyes off the doorway—the one Jade was supposed to walk through twenty minutes ago.

He fucking lost her when he went to take a shit earlier that afternoon. After checking the ratty motel—why a damn millionaire would stay there is beyond him—he circled the burger joint she likes. Nothing.

She vanished.

Maybe she finally went home. Wouldn't be the first time she vanished mid-storm just to crawl back to Charlotte like gravity dragged her there. Even as a kid—bloody lip, busted ribs—she'd show up at his door, Charlotte flanking her, looking for Harper to patch her back up. A fucked-up little pack, stitched together with spite and survival.

His chest vibrates. His wolf's been restless since Wednesday, still drunk on the scent of her. That one stolen moment was enough to stir him up, not settle him down. And now he's sulking—just like Ryder. Only difference is, Ryder won't admit it out loud.

Last time they were face-to-face, she had him pinned to the floor of her shiny new mansion, one hand around his throat like she owned the air in his lungs. She can have it. She can have all of him.

She doesn't know—probably never will—that he'd die

for her. Didn't even flinch when her blade pressed to his dick. She could take his soul, and he'd thank her for it.

Because it's hers anyway.

That's the day he saw it. The tattoo. A compass inked on her forearm. But where the *N* should've been, it had *RR* instead. Red Rocks. Her pack. Her home. Not him.

Fuck. Finally. There she is.

Something's changed. The doom-and-gloom cloud that has been following her? Gone.

It's been replaced by...

Oh shit. The look.

That is the *"I'm about to fuck shit up"* version of Jade.

Once that fire hits her eyes, all bets are off.

Last time he saw that look...

He hears her before he sees her—boots hammering the dirt like it was the ground pissed her off. He doesn't stop punching. Doesn't need to turn around to know who it is. That energy? Pure wildfire.

The shed door slams open.

"You rejected her?" Jade's voice whips across the room, sharp and shaking. "You fucking rejected Senna?"

He exhales through his nose, fist landing hard against the bag. The chain groans. "Didn't know that was your business."

"She's my sister, you prick."

He finally turns. Her face is flushed, fury written in every tight muscle. Even her damn freckles look pissed off.

"I'm not her mate," he says, low and even.

"Bullshit." She's closing the distance, fast. "She felt it. We all did. She's wrecked. And you're what—just in here beating the shit out of a bag like you didn't just destroy her?"

He shrugs. "Better now than later."

"Why?" she barks, shoving him hard in the chest. He doesn't move. "Why would you hurt her like that?"

His fists clench. His wolf is pacing, pissed and panicked. But not over Senna. Not even close.

"Because it's not her!" *he yells.*

He's never seen Jade flinch with him. Not once. The sound of his own voice echoes between them, louder than it should've been. Too sharp. Too damn loud. And that flinch—it guts him. He hates it. Hates that something he said made her brace like that.

Maybe he can fix it.

Yeah, he and Jade fight—they always fight—but the Sheridans are her safe zone. He just needs her to know he can protect her too. Same as the rest of them.

Ryder shifts where he stands, boots scraping faintly against the concrete. The warehouse not quite coming back into focus. He rolls his shoulders, like the weight of that moment still sits wrong under his skin.

"I don't know what the hell the moon's doing. But I look at Senna and feel... nothing." *He meets her eyes.* "And you—"

The word sticks in his throat. His jaw locks around it like a cage.

She blinks once. Then laughs. Sharp. Mocking. Cold. "You're sick."

"I know."

It was the only truth he had.

"ROUTINE. CONTROL. CAUSE AND EFFECT." She whispers it under her breath like a prayer, elbows braced to her knees, hands wrapped and ready for whatever this night is going to bring.

The rusted metal of the bleachers groans beneath her,

and she imagines all the high school make-out sessions that happened under here.

Her gaze drifts, slow and deliberate, to the door—the one painted to disappear into the wall.

She's been coming here for weeks. Off and on. Almost every night lately. And somehow, she never really saw it. The guards. The door. Even Jim?

That realization hits harder than it should. She's a professional. She *owns* a security company. Details are her currency. Patterns are her gospel. But lately, the edges blur. Her focus drifts. Everything feels like static—loud, constant, meaningless.

"Routine."

She pops her head up, scanning the room. Something's off. The little hairs at the back of her neck are doing a nervous dance—one she's learned not to ignore.

Her eyes track across the warehouse until they catch on the catwalk. Someone's up there. Too still to be casual. Too far back in the shadow to be part of the crowd.

Another guard? Maybe.

A sniper, if things go wrong in the ring?

Her wolf stirs. Not a growl. Not a threat.

Just... *awareness*. A ripple through her chest. A low pulse beneath her skin.

Whoever's up there—her instincts don't mark them as danger. But they're not neutral, either.

Her wolf isn't raising her hackles. Just listens. That alone is enough to make Jade more alert. Her wolf doesn't stir for strangers.

And this place? This night? It's suddenly feeling a lot more crowded than it looks.

Suddenly, Jade isn't sure of anything.

She's here because Tony didn't want her to be. She didn't

throw the fight like he asked. Didn't roll over. Didn't bleed pretty. Now she's a problem in his little profit factory—and problems get tested.

She's here because that Hyde of a man, Jim, made her give a shit about what's behind that door.

"Name?"

Jade looks up. Clipboard girl. Ponytail tight enough to pull thoughts straight. She's maybe nineteen. Maybe fifty. The kind of face built by night shifts and don't-fuck-with-me energy.

"Cortez."

Click of pen. Scratch of paper. A pause. "Right. You're the one from Wednesday."

Jade doesn't answer.

The girl keeps going, voice clipped. "Round robin rules. Five fights. Win clean or dirty, you advance. Winner of the final takes the pot—currently sitting at fifty grand."

Jade arches a brow. "That's all?"

"No refs. No weapons. No tapping out. If you kill someone, don't be obvious about it."

She holds back the shock. "Got it."

"And no emotions. Not on Fridays."

Jade's brow twitches. Just barely.

The girl clocks it. "Don't ask. It's just a thing. Leave your heart at the door or get it stomped out. Any questions?"

"Just one. Are these fighters new? I'd hate to waste my precious life on repeats."

"They're new. L.A.'s full of assholes with something to prove. Good luck."

Something shifts inside her. Not quite a growl, but close. Her wolf doesn't like this place. Doesn't like the way that girl said *good luck*. It was too *final*.

She walks off, scribbling something, already moving on.

Jade exhales through her nose. Cold air. Hot lungs.

No emotions. She has that in the bag.

At least, that's what she tells herself.

"Cortez, you're up."

The crowd doesn't cheer. This isn't that kind of venue. It *shifts.* Energy leans in, eyes flick toward the rusted ring in the center of the warehouse. The space clears like smoke sucked through a vent. Bloodstains never had a chance to dry.

Jade pulls her hoodie off slow, deliberate. No performance. No hype. Just control. Her fingers flex once, knuckles popping.

She steps into the circle. Across from her—

Male. Thick neck. Shaved head. Face like busted concrete. His left ear's cauliflowered. Nose crooked.

This is new.

He grins like this is foreplay.

Jade doesn't smile back.

A bell clangs.

He charges first. *Predictable.*

She sidesteps. Fast. Clean. Elbow clips his jaw on the pivot.

He stumbles, surprised, swings wide.

Ducking she sweeps his leg, hitting the floor with a grunt.

The crowd shifts again—small nods, money passed.

No refs. No tapping out.

He rolls and kicks. Wild now. Angry. Sloppy.

Jade lets him graze her shoulder, just to feel it.

Pain sharpens her. Her wolf lets out a deep growl.

She steps inside his reach—knee to his ribs, a crack. Elbow to the throat.

He gags, stumbles.

Then her fist finds his jaw. Hard. Final.

He drops. Out cold.

She stands over him. Chest rising slow. No roar. No victory stance. Just her pulse.

And the stillness that follows. For a moment, she almost feels something.

Then she doesn't.

Her wolf stirs. Unsettled. Not from the fight. From the gaze she *feels* but can't find.

Stepping out of the ring, there's Jim. Almost as if summoned.

She peels the bloodied wraps from her knuckles, the crowd's roar already dissolving behind her like smoke from a cheap fire.

Jim steps up, slow clap echoing like gunshots.

"Winner, winner..." he drawls, head cocked, "but it ain't chicken you're beating next."

She squints at him, breathing hard. "You always this annoying after a win?"

He shrugs. "Just trying to remind you—victory's a slippery thing. One minute you're the hammer..."

He leans in, voice dropping, "Next minute you're the egg."

"What does that even mean?"

Jim's grin widens. "Exactly."

THE SECOND FIGHTER had nearly broken her.

A wall of muscle with dead eyes and fists like anvils. Jade swore the woman smelled wrong—sweet, sharp, earthy. Bear maybe. Hard to tell in a warehouse soaked in blood, sweat, and cheap aftershave. All Jade knew was her ribs weren't healing right, and every breath felt like it might be the last one.

No time to reset. No time to think. Just a muttered "ten minutes" and another number scrawled on her forearm in black ink.

Jade walks to the ring like a soldier to the gallows.

Her hands move on autopilot, unwrapping and rewrapping with stiff knuckles and shaky fingers. The cloth is sticky with old blood, both hers and not. She doesn't feel the sting anymore. She doesn't feel much at all.

The lights overhead hum like they're whispering secrets she's too tired to decode. Her ears ring. Her limbs ache. Her wolf paces, not with rage, but with warning.

She climbs through the ropes. No announcer. No name. Just a shape on the other side of the ring, shirtless, built like regret and revenge, with a fresh set of bruises blooming like art across his chest. Male. Tall. Calm.

He nods once. Respect or mockery—hard to say.

The bell clangs.

Jade doesn't wait. Can't. She lunges, pain buried beneath instinct, landing a jab to the throat that should've staggered anyone else. He takes it like a shrug. Moves like he's studied her. Grabs her wrist mid-swing and twists.

Her knees nearly give out.

The next few seconds are a blur of fists and bone. He doesn't try to humiliate her—he's trying to end it. Fast.

She's not ready to be ended.

Jade drops low, sweeping his legs. He stumbles. She follows with a kick that sends him to the mat. He hits the mat hard, but not hard enough to stay down.

Jade staggers back, chest heaving. Her vision doubles,

then triples. Everything smells like rust and sweat. Her knee buckles, but she catches herself.

He rises slow. Wary. Bleeding from the lip. Waiting for her to charge again.

She doesn't.

Instead, she circles.

Keeps her distance. Makes it clear she's not coming in for the kill.

Confusion flickers in his eyes. Then suspicion.

The crowd grows restless—shouting for blood, for the finish, for the kill. But she doesn't move.

He lunges, testing her. She dodges. Barely. No counterstrike.

Another pass. Another feint. Nothing.

And then—he stops. Arms down. Chest rising and falling like a war drum. He gets it now. She's offering a different kind of win. Not submission. Not surrender.

Stalemate.

Clipboard girl said; *no tapping out. If you kill someone, don't be obvious about it. Nothing was said about a perfect match of strength.*

A standoff that can't be broken without breaking the rules. Seconds drag like hours. No one makes the call.

Finally, from somewhere in the dark—a slow, sardonic clap. And a voice, smug and satisfied, "Well, look at that. The bitch plays chess."

The bell rings. Not official. But final enough.

Jade doesn't wait for permission. She limps out of the ring, bloodied, bruised, and still her. She didn't win by their rules. She won by not becoming them and outsmarting the system.

She knew going into this she'd have to get noticed—

make herself useful, dangerous, valuable—if she was ever going to see what was behind that goddamn door.

But now? She's not so sure. Not going for the kill might've been too soft. Too human.

The crowd's cheers turn to murmurs. Then silence.

And then—

Slow. Measured. Applause. The kind that feels more like obligation than admiration.

"Winner, winner..." a voice drawls behind her, "but I'm afraid the chicken's still clucking."

Jade turns, already knowing.

Jim leans against the chainlink gate like he's been there all along. Grin sharp enough to cut wire. Eyes too calm for a place this loud.

"You got style, Cortez. No pop to tell you its done, but... plenty of flavor."

"Wrong bird, dipshit." Bloodied, bruised, still her. The limp to the bench is slow, but steady. "You here to critique my form, or offer me another fight?"

He doesn't flinch. Just rocks back on his heels like he's got all night. "Neither. You've earned something rarer."

Her gaze flicks to the painted door. Still guarded. Still locked.

Jim follows it with a look too casual to be careless, a smirk curving like it knows secrets she hasn't earned yet.

"No dear, only winners go to that room." He leans in just enough. "But in this case? Being the wrong bird gets you the golden egg."

Jade snorts, pulling a breath between her teeth as pain flares while grabbing her duffel. "And what's the egg? Another fight? A bullet to the brain?"

Jim chuckles. "All life starts with an egg, Cortez."

"Oh, so death's what's behind that door?"

He doesn't answer. Just tilts his head like she's half-right. Like that's the riddle.

Jade's pulse kicks up. "Who the fuck are you? I've been coming here for awhile, why did you just start talking to me on Wednesday and why the fuck would you give a shit about me and my birds?"

His eyes lose their glint just long enough to show something heavier underneath. "I don't. Not often. But once in a while, someone shows up who doesn't just fight. They *show* something."

Jade straightens, slower than she wants to. "What's that supposed to mean?"

"It means some birds break cages instead of building nests."

"And you help those birds?"

"I *notice* them."

He gives a thin smile. "Help's a strong word."

He turns like he's done but pauses, his voice lower now —meant for her alone.

"Careful behind that door, Cortez. Some doors don't swing back the same way."

Then he walks off—no fanfare, no invitation. Just a trail of unease in his wake.

"Cortez."

The voice cuts sharp behind her. Not Jim's. Not anyone from the ring.

She turns.

The same man from Wednesday stands just beyond the crowd's edge—suit too clean for this place, posture too casual to be harmless. The red cord he wraps between his fingers flashes under the low light. Not threatening. Not yet. But deliberate.

"Let's go." He jerks his head toward the painted door. "Someone wants a word about that little stunt you pulled."

Jade doesn't move. Doesn't flinch.

Every part of her screams caution, but she's too raw for pride and too smart for panic. She considers triggering the emergency ping to Luna. A coded message, just in case.

But then—*ugh*, the conversation that would follow. Nope. Not worth the headache.

She shifts the duffle on her shoulder, every muscle aching like glass ground into bone. "Lead the way," she mutters.

He doesn't smile. Just turns and walks like this is routine. Like women who break rules and don't die in the ring are always escorted behind locked doors.

They pass the guards—silent, unreadable, like fixtures bolted into the concrete. No nods. No eye contact. Just the slow, deliberate scrape of a key sliding into place. A pause. Then the final *click*—a soft sound that still lands like a gavel.

The door opens. Not fast. Not theatrical. Just enough to prove it was never really part of the wall.

Up close, it's worse. The layers of paint don't hide the steel underneath—they *highlight* it. Like a wound that healed wrong. The color meant to blend it in now draws the eye, unnatural and pulsing with secrets.

It's hovered at the edge of her vision since Jim brought it to her attention.

Now it's open. And it's quiet.

MEANWHILE, BACK
AT THE MANSION

Turning the corner into the game room, Luna heads straight for the white, fluffy couch where Charlotte and Liam sit—talking quietly like they're the only two people on earth.

Charlotte may be a hard-ass Alpha, but watching her all soft-eyed and mate-smitten nearly makes Luna want to admit Kai is her... boyfriend.

She winces. "Nope. I didn't just think that."

Charlotte glances up. "What was that?"

"Nothing. It was terrible and evil. Don't worry about it." Luna drops onto the couch with her usual flair, the cushion sighing beneath her. "So... remember way back when you asked me to put out a call for she-wolves who needed a pack?"

Charlotte side-eyes her. "That's... not exactly how I remember it."

"Fine. But there was a vibe. A *maybe* vibe. Anyway. I got a hit."

Charlotte stiffens. "You *actually* posted something?"

"Well, yeah. I mean, it wasn't *labeled* 'lost, lonely, and

lupine' or anything. It was a clever pitch that only a shifter would know."

"And she responded."

"Yup. She wants to meet the pack."

Charlotte swings her legs off Liam's lap like battle mode just got activated. "When and where?"

Before Luna can answer, the mansion's digital home assistant crackles to life with its latest update:

"There is someone at the ducking door, fuckers."

Charlotte groans. "Luna, for fuck's sake—"

"What? I've been bored. And stressed. And I miss Jade. I needed a project."

Liam's shoulders bounce with barely contained laughter. In the background, Isabell is muttering a string of Spanish words that *definitely* sound like curses as she makes her way to the door.

Luna glances toward the front. "I'll bring her in here?"

Charlotte nods with her usual Alpha calm. "Bring her in here."

Boots on tile. Slow. Solid. Not hesitant, just... practiced.

Luna leads the newcomer into the room, letting the silence do the intro.

The woman is older than Luna expected—maybe mid-fifties. Face lined, but not in a fragile way. More like tree bark—weathered, sturdy, and unapologetically rooted. Her jeans are sun-bleached, her boots scuffed raw at the toes. Calloused hands grip a canvas duffel that looks heavier than it should be. And still—her spine is straight, her chin lifted. Survivor energy. Farm tough.

"I'm Nora," the woman says, nodding toward Charlotte, then Liam, then Luna. "Slade. Got your message weeks back. Took a bit to get here."

Luna folds her arms. "Where's 'here' from?"

"Nowhere that matters anymore." Nora drops the bag to the floor. "My mate died six months ago. Pack treated me like I died with him. So I left."

Charlotte's expression shifts. Calculating. Protective. Alpha-mode fully loaded. "You run from something?"

"No. I walked. Kept walking until I remembered what it felt like to breathe."

Luna raises an eyebrow. "And you figured *our* little circus might be the right place?"

"You've got a reputation." Nora doesn't flinch. "Rumors say you're building something different. Something with teeth *and* heart. I can work. I don't need much. Just a place where I'm not invisible."

"What kind of work?" Liam asks, his voice softer than expected.

"I raised goats. Patched fences. Pulled calves in the snow with no help but my teeth and a rope. And my wolf is a fighter, not like her—" she nods toward Charlotte, "but she don't quit. And I don't scare easy. Lots of pack politics where I come from and her and I have the scars to show for it."

Charlotte studies her for a beat, then turns to Luna. "Guest room?"

"She gets the one with the ugly quilt," Luna says.

Nora smirks. "Ugly quilt sounds perfect."

"We eat dinner at six sharp in the dining room," Charlotte says, already halfway back to the couch. "Luna will give you the quick tour. Don't be late."

"Yes, ma'am," Nora replies with a tip of her head. "I'm never late, but supper's one thing I'll always be early for."

Luna studies the woman beside her as they move down the hallway. Built like a powerlifter, easily pushing six foot, Nora looks like she could bench-press the SUV parked out front and still have time to wrangle a couple of rogue cattle before breakfast. She's pure power—broad-shouldered, sun-worn, and carrying a presence that says *I don't need to prove a damn thing.*

As they near the dining room, the front door creaks open.

Kai's voice rings out, followed by Ryan's.

"—I'm just saying, if someone puts kale in a casserole, they've given up on life."

"Come on, man, it was one time," Ryan shoots back. "And it was spinach."

Luna groans. "Shit. Come on, Nora. This way."

She quickens her pace, but Nora doesn't follow. Her boots stop short on the hardwood as she glances toward the source of the voices.

Kai rounds the corner first, pink bubble tea in hand. He stops mid-step.

Ryan's just behind him, offering a curious smile.

Nora, hands on hips, grins wide. "Damn, Luna. You didn't say this came with hot dudes too."

Luna keeps walking, muttering, "Abort. Abort."

Kai raises both eyebrows, eyes bouncing from Luna to Nora. "Oh—uh—hi?"

Before anyone can say something *normal*, Kai throws up a hand like he's issuing a legal notice. "Just so we're clear—Luna's my not-girlfriend. Like, she's Luna. But I'm also taken. Spiritually. Emotionally. And occasionally by food."

Nora lets out a deep chuckle. "Relax, pretty boy. I like my men a little more broken-in and a lot less panicked."

Ryan snorts, stepping forward and offering his hand. "Ryan King. Beta of the Humboldt Pack. Welcome."

Nora shakes his hand with enough force to rattle his shoulder. "Nice grip," she says. "You hold a shovel or just leadership positions?"

Kai's expression flickers between impressed and alarmed. "You're terrifying. I like it."

"Good," Nora says, already turning back toward the dining room.

Luna watches the exchange like she's trapped in a sitcom that refuses to get canceled. "This is my actual life," she mutters.

From the hallway, Isabell appears, arms crossed and eyebrows raised. "Dinner twenty minutes. Miss Nora, what you drink?"

Nora looks up. "Coffee. Black. Stronger than the bullshit in this flashy town."

Ryan grins. "You'll fit right in."

SENNA

Not what she expected. No torture chamber. No cages with blood-slick floors. No bear shifter in the shadows with a vendetta.

Just cold air. Clean walls. There is nothing fancy about this room but Just a plain, large office with two more doors behind a man seated at a metal desk that's too polished to belong here.

If the devil wore cologne and kept a calendar, it'd be this guy.

Dark purple suit, grey button down shirt. No tie. A coin rolling over each finger like it's part of his blood rhythm.

"Ms. Cortez," he says without looking up. "Or do you prefer Jade?"

The name lands wrong. Not loud. Not dramatic. Just... precise.

Her wolf goes utterly still.

No one here should know that name.

Fuck. What else does he know?

She says nothing. Silence is safer than denial.

He keeps talking, allowing her time to process and assess.

Control. Cause and Effect.

"You're not like the others." He sets the coin down with a soft *clink*. "You don't fight to survive. You fight to prove you already have."

"Poetic," she mutters, not sitting.

"And dangerous," he replies. "That kind of distinction gets you noticed. Sometimes by people like me."

"Lucky me." She watches him, raw focus. "You brought me here to compliment my trauma?"

A ghost of a smile. "Hardly. I brought you to my office because I heard you were curious."

Fuck'n Jim.

"I'm in the business of opportunities. And you... just upset a very delicate balance."

"And who the fuck are you and why should I care?"

He slides something across the desk—a grainy photo.

A woman. Bound. Bruised. But alive.

Jade's breath catches. Fingers twitch.

Senna?

"What the fuck is this?" Her voice is raw, feral. "Some kind of sick game?"

She's seconds from losing it—her wolf clawing just beneath the skin, begging for blood.

"I've never cared much for games, Ms. Devereaux. Her spine goes cold.

He leans forward, finally meeting her eyes.

"My name is Darcy Vale." The full name settles between them like a verdict. "I deal in leverage," Vale says, voice smooth as silk over razor wire. "And your sister has been quite the asset."

He lets the words linger. A full beat.

A silent hammer dropping.

"Wait... what?" Jade swallows hard, bile searing up her throat.

"Oh. You didn't know she was alive?"

He rises slowly from his black wingback chair, every movement deliberate. "Oh yes, my dear Red Rock Princess, she's alive. Barely. But breathing. She's been *such* a doll—taking care of all our needs."

"You fucker."

Jade lunges, no hesitation—straight for his throat.

She doesn't see the blur until it's too late.

Impact.

Something black crashes into her from the side, breath hot and teeth bared. She hits the ground hard, air knocked out of her lungs. Claws scrape warningly across her skin—but don't pierce.

The panther looms, eyes glowing, breath slow and controlled.

It doesn't growl. It *waits*.

"You want to see her alive again?" Vale's voice floats above it all. "You'll listen."

Jade doesn't blink. Doesn't breathe.

Her wolf rages, fighting to take over, to tear and destroy and end this entire room.

She can feel her teeth sharpening. The shift is seconds away.

But Senna's face flashes behind her eyes.

She forces herself still.

She needs answers.

"You're not a human," she growls. Her voice is rougher now, soaked in wolf.

Mr. Vale chuckles—a smug, deliberate thing.

"Oh, my sweet little fury," he says. "I'm *very* human. One

hundred percent, grade-A Homo sapien."

Her gaze shifts—Vale's fingers stroke the massive cat's head like it's some prized pet.

"Oh, him?" he says, casual as hell. "That's Theo. Your shifter senses aren't wrong. He's one of yours. But I have things he wants. And so, we have an... arrangement."

He leans in, close enough that she can smell the cold on his breath. "Tonight, my dear, was just about introductions. I needed you to understand how valuable I am."

Jade opens her mouth—but doesn't get the chance.

A sting at her neck.

Then darkness.

THE RIGHT SIDE OF THE DOOR

Ryder paces like a caged animal, jaw clenched so tight he hears it crack. That fucking door hasn't opened in fifteen minutes. Maybe twenty. Maybe longer. Time gets slippery when you're this close to burning down the world.

The two guards out front? Statues. Their eyes fixed forward like good little soldiers, no hint of concern that a Red Rock wolf just walked willingly into the lion's den and hasn't come back out.

He growls low in his throat. "She should've been out by now."

Still nothing.

Then he smells it. Faint, but unmistakable.

Fear.

Not the guards. Their nerves are clean. Professional.

This is different. Sour sweat. Bad decisions. The kind that lingers.

Ryder's gaze snaps up.

There he is. The lanky one. Who kept finding reasons to

talk to her. The one who brought Jade water like it meant something.

Shifter hearing truly is a gift in some cases. Ryder heard the name once.

Jim.

The man rounds the corner, trying for casual, but his body betrays him—shoulders tight, steps too quick.

Ryder is on him in a blink, slamming him into the cold wall.

"What's behind that door?" Ryder snarls, forearm pressed across Jim's throat. "What the fuck did you send her into?"

Jim wheezes. "I told her not to go."

"That's not a fucking answer."

The guards don't move. Don't even flinch. Ryder clocks it. The message is loud and clear—Jim's not worth protecting.

The fucker chokes out a laugh. "You think you're the first to bark at the gates of hell? She walked in eyes wide open."

Ryder tightens his grip. "I swear—"

"I warned her." Jim's voice shifts—syrupy and smug, like he's reciting a bedtime story no one wants to hear. "Painted doors ain't for painted girls. But some wolves just gotta learn the hard way."

Ryder slams him again, grabbing the front of his shirt and shoving him against the wall with a thud that rattles the frame.

"What did you just say, asshole?"

Jim winces but doesn't look away. "Easy there, hoss. I'm just the guy with a mop and a memory."

Ryder's breath punches out in a sharp exhale. His wolf stirs beneath his skin, crawling up his spine. Not rage. Fear.

That old, primal kind. The kind that says *we're outnumbered. They know.*

"You said wolves." His voice drops low. Dangerous. "You don't get to say that unless you know something."

Jim tilts his head, eyes flicking toward the painted door, then back to Ryder.

"I know enough to stay out of places that aren't meant for people like me."

"What does that mean?" Ryder snaps, voice rough.

Jim shrugs, like it's out of his hands. "It means I told her not to go back there. What more d'you want from me?"

"Why?" Ryder presses. "What's behind that door?"

Silence stretches. Even the guards don't move. Just keep their eyes locked ahead, like they didn't hear a damn thing.

Jim leans in—not too close, just enough to lower his voice. "Some doors... they're not locked to keep you out. They're locked to keep something else in."

Ryder's jaw tightens. He wants to hit him again, but he can't shake the feeling that Jim's not trying to provoke him. If anything, he looks... *haunted.*

"She walked in on her own," Jim says, quieter now. "Just like I did once. I came back out. Mostly."

Ryder's nostrils flare. His eyes flick to the painted door. Then back to Jim.

"If anything happens to her—"

Jim lifts his hands. "Wasn't me who opened the door."

Ryder steps back only enough to let Jim cough. "I will burn this place to the ground if she doesn't walk out."

Jim adjusts his collar, smirking like a man who's already lost too much to care. "Then I suggest you wait and watch. Fire's coming either way."

Ryder rears back to strike—but something latches onto

him from behind. Two guards drag him off Jim with brute precision. Another crashes into him from the side, driving him into the wall. His shoulder cracks against the concrete, but the pain barely registers.

"Fuck you!" he snarls, fighting the hold. "Where is she? What did you do to her?!"

Jim doesn't answer. Doesn't even flinch.

The guards haul him backward like dead weight, boots scraping the concrete as they shove him toward the steel door.

"I swear to the fucking moon," Ryder growls, "if she's hurt—"

The door flies open. He's tossed out like trash. Hitting the pavement hard—palms scraping, air punched from his lungs.

He rolls, coughing, tasting gravel and blood. When he looks up, it's *him*. The same bastard from Wednesday.

The guy leans out the door just long enough to spit.

Ryder points. "Now you'll fucking die."

The warehouse door slams shut.

He's on his feet in seconds, eyes wild, heart pounding.

No way it ends like this.

Ryder takes off around the side of the building, boots pounding through puddles, dodging old crates and rusted barrels. Every door he finds is locked. Every window blacked out.

Until—

Something catches his eye.

A small loading dock, tucked behind a dented shipping container.

And a shape. Crumbled. Still.

No...

Ryder sprints. It's her.

Jade.

Slumped like a broken doll, half-hidden in the shadows. One arm twisted unnaturally. Her braid matted to her cheek. Her shirt's torn at the shoulder, and her neck—gods, her neck—has a mark. A deep red welt.

His stomach drops.

He crashes to his knees beside her, hands shaking as they brush her cheek.

"Jade," he breathes. "Come on, you bitch. Talk to me."

No response. He touches her neck.

Pulse there. Weak. But there. His breath shudders out of him.

And then—Ryder moves. No hesitation. No second thoughts.

He slips one arm under her knees, the other behind her back, and lifts.

Muscles coil. Flex. His entire frame tenses with restrained fury. His chest heaves, jaw locked tight. Concrete cracks faintly beneath his boot as he rises—not because of effort, but because of *power* held back by a thread.

Jade's head lolls against his chest, her body limp in his arms. But he holds her like she's the only thing anchoring him to the earth.

No more games. No more doors.

He carries her to the car, laying her gently across the passenger seat. Buckles her in—because even now, even like this, she deserves care. His hand lingers on her cheek for half a breath.

Then he straightens. Jaw clenched. Knuckles white as he grips the doorframe.

Looking back once, not at the door but at the building behind it.

Memorizing it. Marking it.

Promising it a reckoning.

The engine growls to life, headlights carving a path through the wet blackness. He turns toward the shadows, toward the road that leads back to the mansion.

Jade doesn't stir.

Ryder glances over—once, twice, again. Each time hoping for a twitch, a groan, a sarcastic insult hurled half-conscious from her lips. Anything.

But she stays silent. Still crumpled in that seat like something discarded.

He grips the wheel tighter, knuckles bleached white.

"Why are you so fucking stubborn? What did you think was in that room?" he mutters, voice cracking in the middle. "What the hell were you thinking?"

No answer, of course.

Only the hum of tires against slick asphalt. Only the tightness growing in his chest. It's taking every piece of human control to keep his wolf caged. If it were up to the wolf, there'd be nothing left breathing in that building.

His jaw ticks. "I know I'm not your damn home, Jade." Knuckles go pale against the wheel. "I'm not the one who makes the darkness back off, or the silence feel safe."

The rain hammers harder, streaking like claws across the windshield. "But you ran to them. You always do."

His voice drops, sharp and bitter. "And now look at you."

A breath. Rough. Like he's swallowing something that won't go down.

"You hate me? Fine. Deserve it, maybe." He glances over, jaw locked tight. "You don't have to want me, Jade. You don't even have to look at me. But I'll get you back to the ones who can fix what I can't."

A pause—then quieter, almost like a vow:

"Just try not to die before we get there."

The rest of the drive passes in silence. There is no peace in it. Just the hum of tires on wet asphalt, the low growl of the engine, and the thunder in his chest.

The lights of Vegas fade behind him, swallowed by desert and night.

He turns off the main road, headlights cutting through the dark as the gravel gives way to the slope he drove up only a couple of weeks ago—but it feels like a whole new lifetime.

The mansion rises like a quiet sentinel against the storm, its Mediterranean arches and pale stone catching streaks of lightning. Rain pours steady. Midnight cloaks the grounds.

But they're not alone.

Eight figures stand at the top of the circular drive—silent, unmoving, backlit by the soft golden haze spilling from the entry lights. The rain doesn't touch them. The wind doesn't sway them.

Charlotte stands at the front, hands planted on her hips, jaw set like granite. Her Alpha presence radiates so fiercely it nearly hums—commanding, unyielding, lit from within by something ancient and wild.

They didn't need a call. Didn't need an alarm. They *felt* it. And still—none of them move. Not yet.

Behind her, Luna shifts uneasily. Charlotte's jaw is tight. And Liam, soaked and tense, stares at the hotrod pulling up with the kind of stillness that only comes from fear buried deep.

Wipers sweep across the windshield in lazy arcs. Ryder kills the engine, hands still on the wheel. His eyes flick up to the house—then to the Red Rocks waiting.

He doesn't look at them long.

His attention drops to the passenger seat. To her.

"Home," he mutters under his breath. Not sure if it's for her or himself.

He's already moving.

The driver's door flings open. Rain hits him full-force. He doesn't flinch. Comes around and throws open the passenger side with a quiet urgency.

Liam steps forward, instinct taking over.

"I've got her—" *Ryder growls.*

Low. Primal. A sound ripped from somewhere deeper than instinct.

Liam freezes. So does everyone else.

Charlotte's eyes narrow. Luna tilts her head. Isabell...smiles. Just barely.

Ryder doesn't explain. He doesn't owe them one.

He slides his arms under Jade like she's already part of him. Cradles her tight against his chest. The rain hits harder, soaking through his shirt, but he doesn't care. Her head rests under his chin, and for the first time since he found her, he lets out a breath.

Not relief. Possession.

The kind that's unspoken but loud as hell to anyone watching. And they are watching.

A ripple of something unspoken passes between the women. Suspicion. Curiosity. Realization?

But none of them speak.

Ryder doesn't look at them. Doesn't offer an excuse.

He just walks—past them, up the slick stairs, and through the mansion's waiting door.

Inside, his gaze drops to the gold-and-black compass inlay on the marble floor. It gleams in the low light, still and steady. Something in his chest cracks open. His wolf howls —not in rage this time, but in raw, unfiltered relief. For the first time in days, the storm inside him stills.

She's safe. Finally.

Then the silence shatters.

"Is she breathing?"

"Where the hell was she?"

"What happened to her neck?"

"Who did this?"

"Why the fuck didn't you call us?"

"Why you?"

"Is she—?"

"Enough!"

Ryder's voice snaps across the foyer like a whip. He's still carrying Jade, boots tracking water across the tile, but every head turns toward him—frozen mid-question.

He doesn't break stride. Doesn't spare them a glance.

Straight to the game room.

He kneels and lowers her carefully onto the couch, arms lingering longer than they should. Fingers tremble before they release her shoulders.

Then he stands. Jaw tight. Eyes untamed.

"I'll answer every damn question," he growls, scanning the room. "But not until you answer mine."

Tension grips the air like a second skin.

Charlotte steps forward, slow and deliberate. Her Alpha energy coils around her like a warning—silk over steel.

"I'll forgive you this one time for raising your voice in my house," she says, cool and measured. "But only because you brought her home."

Her gaze flicks to Jade, then back to him—sharper now, calculating. "But don't mistake gratitude for grace."

He gives a tight nod. One. Nothing more.

Then Maddy steps forward, voice thin but urgent. "Charlotte, Liam... do the light thing. She needs it."

Liam reaches instinctively, hand halfway to Charlotte—

"No." Isabell's voice cuts through the room like a blade.

Ryder turns. She's still by the door, soaked from the rain, unmoving. Like she'd been waiting for this moment. Her gaze is locked on Jade, eyes sharp, unreadable—and entirely certain.

"She wake," Isabell says, not loud—but final. "No power needed."

Maddy blinks. "But she's—"

"Miss Jade strong. She hurt," Isabell cuts in, her accent thicker, firm. "But not broken."

Even Charlotte hesitates. No one argues when Isabell speaks like that. Not even Alphas.

And Ryder?

He just watches Jade's chest rise, barely moving beneath the throw someone had draped over her.

She's alive. Still breathing.

"Okay, Ryder, I need answers. So let's work this out like civilized shifters. You go first."

Charlotte's voice is calm, but the steel underneath it leaves no room for argument.

The two packs settle in—Red Rocks close together, the Humboldt loaners hanging back, wary but curious. The tension shifts, morphing into a strange, collective focus.

Ryder notices one male break from the group, slipping into the corner nearest the door. The way he stands—silent, arms crossed, eyes tracking every movement—feels practiced. Protective. Like this wasn't his first time guarding a room.

Ryder's hands curl into fists at his sides. He glances at Jade, unconscious but breathing, then turns back to the room full of waiting wolves.

"Fine. First question." Ryder's jaw ticks, voice low and rough. "Why were you all already outside?"

The room tightens.

Charlotte shifts her stance ever so slightly—barely a movement, but enough. Maddy's gaze flicks toward Isabell. Liam's brows draw tight. No one answers.

Ryder doesn't wait.

He shakes his head, scoffing under his breath. "She looked like this when I found her. Beat to hell." His hands clench at his sides. "So you'll forgive me if I'm not exactly in the mood to play twenty questions."

Charlotte steps forward, power curling around her like smoke.

"How is it that you found her, Ryder? And where exactly did you find her like that?"

His eyes cut to hers.

"That's two questions, Charlotte. And you didn't even answer mine."

Silence stretches.

They stare each other down—two storms waiting to break. Her eyes, unreadable. His, wildfire.

Then Charlotte exhales slowly. A crack in the armor.

"We were outside because Isabell said to wait."

Ryder's eyes narrow. He glances toward the tiny Latina— soaked, calm-eyed, that eerie sense of knowing too damn much.

"Why would she say that? How did she know you needed to wait? That doesn't make sense," he mutters.

Charlotte lifts her chin, a flicker of challenge in her gaze.

"That was two questions, Ryder—and you still haven't answered mine."

"Touché, she-wolf."

The tension in his shoulders doesn't ease, not fully, but something in his face gives—just a fraction.

"I found her because I've been following her." His voice

is lower now. Rough. Like the truth tastes like blood. "I always follow her."

He drops his gaze. It's not shame. It's something heavier.

And then—Luna's laugh cuts through the silence like a whip.

"Ha! I fucking *knew* it."

Ryder's eyes snap up.

Luna springs off the couch in celebration. "I told you, Maddy! That was *definitely* sexual tension." She throws a hand up to Maddy for a high five.

Ryder doesn't move. Doesn't breathe.

He's still standing there. Rain-damp. Jaw clenched.

She's hurt. And they're making jokes.

A growl rips from his throat before he even realizes it— low, feral, the kind that silences a room.

Maddy's face drops. She quickly shakes her head, wide-eyed, mouthing to Luna, *"Not now."*

But Ryder isn't looking at them. His focus is locked on Jade, unmoving on the couch. Every bruise. Every scrape. Every shallow breath. His wolf claws just beneath the surface, demanding blood, demanding silence, demanding—

Snap.

A jolt, like lightning cracking down his spine. His muscles lock. The growl dies in his throat.

What the hell—

He staggers half a step, blinking. It wasn't pain. Not quite. But it *was* power.

He turns, slow, confused—eyes locking with Charlotte.

She hasn't moved. Barely lifted a finger. But her Alpha command wraps around him like a noose.

"Not in my house." Her voice is quiet. Measured. Dangerous.

The hum of dominance lingers in the air like ozone.

Ryder's heart kicks in his chest. He's been around Alphas —fought them, bled with them—but this? This was different. He wasn't hers. But for a second, it felt like he might be.

He doesn't move. Doesn't speak. Not because he's afraid. Because he's trying to understand what the hell just happened.

Charlotte studies him. Not with judgment, but... interest. Like she's weighing a decision.

Then, she tilts her head. Just slightly. "You felt that," she says, more statement than question.

He doesn't answer. His jaw ticks. He *really* doesn't like being read.

Charlotte crosses her arms, gaze drifting toward the soaked figure still standing by the door. "You asked why we were outside. Why we knew."

Another pause. "Because she told us to wait."

Ryder follows her gaze. Isabell hasn't moved. Still watching Jade with that unnerving stillness.

"She's a witch," Charlotte says, voice even.

Ryder's eyes snap back to her.

"You're joking."

"Do I look like I'm in the mood to joke?" Charlotte asks dryly. "She's the reason we didn't panic. The reason I didn't send out a hunting party when our pack bond began to feel like we were laying on a bed of nails. Because *she* said Jade would find her way home."

Ryder's stomach turns.

Not in fear. In instinct.

Witches were supposed to be all but gone—whispers of a bloodline forced into hiding. Just like shifters. Hunted. Erased. Forgotten.

Humans tend to do that. When something scares them.

When they can't control it. The stories he grew up on didn't end with mercy.

Charlotte must see the flicker behind his eyes. "She's not what you've been taught to fear, Ryder," she says, voice softer now. "She's saved every one of us at some point."

Charlotte eases down next to Jade. Her fingers graze Jade's arm—gentle, reverent.

"Now," she says, eyes lifting, meeting his. "Where did you find her, and what do you know about how this happened to her?"

He doesn't answer right away. He can't. Because the words taste like rust in his mouth.

The image of Jade...

His jaw tightens. A slow, deliberate inhale fills his lungs. When he finally speaks, the truth tastes like iron. The secrets he's kept—following Jade into the dark, not only this time but the others—are out now. *And she's going to be pissed.*

He finishes talking, but the room stays quiet. Not the kind of quiet that settles. The kind that listens.

Charlotte's face doesn't change, but something behind her eyes does—a calculation, a shift he can't name.

Luna looks like she wants to say something but doesn't. Even she knows better now.

The only sound left is the steady tick of the rain against the windows.

Ryder drags a hand through his hair, water dripping onto the floor. The scent of blood and ozone still hangs heavy, clawing at his nerves.

He wants to move—wants to *do* something—but all he can do is stare.

Jade's breathing steadies, faint but real. That's all that matters.

He turns toward the door, the floor squeaking beneath

his boots. Every muscle feels wired tight, one bad thought away from snapping.

He pauses but doesn't look back.

"She'll come for me when she wakes," he says finally, voice low.

"Let her."

DREAMS SUCK

D arkness hums. Heavy. Familiar.
A sound like wind—or breath—pulls her under.
The fields.

Wheat swaying chest high.

Senna's laughter chasing dragonflies through gold light.

Bare feet pounding dry earth.

"Senna, hurry—" breathless, urgent. "We need to find our clothes before he gets back. He's going to be mad we tried to shift without his permission."

Senna just laughs, sun in her hair. "He won't know, Jade. No one will."

But Jade knows better. He always knows.

The air stills.

A crow cuts the sky—black wing, black omen.

Then—

A door slams. The sound folds in on itself. Light turns to concrete. Air thick with copper. The smell of blood and burnt leather.

Senna screaming. "Save me, Jade. Please, it hurts."

Running—walls that repeat, corners that trap.

"Jade! Why aren't you stopping him?"

Can't think. Only run.

Skin hits skin.

A sharp crack.

Pain blooms bright, but Senna's face stays behind her arm.

"Stop!" Senna's voice, small.

"He'll kill you this time."

Blink—

The field again. Lying on their backs, watching clouds.

Senna points at one shaped like a wolf. "That one's you," she says. "Always fighting storms."

Jade rolls her eyes, smiling anyway—until the light fades.

The wolf unravels, edges darkening, stretching.

Its open jaws blot out the sun.

Then—

The cellar.

Chains. The hiss of flame.

Her father's voice, low, patient, cruel.

"You think you're strong?"

No face—just a shadow that breathes.

"No, Father. I'm weak. I'm only good for one thing."

"That's right. I want to hear your weakness."

Metal meets skin.

The scent of burning hair.

Senna's screams dissolve into wind—

Long grass brushing her fingers, fingertips red. Blood-stained wheat sways around her.

A storm building on the horizon.

She feels it even then. The pull. The change.

"You'll always have me," Senna whispers. "No matter what he does."

Lightning—white. Jade's chest jolts.

Voices blur at the edge of hearing.

Not Senna this time. Someone else.

Calling her back.

She fights it, clinging to her sister's face until it fades into static.

Then—

Silence.

LOST

"Senna!"

Her own voice rips her out of the dark. She's upright before she understands why, heart hammering, lungs clawing for air.

Tiny, pale hands grab her shoulders. The world tilts, catches, steadies. Voices blur around her—startled, urgent.

"Easy—easy, you're safe—"

Safe. The word doesn't fit. Nothing feels safe.

Light burns through her eyelids. Walls, not stone. A blanket, not chains.

Not the cellar. Not the field.

"Senna," she whispers again, smaller this time. It barely makes it past her lips.

No answer. Just the faint hum of a fan and the rustle of movement nearby.

Her pulse won't calm. Her wolf stirs under her skin.

A shape moves at the edge of her vision.

Luna. Eyes ringed red, snow-white hair a tangled halo, her fury barely contained.

"Fuck you, Jade!"

A jolt explodes through her bicep.

Jade blinks, stunned. "What the hell—?"

Luna glares down at her, chest heaving. For someone barely five foot, she hits like a freight train.

"Damn, Luna. I don't even know where I am right now. Why are you hitting me?"

"You scared the shit out of us!"

Jade lifts her head just slightly with a hiss, there stands Charlotte, Liam, Maddy, Kai, Ryan, Jaxson, a very pissed off Isabell, and...

"I'm sorry, who are you." Jade throws her head back down on the pillow.

The stranger straightens, chin high. "Oh, I'm Nora, ma'am. Came to see if I could help the Red Rocks, in turn I get a pack that knows I'm breathing."

"How sentimental." Jade's tone is flat enough to sand wood.

Luna's voice cuts through before anyone can reply. "Okay, everyone out." She starts herding the group like a corgi on a caffeine rush. "You heard me. Jade needs to clean up and get her bearings."

Watching from the bed, Jade doesn't need a crystal ball to predict what's coming next.

Everyone single-filing toward the door. Everyone except Charlotte.

And there it is... Charlotte stays at the foot of the bed, waiting until the last boot crosses the threshold. She doesn't even look up when she speaks. "That means you too, Luna. Out."

"But Char—"

"No buts. Give us a minute. I'll be down in a minute. Get everyone in the game room."

No sound comes from Luna, but even the King of

England knows she's pouting. The door shuts, and the silence that follows feels too still.

Charlotte steps closer, the weight of her Alpha energy pressing into the space between them. "We have a lot of questions."

"Yeah," Jade says, throat dry. "I'm sure you do, Alpha."

"But I'm guessing you're pretty confused right now too. So—clean up, then meet us downstairs. We'll play twenty questions while Isabell finishes dinner."

"Okay, I've got an easy one for now." She winces, pushing herself upright. "What day is it?"

"Sunday."

"Fuck me."

Charlotte turns to leave, then hesitates. "Jade."

Looking up she sees something she doesn't see in Charlotte's face very often. Fear.

"There was something different in the bond's pain this time," Charlotte says quietly. "So I expect truth. Pure truth. No bullshit."

Jade swallows hard. Her wolf shifts restlessly inside her, uneasy.

"Yes, Alpha."

The '*Oh Shit*', that comes with the soft click of the door, is jarring.

Jade exhales, long and shaky. The kind of breath you only take when the room finally stops spinning.

Her muscles ache like she went twelve rounds with a boa constrictor.

Maybe she did. Her wolf stirs beneath her skin, restless, pacing—angry she let herself get this broken. "Yeah, join the club," she mutters.

The ceiling blurs in and out of focus. Every inhale reminds her she's still here, still bleeding, still human enough to hurt. The thought annoys her more than it should.

Dragging her fingers through her hair, she catches the tremor in her hand. Weakness. She hates it. Hates what it means.

"Invincible my ass."

Her wolf presses against the edges of her mind—defensive, protective—but there's no fight left to give. Just the dull burn of being alive when maybe she shouldn't be.

She glances at the door Charlotte disappeared through. The Alpha's words still hang in the air like a challenge.

Truth.

Pure truth.

"Yeah," she whispers. "That'll be a first."

Swinging her legs over the side of the bed, she winces. Everything hurts. Standing takes more effort than it should. But she does it anyway. Because that's what Jade does—she moves, even when it's ugly.

The voices hit her before the door does.

Low, sharp—pack voices trying to sound calm but failing miserably.

Jade leans her shoulder into the frame, eyes sweeping the room.

Every set of eyes lands on her like she's a ghost that forgot to stay dead.

"Well," she mutters, "either you missed me, or I walked into an intervention." Her gaze slides to Charlotte, voice sharpening. "So, let's skip the small talk. Who dragged me out of that hellhole?"

No one answers at first.

Charlotte exhales through her nose. "You're not going to like it."

"Fantastic. My favorite kind of news."

"It was Ryder," Charlotte says finally.

For a heartbeat, the room disappears.

The floor tilts. Her pulse spikes, wolf snarling under her skin.

"Come again?"

Luna winces. "Yeah. That was our reaction when he pulled up here."

Jade freezes. "He's here?"

Charlotte's quiet for a beat.

"Was."

The word lands heavier than it should.

Jade's stomach twists. "Define *was*."

"He brought you in, stayed long enough to make sure you were breathing, then left." Charlotte's voice is even, but there's something behind it—curiosity maybe, or caution.

"Ooookay," she says slowly. "That answer only brings more questions. How the hell did he even know where I was? I can't even process this."

She starts pacing in front of the pool table, every step a coil of frustration. Worst-case scenarios slam through her head, one after another.

That fucker's working with Mr. Vale.

Oh god. What if Ryder took Senna during the battle?

Her pulse spikes.

Jade's pacing picks up, sharp, uneven steps on cold tile.

"Okay, so he magically knew where I was. That's not suspicious at all." She feels her world darkening. She feels like she is going to pass out.

Her wolf howls under her skin.

He worked with Vale? The thought burns through her like acid.

Then another hits, worse.

Senna.

Her throat tightens. The memory of that night—the screams, the fire. Could Ryder have been there? Did he work with the Cascade's?

She never saw Senna again after that. Her pulse spikes, chest heaving.

"Oh, you son of a bitch," she whispers.

Luna's brows knit. "Uh, you okay there?"

"No." Jade's jaw locks. "But I'm about to be."

Jade's done pacing. Every muscle buzzes with the urge to kill that fucker.

"I'm going after him," she says, already halfway to the door.

Charlotte's voice cuts through the air like a blade. "Oh no, no. You'll get your time to go after him, but not right now."

The Alpha command hits before the words even finish— low, invisible pressure curling around Jade's spine, forcing her to still. Her wolf snarls in protest but can't push through it.

Charlotte steps closer, tone unshakable. "Right now, we need answers. We need to know what you got yourself into, what you brought through our door."

Jade's jaw clenches. "You think I planned this?"

"I think you couldn't get out of your own head long enough to realize how many people you put in danger," Charlotte says, voice firm but not cruel. "I think things got out of your control, and now here we are."

Routine. Control. Cause and effect.

The words hit harder than any punch she's ever taken. Jade's gaze drops to the floor, shame pressing in like gravity. The realization that she put others before the safety of her own pack burns through her chest.

Even if this trail could lead to Senna... she should've called Charlotte.

Charlotte's gaze flicks toward the ceiling. "We still have a young one in this house to protect."

Jade follows her line of sight upward—toward the second floor. The hall where Ivy and Henry's room sits.

Her anger falters for half a heartbeat, just long enough for guilt to slip in.

"Right," she mutters. "The kid."

Charlotte doesn't soften. "This isn't just about you anymore, Jade. So start talking."

Jade's jaw tightens. Then she exhales, long and shaky. "Fine. You want pure truth? You got it."

She lays it all out—the fights, the spiral she was slipping into, the anger that made her reckless. She admits she doesn't even know what triggered it, only that her wolf would finally move *when they bled in the ring*. It was like the bond between them went dead—silent—until she was in danger.

Now the hard part—*Senna*.

Her throat goes dry. "Vale mentioned Senna. He had a picture—she looked thin, frail—but it was her." The words sound like glass breaking. "He said if I wanted to see my sister again, I needed to play his game. I thought he was lying. I *need* him to be lying."

Charlotte and Luna go still.

The rest of the room follows, eyes darting like they all felt the same invisible snap.

Jade doesn't need to guess what it is—she feels it too.

The bond just shifted. And not in a good way.

Luna's voice is small. "You think she's alive?"

"I don't know." Jade rubs her temples, forcing herself to keep talking. "But I have to find out."

She tells them about Jim, the little man who kept showing up—too helpful to trust, too informed to dismiss. About the painted door, the rush, the blackout. Not every detail—just enough to make the air heavy. Saying it aloud feels worse than living it.

"Senna?" Charlotte's voice cracks. "How, Jade? We didn't recover her after the battle. We assumed she burned in the fire, but now..." The question hangs. It takes a lot to rattle Charlotte. This does it.

Jade scans the room. The males remain silent on instinct, tension rippling through them.

Liam clears his throat, the sound breaking the stillness. "Ladies," he starts carefully, voice calm and diplomatic, "clearly this is a big deal—and we're ready to help however we can—but could someone catch us up? Who exactly is Senna?"

Charlotte runs her hand over the blue flame of the water vapor fireplace—the same nervous tic she always has when things turn bad. "Senna is one of our pack sisters." A quick breath. "But she's Jade's biological sister."

"Oh, fuck."

Jade turns to see Jaxson already half-standing, ready for battle.

"Not yet, Jaxson." Charlotte throws out a hand, stopping him mid-step. "We need to do this smart. If this guy was able to get Jade in a vulnerable spot, there's no telling what he's capable of."

"Jade," Luna's voice softens, careful. "If they'd already drugged you... why are you this beat up?"

Jade glances at her arm, "Oh, these? Textbook intimidation. They wanted me to remember that they could beat me." then pointing at the split in her lip. "That I was theirs even when I couldn't fight back."

A bitter laugh escapes her. "I'm used to it. My father used to do this shit all the time."

The sound of boots on tile slices through the heavy quiet.

"Always such warm welcomes in this house," a familiar voice drawls.

Every head turns.

Jase leans against the doorframe like he's been there for half the conversation, rain still clinging to his jacket. His badge hangs from his belt, but he wears it like decoration, not authority.

Charlotte exhales hard. "You have got to be kidding me."

"Miss me?" he asks, stepping fully inside. His eyes flick to Jade, scanning the bruises with the detached precision of a man who's seen too many bodies. "Heard the Red Rocks had a little excitement. Figured I'd check in before you burned down Sin City."

Charlotte crosses her arms. "Cut the charm. How the hell do you keep showing up at the exact wrong time, Jase?"

He grins. "It's a gift."

"No, it's creepy," she fires back. "You knew about Liam in Vegas. You knew when Ryder showed up here with Ivy and the kid. So unless you've got trackers on my people—"

"Wouldn't dream of it." He steps closer, lowering his voice. "Let's just say I've got sources. And those sources tell me your favorite psychopath, Miles, is walking free tomorrow morning."

The words hang heavy, but Jade's attention snags on something else—Luna.

The tiny hacker goes statue-still, eyes locked on Jase like she's trying to read the code behind his face.

And Jase... doesn't look away. Not right away.

Interesting.

That's the second time Jade's caught that kind of static between them. Luna once mentioned that Jase was there on her darkest day. There's something between them—something only they know.

The shift in the room pulls Jade back—growls ripple under breath.

Luna mutters, "Oh, that's just fantastic."

Jade pushes off the table. Fire shoots through her ribs, sharp enough to steal her breath.

Her wolf should've started healing by now. Should've dulled the ache, closed the bruises. But nothing. Just pain and the weight of it.

She grits her teeth. "What about the Cascade Pack? Did you warn Lucas and Harper?"

He nods. "Already done. They're tightening their perimeter and expecting trouble."

Ryan's already halfway to the hall. "I'll call Spencer. I'm sure we can send a couple pack over there. Make sure they've got coverage."

Jaxson stands. "I'll go."

"Maybe not a bad idea. I'll run it past him."

Jase's gaze lingers on Jade. "You should probably sit this one out until your ribs stop protesting."

Jade narrows her eyes. "You keeping tabs on my medical report now too?"

He smirks. "Let's just say I read fast."

Charlotte steps forward, closing the space between them. "You can drop the cryptic act anytime, Jase. Because if you're playing both sides again—"

"Relax, Alpha." His tone softens just enough to sound sincere. "I'm on your side."

He turns for the door, tossing a half-smile over his shoulder. "Oh, and Jade? Next time you go off the grid, try not to start an underground war."

Jade's voice cuts through the room. "What's that supposed to mean?"

Jase pauses mid-step, clicks his cheek, and turns just enough to meet her stare. "Remember when I told you I was looking for a mole?"

The air shifts. Growls rumble low from the pack.

Jade folds her arms, ignoring the sting in her ribs. "You planning on sharing with the class, or are we doing the whole cryptic-asshole routine again?"

He smirks. "You're feisty for someone still limping."

"Answer the question, Jase." Charlotte's voice slices clean through the noise.

He sighs, like he's tired of being the smartest man in a room full of wolves. "Let's just say you stumbled into a hornet's nest. And the queen?" His mouth curves into something that's not quite a smile. "She's pissed."

Luna leans forward, curiosity flickering behind her caution. "Who's the queen?"

"That's what I'm trying to find out." His tone goes flat—unreadable. "All I know is they call her *The Shadow*. When people talk about her, they literally whisper. It's the weirdest fucking thing."

Jade folds her arms, ignoring the dull ache in her ribs. "So what does that have to do with me 'starting an underground war'?"

Jase's eyes cut to hers, sharp. "Most women who go into that room off the ring, don't come back out breathing."

He lets the words settle. "But you did. And my sources say Vale's in trouble for playing cat and mouse with you."

Jase's words hang in the air like smoke.

The Shadow.

The air shifts.

Not just tension—*the bond.*

It hums low in Jade's chest, crawling through her veins like static. Her wolf reacts first, ears pricking, ready. Then it ripples outward. She feels it brush through the others— Charlotte stiffening, Liam's hand pausing mid-gesture, Maddy's pulse spiking faintly through the thread that ties them all.

Across the room, Luna freezes. Her scent changes—fear, sharp and cold. Whatever this is, it's inside her too.

No one speaks. No one moves, except Kai.

He shifts from his spot by the wall, crossing the room in two strides, and drops into the seat beside Luna. His arm rests on the back of the couch—not touching, but close enough to steady her if she shatters.

The bond thrums once more, like a warning, then stills.

Jade's heart kicks against her ribs. Whatever that was—it wasn't just her wolf reacting.

They all felt it.

Jade narrows her eyes. *What the hell was that?*

Charlotte's voice slices through the quiet, steady and sharp enough to make the air move again.

"So who's pulling her strings, Jase? Names. I don't need myths. I need targets."

Jade feels her pulse in her ribs—each beat a throb of dull pain. Her wolf should be healing her by now. It's not. The ache is a reminder that something's still off.

Jase gives a slow shake of his head. "That's the thing, Charlotte. Nobody seems to know who she really is. Every lead dies two steps in. Anyone who digs deeper either vanishes or suddenly stops talking."

Jade folds her arms, ignoring the fire under her ribs. "So what—you're saying she's running Vale?"

"I'm saying she doesn't run anyone," Jase replies. "People orbit her until they burn up."

Across the room, Luna goes still, shoulders tightening, jaw locked.

Jade feels it again—that ripple through the pack's link. Fear. Not hers.

It hits and fades just as fast, leaving an ache where it shouldn't.

Jade's gaze cuts back to Luna, watching Kai now rub her tiny shoulder. Silent questions forming. Luna doesn't meet her eyes.

Jade exhales through her nose, pulling her eyes back to Jase. "Vale said something about my sister."

That gets his attention. "I'm sorry. Did I hear that right?"

"Senna." The name tastes like rust. "He had a photo. Said she's alive."

For once, Jase doesn't have an answer waiting. His brow creases, genuine surprise flickering through. "That's not in any report I've gotten."

Charlotte studies him. "So even your *sources* missed that."

Jase meets her gaze, steady but softer than usual. "Our files say she was—" he hesitates, the words catching in his throat, "—burned in the fire."

His jaw tightens. The shake of his head isn't just disbelief—it's *genuine shock*, the kind that ripples through the bond like static.

"If Vale's keeping a woman alive," he says finally, voice low, "it's not for charity." His eyes lift, meeting Jade's. "What's she to him?"

Jade's jaw tightens. "She's what he thinks he can use to control me."

He nods slowly, assessing. "Then he's already miscalculated. If she's alive, she's leverage—but only if you let him think she matters more than he does."

Luna leans forward, voice quiet but cutting. "You're talking about people like chess pieces again, Jase."

He shrugs. "That's the game Vale's playing."

Jade's wolf pushes under her skin, restless. *Then maybe it's time someone flipped the board.*

"So let me get this straight." She pushes off the table again, slower this time. "There's some invisible puppet master out there killing women in the ring, and Vale's scared of her?"

"Scared," Jase echoes, clicking his cheek thoughtfully. "Obsessed might be the better word. That's just what I've pieced together during the investigation."

"Then why let Jade go?" Maddy asks, almost too quietly —but it's there, steady. "If Senna's been alive this whole time, why use her now?"

She doesn't look up, shoulders curving inward like she's bracing for being wrong—but she doesn't take it back. Doesn't retreat. Jade watches the moment like it's something sacred. Small, but brave.

She's proud of her for asking.

A pause settles. Jase studies Maddy, his expression unreadable. Then his gaze shifts to Jade.

"He was playing a game he thought he could win," Jase says, voice low. "You ruined that."

Jade feels the weight of every stare swing her way.

She blinks. "What? The one time I don't kill someone, I'm still in trouble?"

A beat.

"I went into that ring ready to kill. Ready to meet my end, if that's how it went. But I didn't. I chose neither. And my wolf agreed."

"Jade," Luna whispers.

She hears the worry in it. The knowing.

They'll talk later. And Jade knows it'll hurt worse than any punch she took in that ring.

Charlotte crosses her arms, jaw tight. "Ok, we'll go into that more later."

The room sits in stunned silence. Shocked faces. Shaking heads.

Kai just looks confused, like someone handed him a jigsaw puzzle with half the pieces missing.

"Okay. Time out." He stands, starts pacing like that'll help. "So let me get this straight. Jade stumbles into some underground fight club where she meets a bad guy. A *really* bad guy. Who, for some fucking reason, is holding her sister hostage."

He swings a finger toward Jase. "Then you tell us that same asshole's in trouble with some 'Shadow bitch' because he didn't kill Jade when he had the chance?"

Kai throws up his hands. "And now somehow this ties back to your powder dealer?"

He stops, scanning the room. "Am I high? Or did we all just start living in a damn soap opera?"

"You missed Miles getting out of jail tomorrow," Jase adds casually.

"Fuck! Of course I did."

Jade almost smiles. Almost.

It's not humor—it's the insanity of it all. The sheer, spiraling mess of it.

Then Charlotte rises to her feet, serious in all the ways Kai isn't. The room shifts.

Charlotte crosses her arms, her voice steady but sharp. "If this woman's real, she's not just dangerous—she's powerful. Organized. We need to find out how deep she runs, how long she's been building this."

She nods to Jase. "When Miles gets out tomorrow—does he have to report where he's going? Any restrictions tied to his release? Or does he just walk?"

Jase doesn't answer right away. The weight of the question settles over the room.

And then Luna speaks.

"The Shadow isn't just a name, Char." Her voice is softer than usual, almost reluctant.

Everyone turns.

"She's an idea. Something people feed when they're desperate enough."

Jase tilts his head, eyes narrowing. "Funny. You say that like you've met her."

Luna's lips twitch—something caught between a smirk and a flinch. "Maybe I have."

Jade's stomach tightens. The room shrinks around them.

The air, thick with a truth no one wants to say out loud.

There's still so much they don't know—and some answers feel like they leads straight back to Luna's past.

OOOOKAY

R yder kills the headlights long before he turns onto the narrow road leading to the mansion.

He shouldn't be here.

He knows that. But he's never been good at staying away. Not from *her*.

It's probably why his pack hates him. Why they stopped pretending he'd ever choose anything over Jade—not duty, not blood, not logic.

He'd tried to get over her. Tried to bury himself in Sidney Pack business, in training, in endless patrols—anything that wasn't her face. Hell, it's why he got so damn good at tracking. He figured if he was going to be a stalker, he might as well put the skill to use.

Never worked.

Never lasted.

Even if she hates him... she's still the gravity he keeps falling toward.

A gust of wind rattles the branches overhead, and his jaw tenses. The last time he felt this kind of pull—this sick mix of want and dread—was the day he let Senna down.

Sweet Senna. He'd tried to be gentle. Tried to make it clear without breaking her.

She was standing there with her hands loosely clasped, like she didn't know what to do with them. Hay bales behind her. Dust in the air.

She looked... neat. Polished. Senna always did.

Classy, old-Hollywood pretty in a way Jade never tried to be.

But Ryder didn't think "beautiful." Not even then.

He just thought, *shit, she's really going to say this out loud, isn't she?*

"Ryder... I think— I mean, I feel like we—"

He'd cut her off gently. Or tried to.

"Senna, you're sweet. You really are. But I'm not—"

Her smile shuddered, then froze.

Something tightened behind her eyes, sharp and fast.

"You don't choose me," she said quietly.

"It's not about choosing—"

"But it is," she snapped... then immediately softened. "I mean... true mates are supposed to choose each other."

"That's what I'm trying to tell you, Senna. I'm not your true mate."

"How do you know? We're still young. Maybe your feelings haven't kicked in yet."

He remembers the hope in her eyes—too much of it, too bright.

"I do have feelings for my true mate, Senna."

He hesitates. Saying her name feels like stepping on glass.

He's doing everything he can to let her down easy. She's a good wolf. A kind one.

"But she's not you."

Her shock guts him. He drops onto the weight bench, needing something solid under him. He knows that saying who he does care for would push her straight over the edge.

"Oh. Oh—okay." She swallows hard. "It's fine. Really. I get it."

Her wolf flickered then—just a flash. Black behind gold. Almost too quick for him to be sure.

Ryder remembers stepping back.

Just a half-step.

And Senna noticed.

"It's okay," she whispered. "Just... forget this. You don't owe me anything."

When she ran, something ugly twisted in his gut.

Ryder swung at the bag hard enough to rattle the chain and send the whole rack skidding across the dirt floor. The echo cracked through the barn like a warning shot.

Not because he wanted her back. Not because he loved her.

But because watching her break felt like getting dragged behind a truck, and he hated that it bothered him at all.

He'd thought about going after her. About fixing it. About saying something decent for once in his life. But that would've been a lie. A betrayal—to her, to himself. And Ryder might be a selfish asshole, but he's not that kind of liar.

Now, parked outside the Red Rock mansion, gut knotted and breath shallow, Ryder knows he did lose his true mate that day. Jade never forgave him for not claiming Senna as his true mate.

He watches the mansion as the lights blink out one by one, each one hitting like a door slamming shut.

He should drive away.

Every rational part of him says to but he doesn't move.

He never does.

WHAT NOW?

The air shifts before the sound.

Soft. Subtle. A ripple in the night.

Jade's body tenses under the thin sheet. She doesn't open her eyes—not yet. Doesn't need to. She *feels* him.

The weight of him, standing over her bed like a storm that's finally found its way home.

She breathes in slow.

Cedar. Rain. Rage. Lust. *Him.*

It coils low in her belly like a match waiting to be struck.

When her eyes finally flutter open, the room is bathed in shadows. Moonlight filters through the corner window, slicing him into halves—predator and man. Her mouth goes dry.

"What the fuck are you doing in my room?" she murmurs, voice rough with sleep. "Sneaking in like a thief? How'd you get past all of Luna's traps?"

He doesn't move. Doesn't flinch. Just watches her with eyes that burn.

"I shouldn't be here," he says, voice low—so low it hums

inside her bones. "I came to make sure you were okay. That's all."

Jade rises, slow and fluid, the sheet slipping down her bare shoulders. Her feet touch the floor without sound. She's still in a sports bra and boyshorts, but the chill isn't what makes her shiver. It's *him*. The fact that he let her *feel* him.

"You've never done 'that's all' a day in your life."

Her hand goes to the button of his jeans.

He catches her wrist. Not hard.

Not enough.

"You don't want this."

Her gaze lifts. Cold. Knowing. "You don't get to tell me what I want."

His jaw tightens, that beautiful rage simmering under restraint. "I came to take care of you. That's it. Just tonight. And then you'll never have to see me again."

She smiles—sharp and dangerous. "Perfect."

Her fingers work his zipper down with maddening precision. He doesn't stop her. *Good boy.*

The sound of denim sliding open is louder than it should be. The only sound in the room aside from the ragged hitch of his breath.

She doesn't break eye contact. Not once.

Her fingers find him—hot, hard, already betraying every word from his mouth. She frees him from his jeans, her hand wrapping around the base like she owns him.

Because maybe she does.

Ryder exhales through clenched teeth. "Jade..."

She doesn't answer.

She drops to her knees and takes him in one smooth motion, never once looking away. Her mouth is hot, lips soft, rhythm merciless. His hands twitch at his sides, then fist in the air like he's trying not to grab her hair and lose all sense of himself.

"Fuck—"

It's barely a whisper, like the word escaped without permission.

She sucks harder.

His head tips back—just for a second—like he's unraveling. Like her mouth stripped him down to something primal. But then his gaze crashes back to hers—amber eyes wild and glassy, clinging to the last threads of control like a man about to drown. His curls—darker now, streaked with silver—cling to his forehead, damp with sweat. Still infuriatingly beautiful.

She sees it.

The war behind his eyes. Hunger battling guilt. Restraint shredded by need. His body fights the pleasure like it's betrayal—but it's losing.

Fast.

He trembles now, a sound tearing out of him—half groan, half growl—raw and involuntary. It hits her deep, coiling hot and low, curling her toes against the cold floor.

She doesn't stop.

God, she *won't* stop.

The way his fists slam the edge of the dresser, bottles rattling from the force, makes her stomach flip. Like he's trying to hold onto the world with splintering hands.

It's intoxicating.

The way he's breaking.

For her.

She watches the storm in his eyes, the panic, the lust, the pleading. His jaw clenched like he's fighting to keep breathing. And through it all—he keeps looking at her.

And she doesn't blink.

Not once.

She moans low in her throat, sending vibration after vibration through him, and his knees nearly buckle.

"Jade…"

It's broken now. Pleading.

And she likes it that way.

Her eyes snap open.

Room still.

Bed cold.

Sunlight crawling across the ceiling.

A beat of silence. Then—

"JADE!"

The voice rips through her head like a paper shredder.

Jade blinks. Hard. Bolting upright, heart slamming against her ribs. Sweat slicks her spine. Her thighs are damp. Her jaw aches. Her pulse refuses to settle.

She drags a hand down her face.

"Motherf—"

"I am so pissed at you!"

Luna's voice again, sharper this time—like she *knows*. Like she just yanked Jade out of sin and smoke on purpose.

"What were you thinking?"

Jade flops back against the mattress with a groan, dragging a forearm over her eyes and throwing daggers at the ceiling.

"Luna, give me a damn minute. You can't just bust in and rip a girl a new asshole straight out of a dream."

What.

The.

Fuck.

Because in this moment, she doesn't know what's worse —that it was a dream. Or that she wants it to be real.

Silence. One beat. Then another.

Luna's voice drops, still annoyed but curious now. "Was it *him* again?"

Jade doesn't answer. Doesn't move. Just lets the question hang there like smoke she doesn't want to exhale.

Luna scoffs, "You've got it bad."

"What the fuck are you even talking about," Jade fires back, too fast, too defensive.

"You're sweating and your hair looks like sex happened."

"No one's hair looks like sex *during* sex," Jade mutters. "This is post-combat dream trauma. Not the same."

Luna's footsteps approach. "You moaned his name."

Jade bolts upright, pillow flying. "I did *not!*"

"You *did*. It echoed." Luna leans in the doorway, arms crossed. "I was downstairs."

Jade glares at her. "You were not. And I did not."

Luna smirks. "Nah I wasn't, but you did."

Jade mutters under her breath, swinging her legs off the bed. "If I punch you, it's because I love you."

They both know this isn't the first Ryder dream.

And considering the years they spent sharing a room, Luna is *fully* aware that Jade's deep-rooted hate for Ryder has always come with a side of something else. Something hotter. Messier.

"You're just mad I interrupted the Ryder Show," Luna says, grinning like the smug little shit she is.

Jade glares at her. "I swear to God, Luna, one more word and I will make you pee glitter for a week."

"Ohhh, I love glitter."

Jade grabs the nearest pillow and launches it. "OUT."

But there's color in her cheeks. And her heart's still not slowing down.

"Don't we have bigger fish to fry?" Jade grumbles, dragging herself toward the closet. She yanks open the door and reaches for the comfort section—yoga pants and an over-sized T-shirt. The combat gear on the other side can fuck right off.

"Yes," Luna says, already following her with way too much pep for someone who just kicked in the door to Jade's orgasm. "Charlotte said we're going over everything at breakfast."

Jade freezes halfway through tugging on the shirt.

Luna smirks. "Isabell made your least favorite. She says she's mad at you too."

The smell hits her halfway down the hall—melted cheese, caramelized onions, a hint of crisped tortilla.

Jade slows her pace. "You said *least* favorite."

"I lied," Luna chirps, smug as hell.

Jade's glare could crack tile. "You're dead to me."

"Mm-hmm," Luna hums, unfazed, already rounding the corner toward the kitchen.

The dining room is alive with motion. The lazy Susan spins slow and steady, dishing out piping-hot breakfast quesadillas on mismatched plates, each one cut into perfect triangles. Someone's already taken a bite out of one—probably Kai. A fresh pot of coffee gurgles in the corner like a damn siren song, and the air is thick with the smell of roasted beans and frying butter.

Jade's stomach growls on cue.

Isabell stands at the head of the table like a culinary war general, arms crossed, eyebrow arched.

"No pienses que te libras," she says flatly, nodding at the plate already marked with Jade's chipped green mug and a napkin folded like a peace treaty.

Jade flops into her chair, rubbing at her face. "I won't even ask what you said Isabell. You didn't have to make my favorite."

"I *didn't*," Isabell snaps, turning away. "I make their favorite. Sit down. Shut up."

Luna plops down beside her, spinning the lazy Susan like a roulette wheel. "She loves you."

Jade grabs the coffee pot before it can be moved, fills her mug to the brim. "I know."

Steam curls upward. She breathes it in like it might fix her. And for a second, it almost does.

She lifts a quesadilla wedge from her plate, hot and greasy, cheese stretching just long enough to make a mess of her fingers. She bites in, and it's perfect—crunch, heat, spice. A distraction wrapped in carbs.

Her eyes meet Isabell's across the table. The witch nods once. Just once.

It's not forgiveness.

It's relief.

The second quesadilla wedge is halfway to her mouth when the room quiets.

Not in a dramatic, slam-your-glass-down kind of way— no, Charlotte doesn't need theatrics. She just straightens in her chair, clears her throat, and somehow the volume cuts like someone hit pause.

Jade doesn't even have to look. She feels it—Charlotte reclaiming gravity like a goddamn planet.

"We'll keep this quick," Charlotte says, voice smooth but firm. "We've got a long day ahead of us, and I want everyone clear on where we stand."

Jade chews slower, her appetite shriveling a little. There's a tension crawling under the table now, quiet but alive—like something's about to shift.

Charlotte's eyes sweep slowly around the table, taking in each of them before she speaks.

"We don't know what Miles will do or where he'll go.

The mansion needs to stay protected, but we also need Harper and Lucas covered." She sets her coffee cup down with a quiet tap, the sound cutting through the hum of the Lazy Susan.

"Jaxson will head out after breakfast to the Cascade territory. Spencer is sending four more guys as well. They're still trying to stabilize the pack, and Lucas is worried there may be defectors... maybe even traitors if Miles shows up."

She inhales, steadying herself. "And that's just the first order of business."

Jade sets the quesadilla wedge down, fingers sticky with cheese...and guilt.

She already knows where Charlotte is heading next. Her selfishness. Her silence. Every one of them has a reason to be pissed at her.

But fuck. All that could be leading to Senna.

A gentle nudge taps her knee under the table—Luna. Light, steady, grounding.

Jade doesn't look up. *Not yet.*

She keeps her eyes pinned to her orange juice like it might have the answers she refuses to say out loud.

Thanks orange juice.

A flicker of something cold brushes her spine—memory or warning, she can't tell. Senna's name sits heavy behind her ribs, right where it's been since last night.

"As for the other business..." Jade exhales, the words tasting like sand. "I owe all of you an apology. I went to a place I couldn't take you with me. Hell, I didn't even want to be there myself, but I guess that's what spirals do. They grab you, and every spin pulls you into a darker level."

She forces herself to look up, meeting each set of eyes before landing on Ivy.

"Ivy... I feel the worst about putting you and Henry at

risk. You came here for safety, and somehow I've dragged us into something none of us can explain."

"I think we're okay. We live with a witch now."

Ivy's soft, lighthearted voice slips into the tension and cracks it open just enough for air.

Jade pulls in a slow breath. The tight burn climbs up the back of her jaw, threatening to spill into something she refuses to feel.

Crying is for humans. Not her.

Not today.

Luna's chair screeches against the floor as she shoves it back. "Fine. I accept your apology. But all this means you have to go back there, Jade—and I'm still fucking pissed."

Pacing in front of the blue coffee credenza , energy snapping off her like sparks. "I mean it's Senna. We have to go get her right Alpha?"

Charlotte goes silent, but Jade feels her looking. That sharp, Alpha-assessing stare crawls down her spine, measuring every cracked edge Jade hasn't managed to hide yet.

Jade's stomach drops. Of course this was coming.

Senna changes everything—and it pisses her off.

There's no snapping out of the spiral, no "lesson learned," no clean reset.

Senna's name doesn't pull her up from the dark—it welds her to it, locks her right back inside the place she's been clawing her way out of. She's not in the ring anymore, but she's still fighting.

Different cage. Same teeth.

And Vale?

He opened a door she didn't ask for, didn't want... but now she can't unsee what's behind it.

Can't *unfeel* the pull.

There is no pretending she isn't part of whatever game he's playing with her sister.

That truth sits hot in her chest—anger, fear, and something sharper, something stupidly close to hope—all of it snarled together and impossible to shake loose.

Her chest grows tight with her wolfs howl. *Yeah I know wolf.*

Charlotte finally speaks.

"Charging in isn't an option. Vale isn't some street-level thug. He's controlled, meticulous, and we still don't know how deep his operation runs." Charlotte's voice stays steady until it doesn't. "We have no idea who this Shadow bitch is or how she ties into any of it—and is the powder in play?"

Her voice spikes on that last part, fear bleeding through the Alpha calm. Her eyes cut to Jade. "Is that what took you out?"

Luna whirls around. "So what? We just sit here while he has her?"

"No," Charlotte says, firm enough to freeze Luna mid-step. "But we're not sending Jade back in blind."

She flicks a look at Luna—pointed, knowing. "What hacking have you already done?"

Luna opens her mouth, but Charlotte's hand snaps up.

"And sit the fuck down. You're making my hair nervous."

Luna drops into her chair with a huff, legs bouncing immediately. "I dug as much as I could. There isn't much out there. I mean—it's underground shit. No clean data trail, no obvious network, no chatter on the boards I usually scrape." She runs a hand through her hair, fingers twitching. "The Shadow keeps everything off-grid. Like, obsessively. Whoever she is, she knows how to stay unfindable."

Charlotte's gaze slices back to Jade. "Great."

Jade exhales through her nose, jaw tight. "So we're going in blind."

"No," Luna snaps, leaning forward. "Just blind-ish. There's enough smoke to guess where the fire is. The disappearances, the backdoor broker deals, the shifter trafficking threads—Vale's name pops up around all of it. The Shadow pops up but not with him or any of it just... Around."

Maddy murmurs around her eggs, "She's the center, like Jase said."

Luna nods hard. "Exactly. It's like she moves through his world but never leaves a footprint."

Charlotte folds her arms. "So what you're telling me is we have two ghosts—Vale and this Shadow—and Jade has already walked straight into one of them."

Luna's jaw ticks. "And we have to walk in after her. We have to go after Senna."

Charlotte doesn't flinch. "Yes. But not stupidly."

"Define stupidly," Jade mutters.

"Letting you charge in alone," Charlotte fires back.

Jade bristles. "She's my sister."

"And Vale is a professional," Charlotte says, voice steady.

"And so am I!" Jade's shout cracks through the dining room, ricocheting off the walls.

Everyone freezes. No one breathes—except Charlotte.

Jade watches as Charlotte gains composure. "He clearly sets traps Jade. And now we know Senna was bait in one of them. We need to know everything we can, so we can safely bring her home."

Luna flinches, but it's Jade who goes still.

Charlotte softens—barely. "What we need is intel. Real intel. More than pops on a screen. More than shadow-chasing, no pun intended. We need an entry point that isn't walking ourselves into a cage."

Luna leans forward. "So what's the move?"

"No one in Vegas knows me."

Jade glances at the stranger—blond-gray hair falling in a messy frame around her face. She hadn't noticed it before, but the woman's pretty in that *I'll fuck you up and then bake you cookies* kind of way.

"Vale expects me. That's the problem." Jade pushes, needing this to be *her* fight.

"Or the advantage," Ryan murmurs from across the table. "He already opened the door for you but if Nora goes too, he wouldn't see Nora coming."

"If he's any good at all, he already knows everything about the Red Rocks—who each of us are and what our strengths are. So sending a stranger..." Liam finally interjects, "is a good call."

Jade stiffens. "I'm not letting anyone else walk into that place for me."

Luna snorts. "It isn't for you. It's for Senna. And for the record? You're the one person who *shouldn't* go in alone. You can barely say her name without folding."

Jade's jaw ticks. Hard.

Charlotte lifts a hand, silencing them both.

"We have two paths," she says. "Either Jade goes back and plays Vale's game—controlled, with Nora as backup, and with a clear exit strategy..."

Her gaze slides to Nora. "Or we send Nora. You volunteered. He won't connect her to Jade, and he'll underestimate you."

"Thanks for the confidence, Charlotte." Nora nods once. "And most folks underestimate me. City people don't know what it takes to run a ranch through winter."

"That's for damn sure." Charlotte gives her a respectful nod.

Luna folds her arms. "Well, we all know option one is exactly what Jade wants—minus the Nora part."

Jade's glare is immediate. "You don't get to speak for me."

"Why not?" Luna snaps. "Someone has to. Your silence is how we ended up in this mess."

Jade inhales sharply. Senna's name pulses behind her ribs like a bruise.

Charlotte leans forward, voice low.

"We're not deciding this on emotion, Luna. Not yours... and not Jade's."

Silence drops. She lets it hang.

MURDERED QUESADILLA

The tray balances against her hip as she nudges the door open with her elbow. Breakfast quesadillas, extra crispy.

Are they supposed to be 'that' black? Hmm, *Probably not.*

But she cooked them herself—a peace offering she probably should've left to Isabell—and the mug of black coffee sloshes dangerously in its cup. Figures. She could never carry a tray right at the diner either.

Chill air rushes out to meet her, the mild hum and flicker of Luna's neon setup washing the hallway shadows off her skin.

The office is exactly how Jade remembers it. The last time she stood in this room was the night Lucas was taken. It was intimidating watching her tiny friend do what she does. Jade forgets sometimes how powerful Luna really is—and the source of that power doesn't comes from the mess of monitors in front of her.

Glowing screens are stacked like a hacker's altar. Four mounted high, four smaller below, each running something different—security feeds, scrolling code, some grainy news channel no one actually watches. A restless swirl of motion and light, all orbiting around the tiny, furious woman in the oversized pink swivel chair.

Luna doesn't look away from the main monitor when Jade steps in. Her white hair spills over the backrest like moonlight, arrow-straight. Her purple eyes stay fixed forward, jaw tight enough Jade can *hear* the clench.

Jade exhales and shuts the door behind her. "Hey, bitch. How long are you going to be mad at me?"

Luna's fingers freeze above her keyboard.

The silence that follows is brutal.

Slowly, Luna swivels just enough to glare over her shoulder—small but sharp, like a blade made of sugar and spite.

"Oh, I don't know," she says. "How long were you planning on disappearing without telling me? Should I match that? Because if we're keeping score, I think you still owe me several days."

Jade sets the tray down on Luna's desk, the mug rattling lightly against a stack of hot-pink sticky notes. "I didn't disappear."

"You didn't *not* disappear," Luna fires back. She flicks her hand toward one of the screens, where a map pulses with red dots. "Do you know what it's like tracking everyone else's drama except the one person who actually needed help?"

Jade rubs the back of her neck. Her wolf rises just enough to press against her ribs—a quiet, guilty presence she hasn't felt in weeks.

"I didn't want to drag you into my shit."

"Bullshit." Luna pushes her chair back and stands up—shorter than Jade by almost a foot, but somehow taking up twice the emotional space. "You didn't tell me because you didn't want to be *seen*. Not by me. Not by anyone."

Jade swallows hard. The words hit clean, no mercy.

Luna folds her arms. "You think I'm mad because you went to the fights?" A shake of her head. "I'm mad because you didn't trust me enough to ask for help. Jade... you didn't even trust me enough to say where you were, even when I asked point blank."

The coffee's steam curls between them.

"And that's what hurts."

Jade twists and sets the tray down with a clank. Before she can second-guess it, she pulls Luna into her arms.

Jade isn't the touchy type—never has been—but damn if this doesn't feel good. Luna melts into the hug, small and fierce and familiar. Hurting her... that's worse than anything Jade faced in that underground darkness.

"Okay, okay—fine." Luna's voice is muffled against Jade's chest. "I'll only be mad for... two more minutes."

Jade still doesn't let her go. Instead she pulls in a deep breath, letting the familiar scent settle her. Luna. Safety.

"Bitch, I can't breathe through your tits."

Jade snorts and finally loosens her hold. "Right. Sorry."

Luna steps back, smoothing her hair with exaggerated offense.

"So... what was decided?"

Jade exhales, jaw tight. "I guess I go with Nora as backup. I don't like it, though. I don't want someone else getting hurt. Especially someone we just met."

Luna stares at her for a beat, then lifts a brow. "Interesting."

"What?"

"You're saying all the reasonable words," Luna says, circling a finger in the air, "but your face? Your face is doing... feelings."

Jade snorts. "I always have feelings."

"No," Luna deadpans. "You have reactions. Violent, impulsive, sometimes... concerning reactions."

Jade shrugs. "Still feelings."

"Mm-hmm." Luna's lips twitch. "Not even remotely." Luna gestures at the tray like it personally attacked her. "And what is *this*? Because I'm not eating that. That looks like a crime scene."

"It's a quesadilla."

"It's a *murdered* quesadilla."

"I did the best I could," Jade mutters.

"I love you, babes, but your best is a hate-crime against tortillas."

Luna pokes the plate with one finger, then points at the mug. "And where is the creamer? You know I take my coffee as pale as *me*. This is... black. Like actual black."

"You drink caffeine," Jade says. "I brought caffeine."

"Yeah, but I'm not trying to summon demons with it." Luna shoves the mug into Jade's hands. "Fix it. I can feel my soul shriveling."

Jade laughs—actually laughs—and the tension between them cracks, just a little.

OH, FOR FUCKS SAKE

The bell over the diner door gives its usual half-hearted jingle as Jade pushes inside. Same cracked red vinyl booths. Same fry-scented air. Same server who pretends not to notice Jade's bruises but always brings extra napkins anyway.

It's not comfort food. It's ritual. Neutral ground. The last square of normal before everything tilts sideways.

She orders the burger and fries without thinking.

The server pours her coffee and hesitates. "Rough day?"

"Wednesday," Jade says simply.

The woman nods like that's explanation enough.

Luna had pushed—hard—for Charlotte and Liam to do their little light-dance healing thing on her. But everyone else agreed the bruises should stay.

No glowing miracles. No suspiciously perfect skin.

Vale can't suspect she's anything other than a tough woman who knows how to take a hit.

She flexes her fingers around the cup, feeling the stiffness pull through her knuckles. Good. Real. Believable.

The server slides the plate in front of her—burger, fries,

extra napkins like always. Jade murmurs a thanks she doesn't actually feel but knows the woman deserves anyway.

A beat of quiet settles. Neon buzzes outside. Someone laughs too loud at the counter. Jade lets the noise wash over her, pretending it fills the cracks she's been ignoring.

Any other Wednesday, this would be the part where she finishes her meal, pays her tab, and walks into the underground ready to bleed a little.

But now there's Nora.

And Jade hates—*hates*—that she's responsible for someone else getting dragged into her spiral.

She pops a fry into her mouth, jaw tense.

Routine. Control. Cause and effect.

She repeats it like a mantra, hoping it still works.

Routine. Control. Cause and effect.

The drive out toward the warehouse of pain and suffering should feel automatic by now. Same turns. Same busted streetlights. Same pothole she steers around without thinking.

Tonight, her brain doesn't cooperate.

Senna's face keeps flashing in the windshield reflection. Not the way Jade last saw her—blood, smoke, and chaos—but younger. Laughing. That shy, guarded smile Jade used to bully out of her with stupid jokes and shoulder bumps.

You promised I'd be safe.

Jade tightens her grip on the wheel until her knuckles ache.

Routine. Control. Cause and effect.

If she'd pulled Senna sooner, pushed harder, done... something different...

The thought snags like barbed wire, tearing as it goes. She shoves it down deep, where all the other useless what-ifs live.

By the time she turns down the cracked side road toward the warehouse, her heartbeat has settled into that familiar pre-fight thrum. Not calm. Never calm. Just focused. Contained.

She parks in the same gravel rut as always. Kills the engine. Lets the silence press in for one breath, then two.

You're not that girl anymore.

You're the one who walks in and walks back out.

Jade climbs out, boots crunching over gravel. The warehouse squats at the end of the lot, all rust and shadows and humming generators. Music throbs faintly under the ground, bass pulsing like a second heartbeat.

Routine.

She moves toward the chain-link gap she always slips through.

Someone's there.

He straightens as she approaches, gaze tracking her in a way that feels... assessing.

Not checking her out.

Measuring.

Jade keeps her expression bored, lazy even. "You're blocking my hole."

His mouth twitches, almost a smile. Eyes stay flat. Sharp. The kind of eyes that catalog things and file them away.

"You Jade?" he asks.

Every instinct flares.

Nobody uses that name here. So he must be one of Vale's guys.

"Depends who's asking," she says, shifting her weight like she's just impatient, not coiled tight.

He looks her over, gaze lingering a fraction too long on her ribs, her hands, her stance. On the bruises everyone voted to keep.

"Tony said to let you through." He jerks his chin toward the gap. "New rules. Fighters get checked in at the door now. Name, weight class, all that."

Her skin prickles. "Since when?"

"Since tonight."

Of course.

Control.

She reminds herself of the word and tries to make it true.

"Sounds official." She steps closer, close enough to smell his cologne under the metallic tang of the lot. "You write it all down in a little notebook or just keep it in that big head?"

He doesn't rise to it. "Just go inside, Jade."

There it is again. Her name. Clean and precise, like it's printed somewhere she didn't sign off on.

She stops just shy of the fence gap, tilting her head. "So you need my info or what? Name? Weight class?" A lazy shrug. "Blood type?"

His eyes flick—barely. But she sees it.

"You?" he says, voice flat. "No. I've got everything I need to know about you."

A chill slides down her spine, slow and unwelcome.

"Yeah?" She forces a smirk. "Hope it's flattering."

He doesn't blink. "It's thorough."

Thorough. Not good. Not safe.

Jade rolls her shoulders like the answer doesn't bother her, even though her pulse kicks harder.

Routine. Control. Cause and effect.

She steps past him, slipping through the gap in the fence, refusing to let him see her hesitate.

Behind her, she can *feel* his stare. Not curious. Documenting. Annotating. Waiting.

The warehouse door comes into view—big sheet metal

thing spray-painted and dented from a thousand fists and boots. Normally George sits on his stool beside it. Tonight? No George.

Jade slows half a step. That's all she allows.

A different guy from the fence—but dressed the same—steps ahead and yanks the door open without a word, like he's been waiting.

No password. No code. No challenge. Just open.

Jade's stomach tightens, but she nods once—neutral, unimpressed—and walks through.

Bright light slams into her first, sharp enough to make her blink.

Seriously—why is it so fucking bright in a place meant for violence?

Floodlights glare down on exposed beams and a chaotic tangle of extension cords. Metal scaffolding towers overhead like a giant got bored halfway through building a second floor.

Sweat. Cheap cologne. Blood already drying somewhere.

Her body remembers it all before her brain does.

Then—across the room—she spots her.

Nora. Sitting on the bench, elbows on her knees, eyes darting but alive.

Relief hits Jade so hard it's almost dizzying.

She's in.

Thank god the password didn't change.

Routine. Some of it is still routine.

Jade heads toward her, weaving through fighters warming up and spectators pretending not to stare at her too long. The energy feels off tonight—tighter, thinner, like the air itself is bracing.

She's halfway to Nora when a shape pops into her peripheral vision.

"Cortez!"

Oh, for fucks sake. Jim.

That little fucker materializes like he crawled out of the vents—hoodie half-zipped, hair sticking up like static, eyes too bright for the low light. He smells faintly of sugar, motor oil, and poor decisions.

Of course he shows up now.

He blocks her path with a grin that's either friendly or a threat. With Jim, there's no real difference.

"You walk in without the magic word?" he asks, voice sing-songy.

"Door was open." Jade keeps her tone flat. "You gonna tell me that means something?"

"Ohhh, everything means something." Jim wiggles his fingers like he's sprinkling psychic dust. "But you already know that. Don't you?"

Jade stares at him. "Jim, if you don't stop talking in riddles, I'm going to staple your hoodie to the wall."

He beams. "See? That's the attitude that keeps you alive."

"Is that a warning?"

He leans closer, lowering his voice just enough.

"Things changed tonight. You feel it?"

"I don't feel anything." Jade deadpans.

Jim tilts his head.

"No feelings? Then why's your heartbeat arguing with you?"

She blinks—and he's gone.

How the fuck does he do that?

Jade forces her shoulders down as she moves through the crowd—slow enough not to look eager, fast enough not to look weak. Bodies shift around her, murmurs rising. A few men follow her with their eyes longer than she likes.

She ignores all of them.

Nora sits on the bench, hunched slightly forward, hands wrapped around her own elbows like she's trying to contain herself. New face. New scent. A quiet kind of fear she's working way too hard to hide.

Good. Jade can work with quiet.

Chaos... not so much.

Nora glances up as Jade approaches, surprise flickering across her features—then relief, though she tries to smother it.

"I really hope I don't have to fight you," she murmurs, tucking a loose strand of hair behind her ear.

Jade sits beside her without touching, elbows on her knees. "Isn't fighting why you're here?"

Nora swallows. "Sure. But... I don't know. You look like you've done this before."

Jade shrugs one shoulder. "And you look like you haven't."

Nora lets out a quiet, shaky laugh. "That obvious?"

"Only to someone who's been in your shoes." Jade studies her—built like someone who's had to move her own mountains, strong everywhere it counts, hands tense, eyes darting like she's memorizing exits. Finally she asks, "Why not me?"

Nora hesitates, then answers honestly. "Because I don't want to get hurt before I even start. And you look like you'd make that happen fast."

Jade snorts softly. "Smart."

Nora's gaze drops to her own fists. "I'm not here to win. I'm here to survive." She pauses. "Sometimes that's different."

Jade's jaw softens a fraction—barely noticeable unless you're watching. "Yeah. It is."

For a moment, they sit in a thin pocket of quiet between floodlights and noise—two strangers choosing honesty because everything else around them is built on lies.

Before Nora can say anything else, the air shifts.

Oh yay. Ratface.

Tony squeezes through a cluster of fighters with a grin that belongs on a rodent stealing someone's leftovers. Same greasy hair. Same too-small eyes. Same fake confidence on a body that's never thrown a punch in his life.

"Ladies." He says it like he invented the word. "Didn't know we were having a two-for-one special tonight."

Nora stiffens. Jade doesn't blink.

Tony's gaze slides between them, lingering on Jade's ribs, her posture, the bruises Luna begged Charlotte not to heal.

Then he smirks.

"You're early," he tells Jade. "Usually you show up right before your name gets called. What's the occasion?" His eyes flick to Nora. "Bringing a friend?"

Jade's voice stays flat. "Never seen her before today."

Nora's jaw ticks—like she clicked into her natural protection mode.

Tony chuckles, rubbing his hands together like he's already counting money.

"Well, don't get too cozy. Looks like the lineup changed." His grin widens. "New rules tonight. New matchups. New eyes watching."

Nora shifts uneasily. "What does that mean?"

Tony shrugs, enjoying the little ripple of tension he's creating.

"Means you two better be ready. You got bumped up the card."

Jade narrows her gaze. "Why?"

That ratty little smile sharpens. "Don't know. Don't care. I just do what I'm told."

Then he points lazily toward the ring. "It won't be long." Turning, Tony disappears into the crowd like a sewer rat that found a new tunnel.

Nora pulls a face—eyebrows up, lips curled like she just smelled old milk. "Is he always... like that?"

Jade watches Tony vanish.

"No. He's usually worse."

From the other side of the ring the chic with the clipboard rattles off names like she's calling inventory, and Nora freezes—not from fear, but from calculation. Her chin lifts and shoulders square.

Jade sees it.

That's not panic. That's someone who's been preparing her whole damn life for things to go wrong.

"Don't overthink it," Jade murmurs. "And don't let them see you flinch."

Nora nods once and heads toward the ring.

The crowd shifts when she steps in—not cheering, not mocking.

Watching.

Jade's stomach tightens.

They're not watching Nora. They're watching *whoever stands with Jade.*

Nora's opponent is a thick, bald bitch with arms like tree trunks. The kind of man who fights because nothing else in his life works. The kind who expects easy wins.

He doesn't get one.

Nora moves like she's been carrying weight her whole life—strong, steady, unshaken.

She takes a hit early, absorbs it, adjusts.

Cautious. Measured. Smart.

Jade finds herself leaning forward, lips parting despite the noise around her.

Nora isn't afraid. She's learning him. She's finding her openings. She's surviving.

The crowd murmurs when she lands her first real hit.

A solid one. Right to the jaw. The man staggers.

Nora doesn't rush. She waits.

The second hit comes clean. The third sends him collapsing.

It's not flashy. It's not violent. It's efficient. Controlled.

Exactly how Nora said she would fight.

Tony whistles low from the edge of the ring, impressed despite himself.

That's right. Take notice of her.

Jade watches Nora straighten, chest rising, eyes scanning the crowd like she already knows she's being observed.

Because she is. Something shifts—subtle but real. A ripple of attention. A hum under the floodlights. Like the room just decided Nora is... interesting.

Nora returns to the bench, sits, and exhales once— steady, controlled.

"Still alive," she says, barely loud enough to register. Jade hears it anyway, threaded under the roar of the crowd. A soft line meant for no one in particular.

No one saw her. That was her whole reason for wanting the Red Rocks.

And now?

People are seeing her in the one place they shouldn't.

Nora is still catching her breath when the crowd shifts again—this time with purpose.

Jade notices first. A ripple. A path opening. Not for a fighter. Not for Tony.

The man pushes through the bodies wearing a charcoal

suit like it's armor, shiny boots, and the same red rope wrapped tight around his right hand.

He walks like he owns everything the light touches. And he's walking straight toward her.

Jade keeps her posture loose, uninterested, even as her pulse punches harder. She knows this is why she's here, why she walked into this hell again—but if the unknown behind that door isn't scary? She has no idea what would be.

He stops in front of her—too close to be polite, too calm to be safe.

"Devereaux."

Fuck. My last name?

Jade doesn't answer.

He nods toward the far wall.

The last time she went through that door she came out barely breathing—and with the first whisper of new information about her supposedly dead sister.

"Come with me." Not a request.

Jade doesn't move. "Oh, tell him not tonight. I'm not in the mood."

He smiles—thin, unreadable, predatory.

"You are now."

Jade breathes once, sharp and steady, then moves.

One step. Then another.

She walks because she refuses to be led.

The painted door waits, humming with old ghosts.

The door shuts behind her with a heavy click. Not a slam—just firm.

Same as before the cold air hits her first, crawling across her skin like fingers dipped in ice. The room is exactly as she remembers it, which somehow makes it worse.

White walls, too clean. The smell of bleach so faint that a human wouldn't smell it.

A gray rug cuts across the floor in a perfect rectangle—no stains, no fraying edges, no sign that anyone with blood on their hands has ever walked across it. Which is bullshit, because Jade knows damn well they have.

At the center sits the metal desk—polished within an inch of its life, the surface reflecting the overhead light like a blade. Files are stacked in a neat, obsessive line. Crisp folders. Sharp corners. Not a single page out of place.

She's pretty sure her name is in one of them. Or all of them.

There's one picture frame on the desk sitting just below the computer monitor, turned away from her.

Jade stares at the back of it and wonders, what horrors it shows.

She doesn't move to quench her curiosity, she won't give him the satisfaction.

The man with the stupid red cord around his hand stands perfectly centered between the two doors behind the desk.

She stands there with her arms loose, weight evenly distributed, body relaxed but ready.

Waiting.

Because Vale wants her waiting. This is part of the game.

Men are so stupid.

The silence stretches, tightens, winds around her ribs like barbed wire.

Jade clears her throat softly.

"So... any chance I can order a quesadilla? Not burnt this time. Last one I had could've won a contract with Kingsford."

He doesn't answer her.

"No? No outside food allowed?"

A soft click to the left grabs her attention. Holding her breath for a split second.

Dark leather boots, worn only where the weight of his body demands it.

Measured steps.

Command dripping with every inch of movement.

Then the suit—dark, fitted, immaculate. This time he carries a black cane with a silver wolf head at the top.

And finally—

Vale lifts his gaze and pins her in place with a look that's too calm, too controlled, too knowing. Like he's been waiting for this.

"Jade." Vale approaches with deliberate, unhurried steps, hand outstretched as if greeting an old friend. "I'm so sorry to keep you waiting, dear."

Her pulse kicks once, hard. *Control.*

"No you're not." Jade doesn't move. She lets the gesture hang there between them — suspended, awkward, meaningless.

Vale's fingers curl back in, smooth and controlled. He withdraws the hand with a soft, amused exhale — like the entire exchange was a test, and she failed it exactly the way he predicted.

Vale steps around her, the cane clicking once against the exposed tile, the next step muffled into silence by the odd gray rug.

He crosses to the polished metal desk, adjusts the files that didn't need adjusting. Jade takes notice of the tick.

Settling into the chair with the kind of lazy elegance only predators have, "Sit, please. We have much to discuss."

Jade stays standing.

"Too proud to sit?" Vale murmurs, flipping open a file

with one precise flick of his wrist. "How will we ever find a smooth working relationship, Jade?"

Tightening her jaw, Jade doesn't respond. Her name on his lips turns her stomach.

Vale turns a page like he's reading something delightful.

Then, without looking up, "You know... you're so different from your sister."

Silence detonates inside her chest.

Deep beneath her ribs, her wolf—quiet for so long Jade almost forgot the sound of her—lashes upward like a trapped storm breaking loose. She's losing her shit.

It's almost poetic, in the ugliest way possible.

Jade only walked back into this place because her wolf went dark.

And now? Now she's clawing at the cage, furious, awake, and demanding Vale's neck.

Full circle.

Vale finally lifts his gaze, pinning her once more with that calm, clinical interest—the kind that feels like hands around a throat.

"Senna always sat."

Jade's pulse spikes so hard she feels it in her teeth.

She doesn't move. "Sat is past tense, fucker. So if my sister is gone, then I truly have no need to have any type of relationship with you." Jade tilts her head in mock-consideration. "Unless you're broke and need someone to pay for your cremation. I'll do that for you."

Vale smiles — slow, thin, satisfied.

"There she is," he murmurs. "The reaction I was looking for."

Vale's smile doesn't falter. If anything, it deepens—curving into something cold and delighted.

"Cremation?" he repeats softly. "My dear girl... you always assume the worst."

He taps the wolf-head cane once against the rug.

A soft hum fills the walls.

Jade's eyes snap to the sound.

The white wall to her right, flickers—then splits into a seamless, hidden panel sliding upward with a mechanical hiss. A screen glows to life.

Jade's heart stops.

Senna.

Locked inside a concrete cell with no windows and one metal cot.

Her hair longer and a ratted mess. Her face bruised. but Jade can see her chest rising and falling. It's shallow but the movement is there.

Jade steps forward before she realizes she's moved. Her breath hits the cold air in a sharp, unsteady burst.

Her wolf screams against her ribs, claws scraping, frantic.

Vale watches her come undone with absolute satis faction.

"She can't see you," he says lightly.

"How do I know this isn't a video?"

"She can hear. Go on. Say hello."

Jade's throat closes. Her voice shreds itself into something raw.

"Senna?"

Senna flinches at the sound—jerks upright, eyes wide, searching the cell.

"Jade?" her voice cracks. "Jade, is that—where are you? Jade?!"

Jade watches as her sister struggles to stand, palms pressed against the far wall, desperate, trembling. Weak.

Jade moves slowly towards the screen. "Senna... I'm here." Her voice is barely a whisper. "I'm right here."

Senna sobs, shaking. "I knew—you weren't—dead. I knew—" She chokes on her own breath. "Jade, please—please get me out—"

Vale clears his throat. "That's enough."

The screen cuts to black.

Jade's snarl breaks the silence.

"What the fuck do you want from me?"

"Oh, Miss Devereaux." Vale sighs as if personally wounded. "All business and no play. Shame. You know that kind of stress leads to heart disease."

"Stop with the fucking games, Vale." Jade's voice is ice. "What do you want in exchange for Senna's freedom?"

"Freedom?" Vale presses a hand to his chest, faux-appalled. "No, no. Not yet. Let's not get ahead of ourselves."

He taps the wolf-head cane against the rug—soft, deliberate.

"A little birdie told me you have a superpower. That you have a beasty inside you. And I hear yours is much stronger than Senna's."

Jade's breath stops cold in her lungs.

He fucking knows.

She forces a shrug. "Yeah? So what's it to you?"

Vale smiles—slow and smug, like he's savoring her denial.

"Miss Devereaux, I only want you to keep doing what you've always done for me."

Jade's voice drops. "Yeah? And what's that?"

Vale leans back in the chair, pleasure curling at the edges of his mouth.

"Fight."

A soft, deliberate knock raps against the door behind her.

Vale doesn't look surprised. Of course he doesn't.

"Enter," he says.

The door swings open.

Jade freezes. Her wolf goes silent.

Miles moves inside like he's limping into a fucking happy hour—relaxed, confident, wearing that arrogant smirk that used to make Jade's blood boil for totally different reasons.

"Well," he drawls, shutting the door behind him. "If it isn't a Red Rock bitch."

Jade's vision tunnels.

Miles. Here.

Working with Vale.

Standing comfortably inside this nightmare like he belongs in it.

She can't breathe. Her vision starts to narrow.

Control.

Vale smiles, pleased.

"Ah. Perfect timing."

Jade takes a step back before she realizes she moved.

Her voice scrapes out low, deadly, shaking.

"What. The. Fuck. Are you doing here?"

Miles just looks at her—and grins.

"Working."

WELL THAT HURT

Jade's wolf hits first.

There's no thought, no warning, no breath between Miles stepping into the room and the black beast inside her detonating outward in a violent, feral surge.

Her vision goes sharp—white around the edges, then darker, darker still.

Her black wolf slams into Miles grey wolf, hitting so hard they both yelp.

Miles's wolf surges up to meet hers—cold, vicious, hungry.

A ripple of power blasts the air between them, rattling the metal desk and making Vale's papers flutter like restless birds.

"Oh now, look what you beasty's did."

Through wolf's eyes, Jade see's Vale nod—and then a red cord whips around her throat.

It yanks her backward, hard enough to choke off her snarl.

Her feet leave the ground for a heartbeat.

The man with the red cord, pulls her back with inhuman strength, planting his boots and bracing her like she's a wild animal being hauled into a cage.

"Hold," he growls.

Jade claws at the cord, but it bites into her neck, burning, cutting, glowing faintly crimson.

Then, a burst of white powder hits her face, slamming into her eyes, her mouth, her lungs.

Jade screams. Not out loud—her voice can't get past the cord.

Her wolf roars, thrashes, rips at her insides—then collapses inward as if someone is dragging it back into a too-small cage under her skin.

Her body hits the floor. Every nerve feels scraped raw. Her skull pounds. She can't inhale—can't exhale—can't think. The world flickers. Her wolf claws once more—but the powder crushes it back down, suffocating her.

Jade gasps wetly, the black wolf curling tight and silent and hurting inside her.

A hand pats her cheek lightly. Vale's voice floats into the fog.

"Now, now. Let's not start the morning with a tantrum."

Jade forces her head up to glare at him, but her vision swims. Her throat burns. Her wolf is whimpering—actually whimpering—in the back of her mind.

Vale sighs softly, as if *she's* the disappointment here.

He lifts a neatly folded stack of clothes and drapes them over the back of the metal chair she refused earlier.

"New clothes," he says, cheerful as hell. "Yours are... well."

He gestures at her torn, powder-stained shirt.

"Rough shape."

Jade doesn't move for them.

Behind Vale, Miles limps forward.

He leans down enough for his shadow to swallow her.

"Now that we're all playing nice," he says, voice low and sharp, "tell me which one of you Red Rock bitches killed my mate."

Jade's wolf claws violently inside her chest—but the powder holds.

Vale tsks softly, almost delighted. "Oh, I *didn't know* the two of you had this much history. How fascinating."

Jade bares her teeth, soft and feral.

"What mate?" she rasps.

Miles's grin is all venom. "You know exactly who."

Jade's stomach drops.

Vale's eyes gleam. "Oh," he says lightly. "This should be fun."

"That fucker died from stupidity."

Something slams into her—fist, boot, elbow, she doesn't know—pain flashes bright as lightning, then everything goes black.

FUCK YOU RYDER

Jade wakes up choking on her own breath. Not pain —not the powder—just panic.

Her eyes snap open to familiar darkness, familiar walls, familiar sheets.

The mansion.

She bolts upright so fast the room tilts. "Nora—where's Nora? Is she—did she—"

Charlotte's calm voice comes from the chair beside the bed. "She's fine, Jade. She's downstairs with Ryan and Kai. She's safe."

Jade forces a breath into her lungs. Her hands shake. Her wolf whimpers in the back of her skull, bruised and silent.

"How," she rasps, "did I get home again?"

There's a beat of silence. Then Luna's voice from the doorway—flat, annoyed, offended by the obvious. "I'll give you one guess."

Jade closes her eyes. *Of fucking course.*

Her voice drops into something cold and quiet. A command wrapped in exhaustion.

"Find him, Luna."

Luna doesn't ask who "him" is. She already knows. And the look she gives Jade isn't playful or chaotic. It's lethal.

"Already on it," Luna says. "I sent the hotel address to your phone."

Jade shoots out of bed so fast the room tilts. Pain slams into her—sharper than she expected. Her wolf is trying to heal her, but sluggish, bruised, still not where she should be.

"Jade, with everything else going on... are you really going after Ryder right now?" Charlotte asks. The tone isn't judgment. It's curiosity—the kind she uses when watching wildlife that might suddenly bite.

"Yes." Jade yanks on a pair of green yoga pants and almost faceplants as her toe catches. "I need to know why that fucker—"

She swears under her breath, straightening as a fresh spike of pain radiates through her ribs.

"I want to know why this fucker knows where I am," she snaps, "and why he always shows up like he's riding in on a fucking white horse."

Jade snatches her keys off the dresser and heads for the garage, every step a reminder that her ribs are still fucked from the powder. Her wolf pushes against her skin, restless, snarling, wanting blood or clarity—whichever comes first.

The overhead light flickers on.

Her Ducati waits in the center of the garage like a loyal beast.

Red. Sleek. Fast enough to outrun bad decisions—fast enough to chase them down, too.

Jade grabs her helmet off the hook.

The weight is familiar. Comforting.

She slips it over her head, the foam brushing her bruised cheek, the visor dropping with a soft, decisive click.

Her world narrows.

Focus sharpens.

Routine. Control. Cause and effect.

She swings her leg over the bike, pain burning hot along her side, but she doesn't pause. Doesn't consider stopping. Hands slide over the grips. Gloves snap into place.

Pushing the ignition button, the engine growls alive— low, hungry, vibrating through her bones. The sound hits her chest like a promise and a threat.

She revs it once.

Her wolf snarls approval.

Then she's flying out of the garage, tires spitting gravel, the cool morning air flooding into the vents of her helmet. The city blurs around her as she cuts through traffic, leaning into turns she has no business taking in her condition.

She doesn't care. Her pulse syncs with the engine.

The hotel pin glows on her screen.

Her wolf whispers one name, over and over, Ryder.

But just as she hits the long stretch of road outside the subdivision—a memory she didn't ask for punches through the darkness.

"Please leave me alone. I don't want to hurt you, but I will."

Jade will never forget the smell of the two humans who tried to corner her behind the convenience store—the sour sweat, the stale beer, the rot in their clothes. She'd been sixteen. Old enough to fight. Young enough to be terrified of losing control.

She could crush them. Shifter strength made that easy.

But controlling her wolf? That was another story.

Her wolf liked the fight. Liked the heat. Liked pushing

against her ribs whenever someone threatened her. And Jade... Jade wasn't fully trained yet. One wrong move, one surge of fear, and she could shift.

Humans had suspicions about shifters but no real evidence.

"Oooh, you think you can hurt me, little girl?" the leader sneered, breath hot and sour, brown teeth flashing when he grinned. He flicked her braid with his fingers as he circled, like she was prey he was testing for weaknesses.

Jade snapped.

"Okay, listen here, fucker. I asked nicely twice. I'm done now."

The second man snorted. "We know you're one of those cult girls from out in the sticks. You shouldn't be talkin' to us like that. It's not proper cultish behavior, right?"

Her wolf surged. She felt her nails sharpen. The world sharpened with them.

And then... a shadow moved. Fast.

Ryder stepped in front of her without a single wasted breath, like his body reacted before his mind could. Broad shoulders blocking her view, posture loose but lethal.

"She's with me."

And yeah... in the quiet of her truck and the privacy of her own mind, she'll admit it now—that was the night she developed a full-blown girl crush on Ryder Sheridan.

But it was also the same night Senna leaned in close and told her, voice soft and certain, that Ryder was her true mate.

Jade jerks her head like she can shake it loose.

The Ducati stays steady beneath her, humming, loyal.

"What the hell," she mutters, opening the throttle.

She refuses to drown in nostalgia—not for him.

The hotel comes into view. And Jade doesn't slow down.

The Ducati's engine ticks as it cools, but Jade's blood is

still roaring when she storms through the hotel's glass doors. The lobby is too polished, too quiet, too... wrong for the chaos inside her chest.

She strides across marble tile, helmet under her arm, ribs screaming with every step.

The front desk clerk opens his mouth to ask something—

Jade lifts a hand without looking at him. "Don't," she mutters. "Not today." She reaches the elevator, jabs the call button harder than necessary.

The doors slide open instantly—empty.

She steps inside, presses the floor Luna texted her, and leans a shoulder against the wall, catching her breath. Her wolf paces under her skin, snarling, impatient.

The elevator rises.

Ding.

The doors glide open—and there he is. Ryder Sheridan is standing there.

Tall. Tension in every line of his body. Hair damp, like he just showered. A towel slung over his shoulder. No shirt and barefoot.

His amber eyes locking on her like she's the last thing he expected—and the only thing he wants.

They freeze.

The elevator hums quietly, indifferent to the storm detonating between them.

Jade's fingers tighten on her helmet. Her ribs flare in pain.

Her wolf lunges at the sight of him.

His jaw tightens, that clean line sharpening, muscle pulsing once.

Jade feels something spark low in her belly before she can smother it. Definitely not helpful.

Jade doesn't get a word out. Ryder grabs her wrist—warm, calloused fingers wrapping around her pulse—and mutters, "Don't yell at me out here."

Before she can bark back, he's already pulling her out of the elevator.

"Ryder—"

"Just—" He glances around the hallway like they're being watched. "Please. Not here. I don't want to get kicked out of another hotel."

"Let me go."

"Not until we're inside." His voice drops, rough and low. "Two seconds, Jade."

He keeps moving, not dragging, but firm enough that her wolf purrs.

What the fuck? Why are you purring?

Pain flares through her ribs, but she doesn't stumble. She refuses to.

They reach his door—only two rooms down.

He swipes his keycard with a frustrated curse under his breath. The light clicks green. He opens the door and steps aside without letting go of her wrist.

"In," he demands.

Jade rips her hand free the second she crosses the threshold, shoving past him with the kind of storm energy that fills the room instantly.

Ryder closes the door behind them, leaning his forehead against it for one slow breath.

"Okay," he says quietly. "Now you can yell."

Head leaning against the door, Ryder's first thought isn't logical. Or noble. He tries to push it out with a deep breath but his wolf is clawing his way out to get to their mate.

Bed. Her. Him. Mate.

Jade fucking Devereaux, ten steps from a mattress big enough to ruin both of them.

He presses his palm flat to the door, grounding himself on the cool wood, because if he doesn't? If he turns around too fast? He's going to grab her. He's going to pin her to that mattress.

He's going to finally let his wolf have the thing it's been pacing for since they were kids.

He squeezes his eyes shut. "Okay. Now you can yell."

Breathe. Don't touch her. Her scent hits him. *Ok, don't breathe either.* Sweat. Pain. Powder burn. And underneath it... the Jade he's always known and always wanted.

"—and don't fucking ignore me!" she's yelling behind him, voice sharp enough to skin him alive. "Are you listening? I asked you a question!"

Ryder drags in a slow inhale that does absolutely nothing to help.

Gods.

Fuck, she's beautiful when she's pissed. He forces his hand off the door and turns.

Jade is pacing the length of his hotel room with her helmet dangling from her fingers like she's seconds away from weaponizing it. Her hair is wild, cheeks flushed from yelling, and bruises peek through her shirt collar like tiny, enraging secrets.

"I asked you *why you keep following me!*" Jade snaps. "Why you always show up! Why you—"

Ryder's wolf lunges, teeth bared, ready to rip the world apart for the bruise on her throat.

He swallows it down. Barely.

Don't touch her. Don't touch her.

Don't—

His voice comes out low, hoarse, dangerous.

"Jade... I need you to stop yelling for a second."

"Oh, do you?" she fires back. "Does the stalker need quiet time? You just said I could yell now."

Ryder's jaw locks so hard he hears something click. She has no idea. No idea the way he feels her in his bones and how close he is to losing the grip he's held for years.

No idea how close he is to crossing a line he can't uncross.

He takes a step toward her. Just one.

Her breath stutters.

His wolf howls.

"Jade," Ryder rasps, not daring to look directly at her— he can't, not without breaking—"if I don't control myself right now... you're not going to be yelling *at* me anyway."

Her eyes widen—but she doesn't back up.

Of course she doesn't.

And he's always been helpless against her.

Jade's stare holds his like a challenge, her chin lifting half an inch.

"Oh?" she says, voice dropping into something smug and sharp. "You think you can stop me from yelling?"

Ryder's lungs forget how to work. Because it's not just defiance. She's taunting. Does she even realize she's doing it?

His wolf *slams* against his ribs in response.

"Jade..." he warns, voice too rough to sound like any kind of warning. "Don't."

She takes a single step closer.

"How did you know I was at those fights? What the fuck are you doing, Ryder? Why are you even in Vegas still? You dropped Ivy and Henry off *weeks ago*. You were supposed to leave."

The words should hit like an attack but they don't. Ryder sees it.

The tilt of her chin. The challenge in her eyes. The way she's practically daring him to react.

She's not afraid to provoke him.

His wolf slams forward, violent and hungry, vision pulsing at the edges as if the animal is trying to claw its way to the surface.

"Jade..." he growls, "don't do that."

She tilts her head. Provocative. Beautiful in a way that ruins him.

"Do what?" she whispers.

He steps closer—too close—and her breath stutters.

He hears it. Feels it. Feeds on it.

"Don't say things you don't understand," Ryder rasps, "when I'm already this close to losing it."

She doesn't move back. Of course she doesn't.

Instead she whispers, soft and devastating, "Then lose it."

Ryder's control snaps like a bone. He doesn't think. He moves.

He slams into her with the force of a nuclear fucking impact, his mouth crushing onto hers like he's been dying for this and she's the only air left in the world.

Jade gasps against him—surprised, furious, hungry—and Ryder swallows it whole.

His hands come up hard, one cupping the back of her neck, the other gripping her hip, dragging her into him like he's claiming space she's been denying him for years.

And the second her body hits his, his cock answers—fast, fierce, impossible to hide. He grinds into her without thinking, a low sound ripping from his chest as the heat of her lines up perfectly against him.

She stiffens—reflex, shock, maybe denial—but he feels the way her thighs tense, feels the jolt that goes through her like he just hit a live wire.

Good. Let her feel exactly what she does to him.

He holds her there, pinned flush to the hard length of him, letting her feel every inch, every pulse, every ounce of barely-contained want he's been swallowing for years.

Her nails bite his shoulders. That shreds his last ounce of control.

She tastes like adrenaline and anger and the kind of trouble he wants to drown in.

Her helmet hits the floor.

Walking her backward, not breaking the kiss for a second—denying her air, but giving her everything else she's been starving for, his grip on her neck, on her hip, locks her into his pace. *His angle. His depth.*

He controls the kiss. He controls her body. He controls

the fucking world as he moves her exactly where he wants her.

Her thighs hit the edge of the dresser, and he exhales a sound that's half growl, half relief—not because he wants to stop, but because now he has leverage.

Ryder cages her there, hips pinning hers, hands spreading along her waist as he drags her up like she weighs nothing.

Her breath stutters—a tiny surrender—and he feels it everywhere.

He breaks the kiss only long enough to murmur against her lips, voice a deep, dangerous rasp, "Touch me, and I stop."

Her eyes widen—that quick flash of panic, the instinct to bolt—and he reads it. He fucking knows her.

His fingers tighten on her hips, grounding her, owning the moment. "Good," he growls. "Stay. Right. There."

Jade tries for a weak, shaky smirk, but he sees the tremble in her thighs.

He leans in again, slower this time, devouring her mouth with a control that feels like violence in slow motion. He kisses her like he's learning her for memory, because this moment needs to be etched for eternity.

Her nails dig into the edge. She's holding on for balance —but he knows she is grounding herself too.

His teeth catch her bottom lip—not gently. A sharp, possessive drag. Her blood blooms on his tongue, sweet and electric, and he's losing it. That mark will heal by morning... but knowing she walked out of this room wearing something of his, sinks deep into his soul.

She inhales sharply, and Ryder feels her wolf finally surge—awake, responding, wanting something other than pain for the first time in too long.

Ryder pulls back just enough to see her face. Her lips are already swollen, her pupils blown wide, her chest rising fast —even for her to pretend she isn't coming apart under him.

A sound rumbles out of him—low, rough, pulled from somewhere deep in his chest. He doesn't even know if it's the man or the wolf that makes it. Doesn't care.

His thumb brushes her lip, slow and deliberate, smearing the tiny bead of blood he left behind.

"Now you're quiet," he murmurs.

He licks her blood from his thumb, and something primitive shivers through her—hips angling into him, thighs tightening as her wolf pushes to the surface.

He smiles at that. Dark. Knowing. The kind of smile that promises more trouble and more pleasure than either of them can survive.

"Good girl," he whispers, voice all gravel and fire.

"Fuck... Ryder." Voice breaks on his name.

His eyes darken instantly.

"Use your words, Jade," he whispers against her mouth. "Tell me what that meant."

She swallows hard but doesn't give an answer.

He smiles—slow, lethal. "That's what I thought."

Even if she claws and fights and lies to herself every damn step of the way, she is his until he releases her.

Barely giving her a second to breathe, one hand clamps around her jaw, tilting her face up to him. The other drops to her waist, fingers digging in hard enough she'll feel the echo tomorrow. She gasps—quiet but sharp—and that sound lights him up.

She shouldn't make noises like that. He doesn't deserve them. But he wants to.

And her wolf pushes forward again, hot and furious and wanting.

Ryder hauls her off the dresser like she weighs nothing. Her legs wrap around his waist on instinct—and fuck, the instinct alone nearly undoes him. Her breath hits his throat, hot and frantic, and he feels her nails bite into his shoulders.

Good.

"I don't even know why we're doing this. I fucking hate you, Ryder."

Her eyes are squeezed shut, her throat bared—offered without her realizing it.

Does she *know* she keeps giving him her throat? Does she understand what that does to him?

"I know." Dropping his voice as low as he can.

Her scent slams into him as he walks—wild, electric, threaded with adrenaline and something darker she tries like hell to hide. It spears straight through him, settling low and hard. Her pulse throbs against his throat, her thighs trembling around his hips, trying to pretend she isn't clinging to him already.

He tightens his grip on her ass, grinding her against him slow and punishing.

"Stop thinking," he growls in her ear. "Drop the hate. Drop the noise. Right now, your only job is to feel what I do to you."

Ryder leans in and takes the small bit of skin behind her ear gently between his teeth—not enough to hurt, just enough to claim. Her whole body jolts.

"I'll take you exactly where I want you," he murmurs, voice like gravel dragged over silk. "And you're going to let me."

She buries a sound in his neck—low, broken, half-growl, half-surrender. Then she bites him. *Hard.*

His cock throbs—violent, instant—and he has to grit his

teeth to keep from coming right there like some inexperi-
enced idiot. She has no idea what that bite does to him.

He slaps her ass, a sharp crack of his hand against her
tight-ass yoga pants, not to hurt her—but to drag himself
back into dominance as he walks, her legs locked around his
waist.

"Not like that," he growls, adjusting her higher, guiding
her hips into a slow, punishing grind against him. "You bite
when I tell you to bite. You take what I say you can take."

Her thighs tighten around him—reflexive, needy, defiant
all at once.

"Yeah..." he growls against her ear, voice rough enough
to scrape. "I feel that too."

He sets her on the edge of the couch—controlled, deliberate—like she's something he's positioning, not placing.
His mouth stays at her throat for one last claiming drag
before he drops to his knees between her thighs.

She tries to close them.

Ryder just lifts his gaze, intentional and predatory, and
shakes his head once.

"Don't," he says quietly.

His hands slide along the insides of her thighs, opening
her again with the kind of steady pressure that removes
choice from the equation. Her toes dig into the floor. Her
legs tense. Her body reacts, instinct before thought.

"Look at you," he murmurs, letting his fingers trail up
her hips, hooking in the waistband just enough to make her
wait. "You don't even know what that little move did to me.
Now lift."

She does—too high, too willingly—and he freezes for
half a second.

Leaning in, dragging the bridge of his nose along her
through the thin fabric, inhaling her like oxygen he's been

starved of. A quiet, wrecked sound escapes him before he can stop it.

"You have no idea," he says softly, "how hard it is not to take everything you're giving away right now."

She stiffens in his hands—then melts—then fights it, just like he knew she would.

Ryder can feel the war inside her, feel the exact moment she realizes her body is betraying her.

"Ryder..."

Her voice cracks on his name, and the sound damn near undoes him.

But then she snaps it back together, sharp as a blade.

"Don't think this changes anything," she spits. "And don't you dare think I'm giving you anything."

Ryder goes still. Not because she stopped him but because the words hit him exactly where his wolf likes them.

She's furious. Ashamed. Lit up. Lying to herself. Lying to him. Trying like hell not to want this.

And he feels every bit of it.

His gaze drags up her body slow, deliberate, savoring the tension coiled in her thighs, the way her hands grip the couch cushions like she wants to shove him away and pull him closer at the same time.

Gods, she's perfect.

"You're right, you're not giving me anything," Ryder murmurs, voice low and dark. "You're fighting me for every inch."

His fingers tighten on her hips, dragging her just a little closer—enough to feel the panic spike in her pulse, enough to feel her thighs tense again. "And you're still losing."

Her jaw clenches. Fury flashes in her eyes. Her body betrays her anyway.

Ryder's smile is slow, feral, carved from the part of him he usually keeps locked down.

"Keep fighting, Jade," he says softly, leaning in just close enough that she has to feel his breath on her skin. "It's the only way you know how to want anything."

"Look at you," he says again, closer now, crowding her space with his shoulders, his heat, his certainty. "Pretending you don't want me every time I get within breathing distance."

"Fuck you, I'm only here for—"

He cuts her off with his mouth tracing heat up her tank, his voice brushing her skin. "Lie to yourself later. Not now."

Her jaw tightens. A tiny, betrayed sound escapes—so small she probably thinks he didn't hear it.

"Oh, that's the one," Ryder murmurs, thumb stroking her thigh. "That's the sound you hate."

"You're imagining things," she whispers.

"No." His tone shifts—lower, rougher, unshakeable. "That was truth."

Her pulse kicks. He feels it under his fingers, sharp and undeniable.

"Say something. Anything," he orders quietly. "Yes. No. A lie. I don't care. Use your voice."

Fully exposed, she's finally honest. Not with her words—with the one part of her that can't lie to him.

And he finds it in an instant. Her breath hitches and her head shoots back the instant his thumb finds the little ball of nerves. Maybe it wasn't fair to ask her to speak and then do that but he doesn't care. This is his game.

Her held breath speaks volumes. "That's what I thought," he whispers at her jaw—owning her reaction, not the moment.

He stands, offering his hand like it's a command, not an option.

She stares at it.

One beat.

Two.

Three.

Then she takes it.

Ryder pulls her up, flush to him, their bodies aligning in a way that steals the next breath from both of them. Watching her, he lifts her tank over her head in one slow, controlled pass.

Her gaze locks on his—furious, wanting, lost.

"Why you..." she whispers, stuttering. "Why do you always do this to me?"

Her question is a spark; his wolf is the gasoline.

Ryder's hand closes around her neck—firm, directing—and he steals her mouth again, a kiss that has more hunger than sense. Then he turns her, positioning her with the kind of quiet strength that leaves no room for argument, only instinct.

His next words come out raw, scraped from somewhere deep in his chest.

"On your knees, Jade."

She moves exactly how he tells her to—slow, defiant, every muscle tight like she hates giving him the obedience she's giving. And Ryder watches all of it. Watches her climb onto the cushions, brace her arms, glance back at him with that furious, wrecking look.

It's the look that destroys him. The last shred of control he'd been hoarding? Gone. His breath punches out of him, his restraint collapses.

He barely registers as the clothes hit the floor. Just the sound of fabric and the rush of heat that follows.

Bringing his fingers to his mouth—Jade still watching over her shoulder—he wets them before entering her. In all his dreams he thought he would take it slow, but here, right now, there is no slow. He has no resolve left.

He slides two fingers inside her, drawn by her warmth, and her breath hitches at the contact. A third joins them, and the sound she makes is low and helpless. He settles into a slow rhythm, deliberate, and she answers him immediately, hips rolling to meet every stroke.

The way her body yields to him does something dangerous to his control. Her arms lock against the back of the couch, muscle and strength on display, her braids pulled into a ponytail that looks like an invitation. Ryder pushes the pace, and her breathing fractures, quick and needy, urging him on.

"I've waited for this moment for years," he says, his voice rough. "And you feel better than anything I ever dreamed."

She arches back into him, offering herself, and he takes the chance, curling his fist in her hair and pulling just enough to make her gasp. His wolf surges under his skin, restless and certain, a low growl vibrating in his chest.

"Mine," he mutters, barely holding it back. "My wolf feels you. He's known you forever."

"Fuck, Ryder." Her voice breaks. "I'm so close. If you slow down, I swear I will kill you."

He doesn't slow. He locks into the rhythm, relentless, drinking in every sound she gives him. Each broken cry tightens the coil in his gut. She bucks against his hand, desperate now, her body chasing the edge.

It's all about her. The slick heat of her skin. The way her breath stutters. The way she trembles when he hits that perfect place again and again.

"Let go, Jade," he growls, control fraying. "I've got you. My wolf's got you."

She drops her head forward, and he tightens his grip in her hair, the mix of pleasure and pain sending her over. In that instant, the world collapses. Past, distance, waiting. None of it matters.

His restraint shatters.

Ryder drives into her hard, the first thrust raw and unforgiving, years of want crashing through him all at once. Her body takes him, tight and burning, dragging a groan from his chest.

She clenches around him, heat and pressure everywhere, and his wolf surges, wild and possessive. Every thrust is deeper now, claiming, demanding.

"More, Jade," he rasps. "All of you."

She meets him without hesitation, arching back, matching him stroke for stroke. He watches her come apart. The way her body moves. The sheen of sweat on her brown skin, the strength in the way she takes him, open and unguarded.

"Ryder," she cries, voice wrecked. "I'm right there."

He pulls her head back, exposing her throat, his mouth dragging down her neck as his thrusts turn frantic. Her body tightens, trembling, stretched to the breaking point.

"Let it happen," he growls. "You're mine."

She shatters with a cry, her body clamping down around him, pleasure ripping through them both. The sound she makes goes straight to his spine.

Ryder follows her over the edge, control gone, the bond roaring as he drives into her one last time and comes undone with her. For a breathless moment, there is nothing but heat, heartbeat, and the echo of each other's names, bodies slick and shaking as the world finally falls silent.

Ryder's lungs drag in air like he's been underwater for minutes. He's draped over her back, her breathing matches his—ragged, uneven, still tangled with everything they just did.

Everything they shouldn't have.

"Jade…"

Her name leaves him before he can shape it.

Too soft. Too raw. Too close to a plea.

And that's what does it.

She pushes him back. Her walls slam up like he imagined they would, but it still hits him like a punch.

She shoves him away. Not hard. Just… final.

She scrambles for her clothes without looking at him, snatching each piece up like proximity alone burns. Ryder's hands are balled at his sides to stop himself for reaching out, chest heaving, trying to understand how everything inside him just cracked open—and she's already gone somewhere he can't reach.

Then she stops. Still bent over her clothes. Frozen. Her gaze drops to her arm. The bruising—gone.

She touches her neck—cut gone too.

Ryder goes cold.

"Jade…" he breathes, again—this time not a plea, but disbelief. "Your injuries—"

"Don't."

Her voice slices through him.

She finally looks at him, eyes blazing, but underneath it he sees it—fear, confusion, something she won't let herself name.

He steps forward.

She steps back.

"Jade, there is something between us."

The words rip out of him, rough, unplanned, dangerous.

Her jaw clenches.

Her eyes shine with hate she doesn't actually feel.

"No, Ryder." Her voice is steady, merciless. "You had your chance to have a Devereaux."

She grabs her shirt, pulls it over her head in one sharp movement. "And you rejected her."

The door slams so hard the frame shakes.

Ryder stands there, still breathing like he ran ten miles, staring at the space she left like he could drag her back with will alone.

For the first time in years—his wolf doesn't growl.

He whimpers.

THE WALK OF SHAME?

The elevator button glows beneath her thumb. She presses it again anyway, because standing still feels dangerous. Feels like thinking.

Behind her, the hotel room door clicks open.

Her stomach drops.

"Jade."

His voice isn't rough now. It's... contained. Leashed too tightly.

She keeps her eyes on the elevator numbers.

Footsteps. Almost silent. Then—

"You forgot this."

She finally looks.

He's holding her helmet.

Not making eye contact, she snatches the helmet from his hand without letting her fingers brush his.

"Thanks," she mutters. It's the closest she'll get to civil.

He nods once, jaw tight. "I'll leave," he says quietly. "As soon as this thing you're doing is done—I'm gone."

Turning to wait for the door to open, helmet hugged to

her ribs like armor. "No," she says. "Today. I want you out of my territory today."

Like that's going to fix anything? Like it's supposed to erase what just happened.

His eyes flick, the smallest crack in the mask. "Jade, please understand... I can't."

His voice drops, rougher. "My wolf won't let me leave you when you've got yourself in real danger."

Ding.

The elevator doors slide open behind her. Relief slams into her like oxygen.

"And stop fucking following me," she snaps. "It's creepy as shit."

He still doesn't move. Doesn't argue. Doesn't even blink.

"Wouldn't dream of it," he lies.

The elevator doors swallow Ryder's face, and Jade doesn't wait a single second. She stomps through the lobby, helmet under her arm, vision blurring in a way she refuses to call crying.

Outside, the air hits her like a slap. She swings a leg over her Ducati, shoves the helmet on, and guns the throttle hard enough heads turn.

She peels out of the hotel parking lot like the asphalt insulted her mother.

Wind knifes under her tank. Her pulse is too loud. Too fast. Too wrong.

What the hell did I just do?

Her bruises—the ones on her arms, ribs, hips—have ached for weeks. She glances down at her wrist at a stoplight.

Nothing. Not faded, just gone.

Her stomach drops.

That's not normal. That's not healing. That's... what the hell is that?

She rubs the spot with her thumb, harder, like she can force the bruise to reappear. Nothing. Just smooth skin and a faint electric hum under her fingertip.

Her wolf has gone quiet, not like before quiet. Like she's taking a satisfying nap. *She's napping?!*

A car honks behind her.

She revs the throttle and shoots forward, turning down a side street she doesn't even recognize. Adrenaline has her shaking. She tries to breathe and it just turns into a choke. Her throat tightens. Her eyes blur.

And then she's pulling over, because she can't see the damn road anymore.

Helmet off. Hands shaking. Breath breaking.

"Get it together," she snarls at herself.

She doesn't.

She grabs her phone and hits the only person who won't make this worse.

Luna answers before the first ring finishes.

"Is he dead?" Luna says immediately. No greeting. No hello. Just pure Luna triage.

Jade opens her mouth and nothing comes out. Then—a sound. Not a growl. Not a curse. A broken, humiliating sob she didn't mean to let loose.

Luna goes silent for *one full beat.*

"...Jade?" she says, sharper now. "I'm pinging your phone."

Jade presses her forehead to the handlebars, trying not to fall apart completely.

"Don't—" she chokes. "Don't come. I'm— I just—"

"Too late," Luna snaps. "Stay on the line. I'm coming."

"Luna—"

"Save it. You only cry when something is really, really wrong or when you get hit by a truck. So unless you're calling me from under an SUV, you're not hanging up."

Jade squeezes her eyes shut. A single tear escapes anyway, hot and humiliating down her cheek.

"Luna," she whispers, "I messed up."

There's a sharp inhale on the other end.

"Okay," Luna says, dead serious now. "You do that all the time."

Jade hears it—the roar of Luna's Lamborghini firing to life like she just punched the ignition with her whole soul.

"You're just down the road, Jade. GPS says five minutes. Want to take bets I make it in two?"

"No," Jade chokes, wiping her cheek with the back of her hand. "I can't lose anything else tonight."

She doesn't have anything left to say after that.

Neither does Luna.

So the two of them just... sit there.

Phones pressed to their ears.

Listening to the city breathe between them—traffic hum, distant horns, a motorcycle somewhere revving too loud, the faint echo of someone laughing on the sidewalk.

It feels stupidly comforting.

Jade loves this city—the life, the rhythm, the way Vegas never really sleeps.

And listening to *it* when the noise in her head is this loud brings a kind of silence she desperately needs right now.

The hum of engines, the distant chatter, the buzz of neon—it all settles around her like a blanket.

After a long moment, "Oopsies. I'll stop at that red light twice next time."

A roar splits the night—deep, throaty, unmistakable.

Jade lifts her head just in time to see headlights whip around the corner way too fast, tires screaming against the pavement as Luna takes the turn like she's trying to drift into the Fast & Furious franchise.

The Lambo slides into the spot beside Jade's Ducati with surgical precision—*and* the subtle hint of "I almost spun out but we're not talking about it."

The engine cuts. Silence drops like a curtain. Then Luna's door kicks open.

She steps out still wearing her club dress, hair wild from the wind, eyes laser-focused on Jade like someone just hurt her favorite person and Luna is ready to commit a felony.

"Okay," Luna says, slamming her door shut with unnecessary force. "Do *I* get to kill him now, and how messy am I allowed to make it?"

Jade tries to breathe. It comes out a hiccup.

Luna freezes.

Her entire face softens. All the murderous intent bleeds out of her at once.

"Oh, babes..." Luna whispers. She crosses the distance in three strides. "Okay. I'm here. I'm here. Just breathe."

And Jade breaks.

It starts with a shudder.

Then another.

Then her whole body shakes like someone pulled the last support beam out from under her.

Her breath stumbles out in harsh, broken bursts—too loud, too ragged, too real. The kind of sound she never lets out in front of anyone. The kind that rips its way up from somewhere deep and raw.

Luna just pulls her tighter, forehead pressed to Jade's temple.

"Hey. Hey," Luna whispers, voice fierce and soft all at once. "I've got you. Let it happen. I'm right here."

Jade tries to inhale—fails—tries again—fails harder.

And then everything pours out of her at once, the heat, the confusion, the fear, the anger, the thing Ryder unlocked inside her that she doesn't want and doesn't know how to shut off.

Her shoulders shake. Her fingers curl into Luna's dress. She can't stop the sounds leaving her throat—messy, unguarded, humiliating, honest.

Luna holds her through all of it. No judgment. No comments. No demands.

Just pure, unmovable presence.

Eventually Jade's breathing stops tripping over itself. The shaking eases. She drags her palm across her face, trying to gather whatever pieces of dignity she has left.

Luna loosens her hold, but only barely.

"Okay," she says, brushing a strand of hair from Jade's cheek, "now do you want to tell me what the fuck happened?"

Jade sniffs—once, hard—and shakes her head.

"No. Not until you tell me why you're in this dress."

Luna straightens immediately, offended in the most dramatic way possible.

"Oh, this ol' thang?"

She rises to her feet and does a slow, unnecessary spin, the tiny black dress hugging every inch of her like it was sewn directly onto her body. She flicks an imaginary piece of lint off her hip like she's on a runway.

"It's classy. It's sexy. It says, 'Yes, I know hacking is a skill, but so is having this body.'"

Jade drags in a breath that's half a laugh, half a choke.

"Okay, but where were you?"

Luna's grin freezes. Then her eyes go huge.

"Oh *shit*. Kai."

Jade blinks. "What do you mean Kai?"

"We were at this club—one of my clients, long story you do *not* care about. Anyway, he went to the bathroom when you called and—yep—he's still there."

Before Jade can process that, Luna's already sprinting back to the car, heels clicking like tiny weapons.

Jade hears Luna launching straight into the call, "Hey, not-boyfriend... No, I'm fine. I had to run out to fix something for a client, it was urgent."

A beat.

Then Luna sighs dramatically.

"Kai, don't cry like a bitch. I didn't *leave* leave. I know, I know. I'm sorry. Yes, I'll make it up to you."

Another pause. Jade can practically *hear* Kai spiraling on the other end.

"No, I didn't leave forever," Luna says, pinching the bridge of her nose. "And that bitch could never take my place. Obviously."

She rolls her eyes so hard Jade hears it.

"No, I didn't leave with him either. Gods, Kai. Just order me another drink, okay? I'm coming back."

She ends the call with a flick of her thumb and looks at Jade like nothing about that entire exchange was unhinged.

"Okay, next," Luna says, waving her hand like she's calling up the next customer at a bank teller window.

"You go get Kai and meet me at the mansion?" Jade scoops up her helmet, wiping the face shield with the bottom of her tank. "I could use a few quiet minutes on the ride back to... think."

"Perfect. Give me an hour," Luna says, already sliding

halfway into the driver's seat. "Then it's PJs and Profanity time."

"Luna, the sun is coming up."

Luna shrugs, flicking her hair like sunrise itself personally inconveniences her.

"Jade, that sun doesn't care if we're in our PJs and we cuss a lot."

Just like before, the Lamborghini growls to life—a low, smug purr of pure horsepower—and in the same breath she arrived, Luna is already gone. Tail lights. Smoke. Vanished like the feral little princess she is.

The Ducati settles under her like it knows her mood.

Jade doesn't gun it this time. She doesn't peel out or scream down the Strip. She just rides.

Vegas glows around her—neon signs humming tired goodnights, casinos emptying out the last of their drunks, the dust on the horizon catching the first hint of sunrise. It should calm her. It usually does.

This morning, it barely touches the noise in her head.

Miles. She saw Miles. She still hasn't told the pack. Hell, she hasn't had time to process that herself.

Her chest tightens, a ghost of panic sliding down her ribs. The others need to know—Lucas, Harper, Charlotte, everyone.

Then Vale flickers through her mind. The office. The door to the left. *But, What's behind the right door?*

The way he said Senna's name like he owned it. Her grip tightens on the handlebars hard enough her knuckles ache.

Senna. Alive.

Gods, if he hurt her—

Jade swallows, fighting back the burn in her throat. She needs a plan. A next step. Something concrete to hold onto before her head caves in. But every time she reaches for clarity, she feels *him* instead.

Ryder. His voice. His mouth. His wolf.

She presses her knees tighter to the tank, trying to ignore the faint spark of warmth in her gut. Her wolf once again purrs. *WTF?*

Jade exhales sharply. "Shut up you bitch," she mutters into her helmet.

Her bruises? Gone. Not faded—gone.

She checks again at the next red light, tugging her sleeve up. Smooth skin. Like nothing ever happened. Like Ryder's hands, Ryder's teeth, didn't leave their mark.

She takes the turn into the Red Rock mansion neighborhood slower than usual. She needs these last few minutes—this quiet space between chaos and questions.

Senna.

Miles.

Vale.

The fights.

Ryder.

Her wolf.

She needs to sort it out.

But there's no sorting anything tonight. There's only driving forward.

The Ducati hums beneath her like it's doing its best to hold her together.

The mansion lights are glowing. Calling her home.

Isabell is probably up making breakfast for the packs.

Jade kills the engine, the sudden silence both jarring and grounding. She swings off the bike, helmet dangling from her fingers, and walks toward the front door with the kind of exhaustion that feels older than she is.

Stepping inside, Charlotte is in the foyer—arms crossed,

hair damp from an early-morning shower, coffee mug in hand. She doesn't say a word.

The irony isn't lost on Jade that Charlotte is standing directly in the center of the inlaid compass.

Charlotte's eyes narrow the second Jade walks in. Then her nostrils flare.

Jade freezes.

Charlotte's eyebrows lift in the slowest, most nonjudgmental arc Jade has ever seen in her life.

Oh gods. She smells it. She smells *him.*

Jade's stomach drops to the floor.

Charlotte takes a long, slow sip of her coffee. "So he's not dead then."

Jade shakes her head immediately, palms up like she can physically shove the questions back into Charlotte's mouth.

"Don't," she pleads. Her voice is raw. "Please. I need... I need a few minutes before anyone says anything. Okay?"

Charlotte stares at her for a long, silent beat, then a short nod, "Sure. Breakfast is going to be really fun today. I heard Luna left Kai at some club, too."

Jade watches, stunned, as Charlotte smirks. A real, honest-to-god smirk.

"I better have Isabell make some popcorn," Charlotte is already turning toward the dining room as her giggle trails off.

"Fuck."

A shower and an entire bottle of wine sound like the only two things that will help this new kind of pain.

Stepping into the game room, Jade grabs the closest bottle without even checking the label, and heads upstairs before anyone else sees her.

Shutting her bedroom door with her foot, Jade toes off her shoes and heads straight for the bathroom. She peels off her tank top on the way, letting it hit the floor, then drops the wine bottle onto the counter with a dull thud.

She's already reaching for the shower handle, turning the hot all the way on and not bothering with the cold. Steam floods the space instantly, thick and blinding — perfect.

Perfect for hiding the kind of morning she's having.

No wince. No ache. Not even a ghost of soreness.

She drags her fingers over her ribs, her hip, the spot on her shoulder where Vale's guy slammed her earlier.

Nothing.

"Great," she mutters. "Now my injuries are gaslighting me."

She steps out of her leggings, kicks them toward the hamper, and grabs the wine.

Thank the gods she grabbed a twist-top—her hands are too unsteady for anything else.

The cap hits the counter, and she takes a long, burning swig straight from the bottle.

A nice cheap Merlot, good choice. It pairs nicely with confusion and regret.

The heat floods her chest, not enough to soften anything, but enough to make her knees stop shaking.

She sets the bottle down and reaches for her phone.

Swipe.

Swipe.

Hidden album.

The folder pops opens to show one photo. The only thing that Jade has really ever felt she wanted to hide from anyone. Even Luna.

Ryder, years younger, hair a little too long, arms crossed in that cocky "I'm pretending not to care but I care too much" stance. Harper took it but Jade stole it. Told herself it was for intel.

It wasn't.

She stares at it, throat tight.

Her chest aches in a way her body refuses to anymore.

Her thumb hovers.

Just long enough to admit—to herself—that she's looking at him like he just broke something inside her.

Then she exhales, hard, and taps Delete.

"Done," she whispers.

Like saying it out loud will make it true. The phone screen goes black.

For a moment, Jade stares at her reflection in it. "Good," she mutters. "One less mistake in my life."

She sets the phone face-down on the counter, turns to the shower, and steps into the steam like she can wash Ryder Sheridan out of her skin.

POPCORN FOR BREAKFAST

"Fuck you, Charlotte." Jade shakes her head, grabbing a handful of the popcorn that Liam just spun towards her. "And you told him too?" She points accusingly at Liam.

Charlotte doesn't even flinch. "I don't keep secrets from my mate, Jade." She lifts her coffee, and Liam meets her halfway—cups clinking like it's a pact.

Before Jade can fire back, Kai flops into his seat like someone stole his puppy.

"Umm, can someone explain to me why there's popcorn for breakfast?" he asks the room. "Because I've had a really bad morning. My not-girlfriend left me at some fancy club alone." His voice hits peak whiny. "You can't abandon someone this good-looking at a bar and not expect women to be all over me."

Jade rolls her eyes so hard she sees yesterday.

"I told you to point them out so I could break their fingers for touching you," Luna's voice comes from the doorway, "but you—"

"You threatened to rip the bones out of a woman's hand

for complimenting my shirt." Kai throws his hands up. "My shirt, Luna."

Luna shrugs. "It was a very flirty compliment."

Luna slides a coffee over to Kai without looking up. "Also, Kai, you're not that good-looking."

He gasps, offended. "Excuse me? I am *absolutely* that good-looking."

Liam nods solemnly. "He kinda is. In a harmless Irish Setter kinda way."

"Exactly!" Kai gestures wildly. "I'm a catch! I'm adorable." Kai stops, "Irish Setter?"

Luna snorts. "Women adore feeding strays too. Doesn't mean they want to keep them."

Jade chokes on a popcorn kernel. "Damn, Luna."

Kai clutches his chest in agony. "You are all monsters."

Luna pats his arm. "Monsters with standards, babe."

The table erupts—Charlotte hides a grin behind her mug, Liam's shoulders shake, and even Jade feels a smile threaten to break through her exhausted face.

Which is, of course, when Charlotte decides she's had enough.

She lifts her hand like a judge about to restore order in a courtroom.

"Okay, enough. We need to focus."

The whole table quiets... mostly.

Kai still mutters, "I'm a motherfucking wolf," under his breath.

Ryan knocks him upside the head as he walks by. "Eat your breakfast, man."

"Okay, Nora," Charlotte says, corralling the energy like only she can. "Let's start with you. How did things go last night?"

Nora sits up a little straighter, oatmeal spoon halfway to

her mouth. "Well, I'll tell you what—I felt alive after those fights." She points her spoon for emphasis. "But I also learned that women fighters? Very chatty."

"Chatty how?" Jade asks, genuinely confused. "They were never chatty with me."

"That's probably because you not only kick their asses, but you bite," Maddy says, not looking up from her plate.

Jade just shrugs. *Fair.*

"I have that grandma aura, I guess," Nora continues breezily. "People always talk to me. But there's definitely a mixture of feelings about that hidden door everybody pretends not to know about."

She takes a bite of oatmeal, totally calm, while Jade notices the rest of the table eating like this isn't about to become a nuclear-level conversation. How are they relaxed when she's holding the *Miles* bomb inside her chest?

Nora swallows and goes on. "One girl said she keeps coming back because she wants to get noticed. Her friend told her celebrities and big names watch from behind that door. She's hoping for an acting gig or something."

Jade snorts. Of course someone thinks the murder door leads to Hollywood.

"Another woman said she's looking for a different fight club because the reputation of that door freaks her out."

Nora takes a sip of juice, still completely unbothered. "I asked if any of them had ever gone behind it. They all said no. But..." She pauses, glancing at Jade. "They've seen one person go through it and then come back out."

Every fork freezes mid-air. Heads turn. Chairs creak.

"They pointed at you," Nora finishes softly, chin dipping toward Jade.

Jade blinks. "Fuck, seriously? None of them have gone in there?"

"Nope," Nora says, popping her lips on the *p*. "Miss Hollywood Hopeful thinks the reason they never see people come back is because they're off filming their big movie roles." She rolls her eyes. "The others say it's all rumors. Fear-mongering brings in crowds, and money people like money people."

Any other shifters in there?" Charlotte asks, looking between Nora and Jade. The Alpha-voice is creeping in—calm, controlled, but sharp enough to slice through bullshit.

"Oh, yeah. Plenty," Nora says, lifting her brows. "But they weren't the ones fighting. The two monsters guarding that door? Bears. I'm sure of it." She crinkles her nose like the smell just hit her again. "Stink to high heaven, bears do."

Jade nods. "Yeah. I've suspected there's at least one shifter in the ring too, but honestly? I couldn't narrow down what he was."

Jaxson straightens, concern written all over his face. "Hang on—wait. You were fighting males too?"

Jade's throat tightens. She can't explain it—not without unraveling why she chose the fights in the first place... or why she didn't care who stood across from her.

She just gives a side shrug—the universal *drop it* signal.

Charlotte picks the reins back up. "Okay, anything else on your side, Nora?"

Jade's stomach flips again. She's barely touched her breakfast. They've battled Miles before... but never *this* Miles—never the broken-mate-bond version with a bad-guy ally who knows he has leverage because Senna is trapped in the middle.

"Nah," Nora says lightly. "Pretty cut and dry. I'll find out more next week."

"Hopefully you don't have to go back next week," Charlotte says, shifting her focus. "Jade. You're next. What happened behind this infamous door this time?"

Jade exhales slowly. Her hands tremble under the table.

"Well... I'm going to start with this, it's confirmed Senna is alive. I spoke with her."

"What—you're just now saying something?" Luna blurts, her face cracking with hurt before she can school it.

"It's not like there's been tons of opportunities before now, Luna." Jade holds up a hand. She needs control of the room before she loses control of herself. "Just... let me get this out. It's going to take a minute."

The whole table goes still.

"She couldn't see me, but she could hear me. I could see her." Her voice softens. "She looks terrible... but alive."

Charlotte's voice stays steady. "Damn. I mean I'm glad she's alive but I hate that she's trapped. Okay. What does Vale want from you?"

"He wants me," Jade says bluntly. "He knows about my wolf, and he wants me to fight. That's all he got out before—"

She stops. Swallows. Her heartbeat climbs up her throat.

"—before Miles walked through one of the doors."

Everything stops. Chairs freeze. Utensils hover. Even breathing seems to stall.

Around the corner, Isabell appears, silent and deadly still, like she felt the shift in the room from down the hall.

Charlotte's voice is measured, but Jade hears the crack beneath it. "Well... I guess we knew he'd pop up somewhere. I won't lie—this has me shocked."

Jaxson leans forward, elbows on the table, every inch of him radiating protective rage. His voice booms, thick with worry. "So is he working with this Vale guy?"

Jade shakes her head, jaw tight. "I got more questions than answers this time."

HOT OLD LADIES

After Jade left the other morning, he tried to leave Vegas—even though he already told her he couldn't. He made it as far as Bullhead City before the pull caught up to him. He ended up crashing at some RV resort where a pack of hot old ladies kept trying to drag him to a potluck by the pool.

He refused. *Obviously.*

So they brought the food out to him instead.

He's not big on giving compliments—but damn, the food was killer.

And honestly? That was the only part of the trip that didn't feel like failure.

He tried to do what Jade asked. He did... but he couldn't stay away. *He never can.*

And especially now with Jade spiraling.

So now he's back in Vegas, leaning against a sun-baked concrete wall, staring at the warehouse across the street. Somehow it looks even worse in daylight. His shifter senses aren't helping either—the smell of rot and bad decisions clings to the place while he waits for something to happen. Some sign of life from the building he's afraid could kill his mate.

Ryder checks the street again before pulling his phone out. He hates calling Harper.

She hates my guts almost as much as Jade.

He decides to text her first.

> Pick up the damn phone.

> It didn't ring fucker.

She picks up on the second ring. "You did that to get a reaction out of me."

He exhales. "Of course I did. I need information."

A quiet clink in the background—Harper setting something down. "About Jade."

"Yeah. She's not alright." He scrubs a hand over his jaw. "And I don't mean her usual pissed-off self."

"Well," Harper says carefully, "there's a lot going on."

"Stop fucking with me, Harp," he snaps. "Because right now I'm standing outside the warehouse she's been sneaking off to, and every instinct I have is saying this is more than her just fighting in some secret fight club like last time. I've carried her home twice now."

There's a beat of silence on the line.

Harper doesn't fill it right away.

When she finally speaks, her voice is surgical. Controlled.

"Before I tell you anything, I want to know why."

He swallows hard, pulse kicking up.

"Why are you following her?" Harper asks. "Why do you know about 'last time'?"

Ryder feels his chest lock up. The walls slam in.

Fuck. He knew this was coming—he'd hoped it wouldn't but he needs information.

He's only said those *why's* out loud once. To one person.

Jade.

Harper waits. Patient. Sharp. He can hear her patience. She's not letting him dodge this.

Ryder drags a hand through his hair, staring at the cracked pavement like it's personally responsible for his suffering.

"I know because I found her last time too," he finally says, voice rougher than he planned. "Bleeding. Alone. On a sidewalk."

A breath.

"A buddy had called me when he saw her."

"That's a lie."

Ryder, shakes his head. "How do you know it's a lie?"

"Ryder. Owen. Sheridan. I'm your sister. I can hear a lie."

"Fine. I follow her... sometimes," Ryder mutters, jaw tight, "because someone has to. Because she doesn't tell anyone shit. Because she won't ask for help even when she needs it."

Harper doesn't react. She just listens—which somehow makes it worse.

"Because something is wrong with her wolf. Because she's... different. And she scares the hell out of me."

The last words scrape out of him before he can stop them.

And then, quieter—the truth slipping through a crack he didn't mean to open...

"Because I can't stay away."

"Why Ryder?"

His voice lowers, barely a growl. "You know why Harp." He takes a deep breath.

"Because she is my mate and I will always do whatever it takes to protect her, even if that means from herself."

Harper exhales, not judgmental—just knowing.

"That," she says softly, "is why I'll tell you what's going on."

Harper is quiet for a long moment—long enough that Ryder's wolf starts pacing, claws dragging against his ribs.

"Ryder... before I say anything, you need to stay calm."

"Yeah, that's not happening. Just talk."

She takes a breath—one of those measured, careful Harper breaths.

He can picture her rubbing her temples, bracing herself the way she always does right before she drops something that changes everything.

"There's a man running the fights," Harper says. "His name is Vale. And he wants to use Jade."

Ryder goes still.

"We don't know how deep it goes yet," she continues. "He's seen her fight. He wants her loyalty for something. And this isn't some underground Vegas hobby-ring. It's organized. It's deliberate. It's dangerous. *And,* he knows about her wolf."

Ryder's throat goes sandpaper-dry.

Every instinct he has—wolf and man—starts screaming the same thing.

"Why would she go back then?" Ryder snaps. "Why—after the first time I picked her up out of the mud, bleeding and shaking—would she go back there for a second round?"

Harper hesitates.

That alone tells him he's not going to like the answer.

"Ryder... there's something else."

His grip on the phone tightens until the casing groans. His wolf goes dead still—a predator scenting shift in the air.

"Spit it out, Harp."

"It's Senna."

Everything inside him locks, like someone flipped a breaker in his chest.

Senna. Jade's sister. *Dead Senna.*

"What about her?" Ryder asks, but his voice is wrong—too quiet, stretched thin.

His skull feels like it's going to split. His wolf rakes claws down the inside of his ribs, frantic. The ghost Jade grieves. The ghost that has lived in the space between him and his mate. The ghost that kept Jade unreachable, even when she was standing right in front of him.

"She's alive."

The words land like a sledgehammer.

Ryder opens his mouth, but nothing comes out. His wolf surges, snarling, trying to make sense of it.

"She's alive," Harper repeats, softer. "Jade saw her. Not face-to-face, but she spoke to her. She's being kept somewhere behind some door in that hell hole."

He presses a hand to the wall behind him because the ground feels like it might tilt.

"What the fuck do you mean she saw her?"

"She's hurt. Weak. They don't know how long she's been there. Vale's holding her."

"Jesus Christ." Ryder drags a hand through his hair. "Does Jade think she can save her?"

"Of course she does."

He squeezes his eyes shut.

He knows exactly what that means. Self-sacrifice. Recklessness. Jade throwing herself into hell without blinking.

"She's going to get herself killed," he mutters.

"No," Harper says firmly. "Because now you know. And you're going to help whether she wants you to or not."

He doesn't fight it.

Can't.

His wolf is already howling under his skin.

Then Harper's tone shifts—gentle, but surgical again.

"There's one more thing, and... I need you to understand we don't have all the answers yet."

Ryder braces. "Just say it."

"Miles is involved."

Ryder's vision tunnels. For a second, all he hears is blood rushing in his ears. He snaps. "The Miles whose pack you're now Queen Alpha of? The same Miles who attacked the Red Rocks—what—three times trying to take your territory? *That* Miles?"

"Yeah, *that* Miles." Harper's voice is dry, edged with bite. "And thanks, by the way, for standing in the shadows while we were getting our asses kicked."

"Hey, sis, you know damn well I couldn't get involved." Ryder grits out. "Pack politics and shit."

He pushes off the concrete wall, pacing now, wolf pacing with him.

"But what the hell do you mean he's involved?" Ryder's voice drops to a low, dangerous rumble. The kind of sound that promises violence the second someone gives him a target.

"He walked through the door while she was talking to Senna."

Ryder stops breathing. Range-finder instinct. Threat assessment. Kill path. Everything snaps into place.

"Miles," he repeats, barely audible. "He's working with this Vale dude?"

"We don't know exactly," Harper says. "Jade only said it

looked that way. We don't know if he's being used, if he's helping willingly, if Vale has leverage... we know nothing."

Ryder presses his fist against his thigh. Hard. Trying to ground himself. Trying to keep his wolf from ripping through his skin.

"And Jade?" he forces out.

"She's scared," Harper says softly. "For Senna. For the pack. For herself."

A pause. Heavy. Weighted.

"She's spiraling, Ryder. Worse than any of us realized."

He closes his eyes. His wolf slams against his ribs like an animal trapped in a burning cage.

"And you want me to go in there," he mutters. "You know she'll try to kill me."

"Yeah," Harper says, perfectly matter-of-fact. "I'm banking on it."

The line goes dead.

Ryder stands frozen against the sun-baked concrete wall, trying to piece together everything Harper just told him.

Jade.

Senna.

Miles.

Vale.

His mate spiraling into hell while he's been pretending to keep his distance.

His wolf shreds what's left of his composure.

Dragging a hand down his face, Ryder forces his lungs to work, and pulls his phone back up.

There's only one person he can call.

Only one creature who moves through shifter secrets like it's his personal hunting ground.

Linus.

The raven who uses information as currency—and doesn't have enough morals to care what he buys with it.

Ryder scrolls to his name. The contact photo is just a black feather. Typical dramatic bastard.

He hits call.

It rings once.

Twice.

Then a voice answers—smooth, amused, like Linus was *expecting* him.

"Well, well," Linus croons, "if it isn't my favorite wolf with boundary issues. To what do I owe the pleasure of you ruining my afternoon?"

Ryder exhales hard.

"I need information," he says. "And I need it now."

Linus hums thoughtfully. "Oh, this sounds fun."

Ryder's jaw clenches. "It's about some underground fight club here in Vegas. Some guy named Vale. It seems he knows about shifters.

A beat of silence.

Then Linus's tone shifts—still playful, but threaded with awareness. "Yeah, you're talking about that fucker in Vegas."

"What do you know about him?"

"I know Vegas has turned into some kind of hot spot for some weird shit man. Do you know those Red Rock got some witch, like —real, alive witch living with them?"

"What?" Ryder blinks hard. This is... not the kind of information he expected.

He's suddenly starting to feel like he's been stalking Jade without knowing a *single fucking thing* about what's actually happening in her life.

"What do you mean a witch lives with the Red Rocks?"

"Yeah, a little while back, a bunch of my raven buddy's

got beat to shit by this witch at their fancy mansion I guess. Some got dead."

"Ok, well I didn't expect that. Moving on from that, what do you know about this Vale guy?" Ryder shakes his head like he can make room for more information. The last ten minutes have been really enlightening.

"That fuck." Linus huffs, "Is doing some super underground shit man. I only know rumors because no one talks in real speak. They just talk like they heard it from a friend of cousin or some shit. But the rumors be, he has underground fight clubs all over the west. Vegas. L.A. San Diego. Reno. The list goes on. The fights are just his hook. Drugs is his real business."

"Drugs?" Ryder's brain is one misfired synapse away from exploding. "He's using shifters? Shifters don't do drugs. Our bodies metabolize them too fast."

"No shit Sher—whatever that dudes name is—this stuff is made for us apparently and it's spreading through the shifter world fast."

"What do you know about the drug?"

"Nothing man. I just know that the word drug is being said. I don't even know what it's really doing. Like I said, no one talks."

"But the fight club I know about in Vegas? It's humans, not shifters."

Linus lets out a low whistle on the other end of the line.

"Ooohhhh, so you're only at the *first* door, man. The shifter fights? Invite-only. Whole different animal." He pauses, then adds proudly, "Ha. I'm so punny."

Ryder drags a hand down his face. "Yeah, you're hilarious," he deadpans. "What else should I know?"

Linus goes quiet for a beat. When he speaks again, his voice has lost the playful edge.

"Run, man. I mean it. I don't like most people—you know that, but for some reason I think you're cool. So run."

Ryder's jaw ticks.

"And on that note," Linus adds, tone snapping right back into business, "what are you gonna give me?"

"No, man," Ryder growls. "You owe me."

"For what?" Linus shoots back, all offended innocence.

"Christine," Ryder says flatly.

There's a sharp inhale on the line. "Ohhhh... dude." Linus groans. "Nuf said."

Silence stretches, then Linus sighs like the world's most dramatic bird.

"Okay, okay. Keep your head down, man. And get out of Vegas as soon as you can. I'm serious. Drugs. Witches. Werewolves... and the vamps are getting *real* nervous with all this witch talk." He clicking his tongue.

"Vegas really is turning into the Sin City of darkness and all the fuckers that go bump in the night."

"Hey, thanks, man," Ryder mutters. "You're alright. I don't care what they say about ravens."

Linus scoffs. "Hey, not all ravens are bad, man."

Ryder snorts. "Yeah? Well, a damn good portion of ravens are douchebags."

"The same could be said for wolves," Linus fires back without missing a beat.

Ryder huffs a laugh. "Touché, my friend. Thanks for the info."

"No problem, wolf," Linus replies. "Try not to die. It's bad for repeat business."

The line cuts out, leaving Ryder staring at the warehouse like it personally ruined his day, trying to untangle the mess of shit Linus just threw at him.

After running through several scenarios he keeps

coming back to the same one. He needs to get into those fights.

> Linus, one more favor man. Get me into those fights?

Ryder watches the three little dots flash.

> I just told you not to get dead but give me a day. I'll see if I can get you in.

BETRAYAL OR FATE

Jade drags herself up the mansion steps, keys slipping in her sweaty palm.

Work was a blur—documents she read three times, conversations she pretended to follow, Sam stepping in like the goddess she is. The girl deserved a damn promotion for taking point while Jade spent most of the day staring through walls.

Charlotte's order has replayed in her head all afternoon: *You're not going Friday. We play hard to get. Make him chase you.*

Friday came and went. Turns out, sitting still hurts more than the battles in the ring.

The house is *too* quiet when she walks in.

Never a good sign.

She kicks off her boots—one landing with a thud against the wall because, yeah, she's in a mood—and heads toward the game room. Voices filter out. Low. Serious.

And then her wolf lifts its head.

Ryder.

His scent hits her before the doorway does—cedar,

smoke, and the infuriating warmth she pretends she can't pick out in a crowd. It snakes under her skin, familiar in a way that makes her jaw clench.

Shoulders tense, her wolf prowling beneath her skin like *finally*—as if this is good news. Jade rolls her eyes at herself and keeps walking.

Jade storms into the game room.

Charlotte sits at the table, elbows on her knees, worry pinching the edges of her mouth. Ryder sitting across from her, arms crossed, gaze tracking Jade like a storm cell rolling in.

Her blood spikes.

"Oh, hell no," Jade snaps. "What is *he* doing here? Charlotte, seriously?"

Charlotte doesn't flinch. Doesn't even blink. Which pisses Jade off more.

"You're late," Charlotte says calmly. Too calmly.

"I was working." Jade shoots back. "But please, go ahead and tell me why my stalker is having family meetings without me."

Ryder's jaw flexes, but he doesn't bite. Which somehow pisses her off more.

Charlotte inhales slowly, then lifts an envelope off the table.

Black. Thick. Blue embossing. Blue wax seal.

Expensive in that unsettling way—like a man who sends roses after breaking your bones.

"This came today," Charlotte says. "Courier. Addressed to you."

Jade freezes. A thin line of cold slides down her spine. "From who?"

Charlotte hands it over. "I didn't open it but I can guess from who."

Jade already knows.

Vale.

The script on the front is elegant. Romantic—even. It makes Jade want to burn the whole house down.

She rips it open.

Jade,

You were missed on Friday. Terribly. I hope nothing... unpleasant kept you away. A certain beasty gentleman, perhaps? I assure you, he will not be invited again if his presence scares you off.

I look forward to seeing you on Wednesday night. We have so much to discuss.

Warmly,

Vale

Jade's stomach flips. Her vision edges red.

"He knows where we live," she whispers.

"Yup," Charlotte says, standing now. "And that's why we need to be smarter than him."

"So your plan was what? Let Ryder into the mansion?" Jade gestures wildly between them. "Is that the big strategy?"

Ryder, shakes his head, eyes locked on her—steady, infuriatingly calm.

"No, Jade," Charlotte says. "My strategy is that someone *else* needs to go in before you do. Someone he won't expect. Someone he doesn't know."

Jade scoffs. "Oh please. Vale knows the Red Rocks. He's clearly watching me. You think he doesn't know someone else is stalking me?"

"No," Ryder mutters. "Because I've been tailing your tail."

Jade whips around so fast the air shifts. "I'm sorry—what? That's creepy as fuck."

Then it hits her. Hard. Jade freezes mid-step, eyes narrowing to lethal slits. "How do you know any of this?" Her voice is low, dangerous. "Vale." She takes a step toward him, shoulders squared like she's about to throw down. "How the hell do you know?"

His jaw tics, but he doesn't back up.

"And what else," she adds, quieter, sharper—like a blade sliding into place, "do you know that you shouldn't?"

Her wolf stirs under her skin, claws scraping—not at Ryder, but at *her*. At Jade.

Agitated. Impatient. Like her wolf is saying, *He's ours, idiot. Stop fighting me.*

But Jade's human side? Oh, she's livid. Confused. Cornered. Betrayed. And beneath all that molten fury, buried so deep she wants to tear it out—a crack of something she refuses to name.

Something that feels like betrayal... but not because of Ryder. Because her wolf isn't on her side this time.

"I know everything," Ryder says. "I even met Isabell before you got home."

The words hit like a blade sliding between Jade's ribs.

She doesn't freeze because she fears for Isabell's safety. It's because something primal and ugly inside her *rears up* at the idea of Ryder anywhere near *her* witch.

"You leave her out of this." It comes out low. Sharp. Almost feral.

Ryder lifts his hands a fraction, but not in surrender—in warning.

"Relax, Deveroux. Her secret's safe with me. But it's already on the streets, and I came to warn her." He lets a slow, infuriating smile spread across his face. "She loves me already."

"How," she spits, "did you even hear about her?"

"I called in a favor." The way he says it—that smooth, deep, gravel-warm voice—only makes it worse.

Her stomach twists. Her wolf prowls. Her fists curl.

Ryder steps closer, his eyes holding hers like he's daring her to breathe wrong.

"A buddy told me about her," he says. "He also got me the password to get into the fights."

He hesitates—*not* like he's unsure, but like he's choosing which landmine to step on next.

Then he lowers his gaze, voice dropping into something rougher, almost reluctant.

"Jade... I know about Senna."

The world doesn't just tip—

it *drops.*

Like the floor tilts out from under her and every bone in her body forgets what holding her up is supposed to feel like.

"You're doing this behind my back?" Jade's voice breaks into a low, dangerous register.

"Everything I do is behind your back, Jade. Trust me, I'm used to looking at your back." Then, quieter—serious. "But this? This is the first thing I've ever done in your face."

"Do you have any idea how bad this could go? He's not some amateur ringmaster, Ryder—he's—"

"I know exactly what he is," Ryder cuts in, voice low enough to vibrate the floor. "Do you think you're the only one who ran away and got trained to become a killing machine?"

That stops her.

Harper never mentioned Ryder leaving pack territory. Never mentioned training. Never mentioned anything that sounded like this version of him.

His words drag her eyes back to him whether she wants them there or not.

"And I'm not letting you walk in blind again," he adds.

"I don't need your fucking permission, Ryder."

"No, you don't." He doesn't flinch.

"But he has mine for this mission. So this is happening." Charlotte's Alpha order slices through the room, cracking at the back of Jade's skull—and Ryder reacts... again. She definitely sees it this time. *Why the hell is he reacting to her alpha orders? He has an alpha.*

"Fine," Jade mutters. "I guess I'll see you tomorrow."

She can't stay another second. If she does, she'll break—either something in the room or something inside herself.

"Be back for dinner or suffer Isabell's wrath," Charlotte calls after her.

Jade climbs the stairs two at a time, pulse roaring in her ears.

Looking down, the compass is there. Always there. A quiet anchor in all the chaos. It calms the pulsing in her head. A reminder that even if she's furious with her Alpha... and even if the man she hates most is breathing her air...

She is loved. She is protected. She is not alone.

For just a heartbeat—just one—she lets herself believe it.

AS THE WOLVES TURN

Jade doesn't last long sitting in her room. She tried. She picked up a book. She took a shower. She folded towels that were already folded.

Gods, she tried.

But her skin felt too tight, her wolf pacing just under the surface, claws scraping, wanting out—wanting distance, wanting *air,* wanting anything that isn't this house full of people she loves and can't bear to face.

Now breathing in the desert air, relief hits her lungs.

She strips, drops her clothes on the porch rail, and shifts fast—too fast. Bones snapping, fur bursting through skin in a rush that's more desperation than control.

Her wolf launches forward immediately. No hesitation. No second thoughts.

Just dark earth and wind and the pounding rhythm of paws slamming into the ground.

She runs like she's trying to outrun her own heartbeat.

Her breath a sharp huff. Thoughts scattered. Her emotions too loud.

I can't do this. Senna. I am so sorry.

A howl tears out of her, raw and cracked.

And then—

Another howl answers. Jade skids to a stop. Not because she's startled—but because her wolf isn't startled at all.

She knows.

Shadows shift behind her. Shapes emerge.

One by one, their wolves step into the moonlight.

Charlotte and Liam lead the way, side by side—both black as the shadow they stepped out of. Liam's wolf is massive, a whole head taller than Charlotte's, built like he was carved from night and muscle.

Charlotte's is leaner, faster, that dangerous kind of stillness that makes the air pay attention.

Maddy slips from the dark behind her, russet fur catching traces of moonlight, her movements quiet and deliberate—like she's approaching a wounded animal she knows could bite.

Jaxson's hulking dark brown wolf steps in beside Ryan, both of them forming the outer wall of the circle. Ryan is laser-focused, gaze sweeping the horizon even now, like danger might break from the shadows at any second.

And Luna...

Luna's white wolf slips out last, lingering at the back— she always does. Not because she's slower. Because distance is safer. Her fur is almost luminescent under the moon, eyes sharp and unsettlingly intelligent.

Watching Jade. Reading Jade. Tracking every emotion Jade tries so damn hard to bury.

Jade's wolf bristles—not at Luna, but at what Luna carries inside her. Everyone knows the white wolf is the *gentler* half... but even she is a mask over the thing that lives beneath.

The thing Luna fights every day. The thing Jade has seen

in glimpses. The thing she knows could tear a pack apart if it ever slipped free.

So the white wolf keeps her space. Always at the back. Never fully joining the circle.

Not out of fear. Out of restraint.

Kai bounces out of nowhere, gray-gold fur bristling with excitement as he practically vibrates with the need to run. He gives Jade a playful shoulder-bump and leaps back— careful enough not to piss her off, loud enough to say *I'm here.*

They didn't follow her. They *ran with her.*

Because Jade might want distance. But her wolf... her wolf wants her pack.

And the pack answered.

Jade growls low in her chest, a mix of warning and gratitude, her fur bristling with too many feelings she can't name.

No. I can't— you shouldn't— why are you—

She hates that they're here. She loves that they're here.

She hates that they can see how broken she is. She loves that they came anyway.

Maddy steps forward—ears low, tail sweeping slow in a peace-offering arc. Then, in the most Maddy-move ever, she flops onto her back with a soft whimper. Pure submission. Pure love. Pure *don't run from us, Jade.*

Charlotte answers with a low chuff.

That Alpha-mother sound—warm and steady, impossible to ignore.

Jade's wolf shudders. For the first time all week, the crushing pressure in her chest loosens—just barely.

But enough. Enough to breathe. Enough to stand without shaking. Enough to feel the pack forming a wide semicircle around her.

Not boxing her in. But guarding her. Standing between her and the world like a living shield wall.

Jade lifts her muzzle to the sky and releases a long, low howl—not pain, not fear, not dominance.

Something else. Something raw. Finally honest. Something she'd never admit in human form.

I need help.

Maddy's wolf pops up instantly, answering with a sharp, bright howl that vibrates through the desert floor. Luna joins next, her voice a warm ribbon in the distance. Liam's deep, thunderous bellow rolls over the ridgeline. Charlotte harmonizes like she's stitching the entire pack together with sound.

One by one, the Humboldt wolves join the chorus—Jaxson, Ryan, Kai's overeager voice cracking halfway through.

The desert listens. The stars lean in.

And together, the Red Rocks and Humboldt's declare the truth in a way only wolves can: *We are one. We protect our own.*

To the death.

The run burns the last of the panic out of Jade's veins, leaving only the good kind of exhaustion—the kind that makes her wolf finally settle.

By the time they loop back toward Red Rock territory, the pack slows, paws digging into familiar earth. One by one they shift, human skin replacing fur with a chorus of grunts, pops, and groans.

Jade shifts last—because of course she does—and finds everyone else standing around in the dark, very naked, very unbothered, and very much not in a hurry to get back to the mansion. Until Charlotte puts her watch back on.

"Shit. It's 6:10."

Jade huffs out something dangerously close to a laugh. It will never not be funny that Charlotte—the most powerful Alpha Jade has ever known, the woman who could break a grown man with a look—is genuinely terrified of being late to dinner.

Liam snorts. "Well... we're dead."

Kai grins, absolutely zero shame on display. "Technically we're late for dinner and naked. So maybe Isabell will kill us first and feed us second?"

"Dude," Jaxson mutters, "she's going to hex your dick."

Kai covers himself instinctively. "What? No—Isabell likes me."

"No she doesn't," Luna says flatly, gathering her clothes. "She tolerates you. On her best days."

Maddy is already giggling as she hops on one foot trying to put her underwear on. "We can make it! The back door's right there!"

"Absolutely not," Jade says. "I am *not* showing up half-dressed to Isabell's kitchen."

Jaxson shrugs and just starts jogging toward the house—completely naked—like a barbarian who fears nothing.

Liam groans. "Pants! We have pants!"

"Do we?" Jaxson calls over his shoulder.

Charlotte throws her head back, laughing. Actually laughing. "Oh my god—fine. Everybody grab your shit. Move!"

And they run.

A pack of grown-ass adults, sprinting across the backyard in various states of undress, clutching shoes and shirts and dignity, hopping over pool noodles and dodging blow up flamingos and unicorns, laughing like idiots who forgot they were emotionally imploding twenty minutes ago.

Jade... actually smiles. She hates it. *But secretly loves it.*

By the time they crash through the back sliding door, breathless and half-dressed—Isabell is standing in the dining room doorway. Spatula in hand.

Eyes blazing.

"You late," she says, voice calm in the way hurricanes are calm.

Kai squeaks.

Jade swears she sees Isabell's nostril twitch.

Just one.

That's how they know they're all screwed.

Maddy steps forward first, still half out of breath, hands raised like she's approaching a wild animal.

"Isabell—we can explain."

"No. You sit."

Every wolf in the room—warriors, fighters, sentinels, an Alpha—immediately drops into their chairs like chastised toddlers caught coloring on the walls.

Isabell flicks her spatula toward them.

"*After* clothes," she says, voice sharp like she's scolding puppies. "Put. Clothes. On."

Half the pack scrambles to tug shirts over their heads and pull pants on under the table.

Kai gets stuck halfway in a sleeve and lets out the tiniest whimper.

Pathetic.

Jaxson pauses beside him, chest completely bare, pants still inside-out, looking like some ancient warrior dropped into a modern dining room.

Jade doesn't see him without clothes very often. He's massive—all broad shoulders and carved-out muscle, the kind of build that belongs in strongman competitions hurling boulders for fun.

"Pants are just a social construct"—then he catches Isabell narrowing her eyes.

Jaxson mutters, "What? I'm putting them on," like he's personally offended by clothing.

Jade catches Charlotte across the table, her lips are pressed together so tight they're practically white. Her shoulders shake once—just once—because she's trying not to laugh in the face of pure witch fury.

Maddy, still wearing her shirt backwards, whispers, "I think she's in a good mood though—she didn't call all of us *eediots* yet."

Kai finally wrestles himself into his shirt and beams proudly. "Guys... I did it."

Isabell turns, spatula in hand.

"Eediots."

"I stand corrected." Maddy folds her hands on the table in front of her.

Kai's smile dies instantly.

Luna is the only one who doesn't bother hiding her amusement. She sits back, arms crossed, grin wide. "This is the best day of my life," she murmurs.

Jade wants to hold onto her anger.

Routine. Control. Cause and Effect.

But, the room is warm. Chaotic. Ridiculous. Familiar.

And for the first time all day, her wolf settles—really settles.

Charlotte clears her throat, still fighting a smile. "Alright. Clothes are on. We're seated. No one's dead. We're ready for dinner."

Isabell lifts one brow. "Good." Then she disappears into the kitchen.

Jade hears the patter of Henry's light-up shoes—Luna's doing, obviously—seconds before he barrels into the dining room, blue lights flickering with every victorious stomp.

"Jade! Look!"

He stomps once. Lights explode under his toes. His grin could power the Strip.

Jade manages a smile. "Very impressive, little man."

He beams harder, then scampers off toward Lucas's old chair—the one he climbed into every chance he got.

A flicker of pain hits. Quick. Sharp. Gone. *I miss you Harp.*

Routine. Control. Cause and effect.

Jade stares at the condensation sliding down her glass. Feels the wolf shift under her skin. Quiet, but not gone. Waiting.

Her gaze drags up—straight into Luna's. Luna's grin softens. Not pity. Not concern. Just... recognition. A silent *you good?*

Jade tips her chin. Barely but enough.

The pack's chatter swells around them—warm bodies, warm voices, warm lights. A space where nothing hunts her. Where no one is taken. Her wolf stretches, pushing into the warmth like she wants to stay.

Then—

A sound. Soft. Fabric. Paper.

The letter shifts in her pocket when she moves her leg— that cold brush snapping everything tight again.

Jade exhales through her nose, reaches into her pocket, and pulls the folded letter free. She smooths the edge with her thumb, hesitating... then slides it onto the table between the bowls and the chaos.

The room dips.

Maddy notices first. Her smile fades. "Jade... what's that?"

Pushing the letter forward. "Something I got today."

Luna leans in like a crow that smells chaos. "Ohhh, is it a threat? A love note? Another bill from the HOA?"

"Just read it," Jade mutters.

Luna lifts the paper, eyes scanning—face tightening, jaw clenching. Maddy shifts, frowning. Kai sits up straight. Even Henry stops kicking his light-up shoes.

Luna plucks the letter from the table, "A certain beasty gentleman?" She snorts. "Vale writes like a Victorian villain trying to flirt with his food."

But then her expression cracks. Just a little.

"Jade... what's underneath the handwriting?"

Jade's shakes her head. Not knowing what Luna is talking about.

Luna tilts the page toward the overhead light.

"She's watching."

A cold ripple moves through the room. Before anyone can speak—the front door opens.

Bootsteps. Two sets.

And then Ryder strolls into the dining room like he owns the mortgage.

Nora is hooked on his arm, her oversized purple flannel *matching his plain purple tee* like they coordinated on purpose. Her smile is bright, beaming, oblivious.

Together they look like the prom king and queen of TwoDot, Montana—all charm, cheap flannel, and bad decisions.

Jade's stomach turns.

Ryder's grin is pure trouble. "Thanks for inviting me for dinner Isabell." Ryder speaks up and towards the opening to the kitchen.

Luna mutters, "Oh good. Dinner AND theater."

Ryder scans the room until he lands on Jade. His smile

widens—not   kind,   not   soft—weaponized   charm.
"Miss me?"

She doesn't move. Doesn't blink.

"Fuck Isabell," Jade mutters before her brain can stop
her mouth. She winces and immediately looks at Ivy. "Sorry.
I'll try to be better."

Ivy waves her off. "Henry knows which words are grown-
up words."

Henry nods with the solemn authority of a tiny judge.
"Yeah, Jade. If *I* can't say fuck, *you* can't say fuck."

Jade stares at him. "You just said it twice."

"Henry." Ivy is trying to hide the humor.

He shrugs. "I just say'n."

Luna chokes on her water. "He's not wrong."

Turning back to her sworn enemy now pulling out a
chair for himself.

"Ryder, I know you get some sick joy out of making my
life miserable, but why are you *here*?" Jade asks, heat rising
under her skin. "I get that you got yourself into the fights—
for whatever reason—but why are you sitting at *my* dinner
table?"

She stops, catching herself right before her favorite word
launches out of her mouth again. A slow inhale. Teeth
grinding. "Why," she says tightly, "are you here?"

Ryder doesn't flinch. Doesn't soften.

Of course he doesn't.

"I know this is a difficult concept for you to grasp, Jade,"
he says, tone lazy, practiced—designed to get under her
skin. "But not everything is about you. After our... little
meeting earlier, I stayed to talk to Nora. I needed more
detail about what she saw. What she heard."

Jade's pulse jumps. Little meeting. That's one way to
describe it.

"And," Ryder adds, tipping his head toward the kitchen, "Isabell informed me I was staying for dinner. Apparently I 'need to get stronger if I'm going to take care of our stubborn Jade.' Her words."

"No, no." Isabell appears with a steaming casserole dish, setting it square in the middle of the lazy Susan. "I not say stubborn Jade. I say strong Jade."

She pauses, considering. "But stubborn work."

Then she winks at Jade.

Jade nearly chokes on air. *Seriously?*

Luna slaps her palms on the table, bracelets clacking. "Okay, as much as I'm enjoying tonight's dinner episode of 'As the Wolves Turn,' can we skip to the last page? What's the letter? And what meeting?"

Ryan move—he sharpens. His posture straightens, eyes narrowing, the kind of stillness that means he's already calculating exits, threats, and who he has to maul first. "I agree," voice low. "I'd like to know what the hell is going on."

Maddy lifts her hand timidly. "Also, um... what the... duck," she says, glancing at Ivy for approval.

Ivy nods once—permitting the modified curse.

Maddy continues, "What does *she's watching* mean?"

The table goes still.

Warm room, warm food, warm noise—and suddenly Jade feels none of it. That phrase crawls under her skin again.

Her wolf paces. Not scared. Alert.

Jade swallows hard. The letter is in the middle of the table now, like a centerpiece no one asked for.

Luna points at the letter with her fork, eyes wide and wild.

"Someone better start talking before I lose my mind and

let Miss Blacky Beast out. She will eat all your faces. Don't test me."

Henry freezes, juice halfway to his mouth.

"No, Una. My face cute."

Luna softens instantly—only for him. "Not you, Henry. Never you. Only these ridiculous adults." She pats his head with the hand *not* holding a fork. "I will always protect you and your mom from any face-eating."

Henry nods, reassured, and goes back to sipping his orange juice like this is all perfectly normal.

Ryder leans back, arms crossed, eyes locked on Jade like she's the only one in the room. "She's watching?"

"Yeah," Jade says, matching his stare, refusing to blink first. "Luna found a hidden message behind the letters."

His eyes flicker—surprise or recognition, she can't tell. He masks it fast. Too fast.

Two can play that game.

And Jade refuses to lose to him tonight.

Finally, Jaxson reaches across the table and scoops up the black envelope. The paper looks wrong in his hands— too elegant, too deliberate, too much like a threat dressed up for Sunday mass.

He unfolds it carefully, the quiet in the room settling around him like a held breath.

Then he begins to read aloud.

The words spill into the air, Vale's cadence smooth and poisonous—every line sliding like oil across the warm, familiar dinner table. Charlotte's shoulders stiffen. Ryan's jaw ticks in time with every sentence.

But Jaxson's voice falters, just for a moment, when he reaches the end. The formal closing. *Warmly? It's creepy AF.* The signature that should have been the last thing on the page.

Except—it isn't.

Jaxson lifts the letter, squinting at it. Then he pulls out his phone and flicks on the flashlight, angling the beam across the page.

"Give me that," Jade snaps, already reaching.

Jaxson doesn't fight her; he just hands it over.

Jade angles the paper herself, dragging the flashlight closer.

And there it is—faint, slanted, wrong. A message Vale didn't write... or didn't bother hiding well enough.

Oh my fucking god. What else can happen to me today?

She doesn't say the words—not yet—but the room feels them anyway.

"'She's watching,'" Jaxson murmurs. His voice is lower now, his worry tone slipping into place. "I don't think those were written by the same hand."

A ripple moves through the room.

Jade's stomach goes cold. Her wolf rises, pacing, ears flat.

Ryder shifts in his chair. Not relaxed now. Not smug. Something she isn't used to seeing on him. Concern? No. She won't give him that. Not even internally.

"Ok so how was this delivered?" Ryan asks.

"Charlotte said a courier delivered this afternoon. That's all we know. But this does mean, that Vale knows a lot more about us than we know about him." Jade feels every gaze in the room land on her—Charlotte's calculation, Luna's worry, Ivy's fear, Maddy's confusion, Ryan's readiness to tear something apart.

But it's Ryder she feels the hardest. Watching her. Waiting.

Charlotte's voice snaps the moment in half. "I called Spencer and asked if Ivy and Henry could go to the Humboldt territory until we get this all figured out." Charlotte starts cutting into the lasagna Isabell set down. "Ryan has agreed to take them tomorrow morning."

"I got a new packpack, Jade!" Henry announces, practically vibrating in his chair.

Jade leans across the table and bumps her fist gently against his. Just because she's scared doesn't mean the little pup needs to be too. His smile is blinding... and gone a moment later as he turns back to his plate now full of cut up lasagna.

The warmth he leaves in her chest barely has time to bloom before the fear rushes back in.

"That puts us one wolf down," Jade says, forcing the tightness in her chest back where it belongs.

"Well," Charlotte says, gesturing vaguely at the universe, "we just wouldn't be the Red Rocks without a Sheridan in it, now would we?"

Jade had no idea her body could handle any more chaos, yet here it is—another wave crashing straight into her skull.

"What? He's joining the pack? He has a pack?" The volume rattles the silverware. She doesn't care.

Ryder shrugs one shoulder like this is all normal, like Jade isn't seconds away from launching herself across the table.

"Actually, I claimed lone wolf status awhile ago, Jade. I don't have a pack." His eyes hold hers. "But no—I'm just a hangout until we get Senna back and get you out of danger."

"Don't you dare say her name." The words scrape out of her. "Not you."

Ryder's expression shifts—barely. A flash of something she refuses to name.

"You think I don't know what she means to you?" he says quietly. Not soft. Not gentle. Just true. "And you think avoiding her name is going to keep you from breaking apart?"

Jade's pulse spikes. Her wolf claws the inside of her ribs. *He doesn't get to talk about her. He doesn't get to breathe her into the air.*

Luna stabs a fork into her lasagna like she's casing the table for weaknesses.

"Okay, great. Loving all this tension," Luna says, making dramatic little circles in the air. "But maybe we don't have a Sheridan–Devereaux death match before dessert?"

Maddy whispers, "Pretty sure this *is* dessert," earning a smack on the arm from Isabell.

Charlotte's tone snaps sharp. "Enough. Ryder, talk. Jade, breathe."

Ryder leans forward, elbows on the table, like he's settling in for the show.

"I'm here because I know this type of shady world. I'm here because I found a way in. And I'm here," he flicks a glance directly at Jade, "because whether you like it or not, I'm not letting Vale get anywhere near you."

Jade's stomach drops. The room tilts again.

He shouldn't know this much. He shouldn't know anything.

"And why," she asks, voice low, controlled, deadly, "do you care whether Vale gets near me?"

Ryder smirks—slow, infuriating, deliberate.

"Oh, sweetheart," he murmurs, "you know exactly why."

The table collectively inhales.

Jade sees red.

THE TRUTH SUCKS

J ade steps into the backyard like the air out here might actually give her lungs a second chance. The pool lights shimmer soft blue across the water, knives thudding into the wooden target with each practiced flick of her wrist.

Routine. Control. Cause and effect.

It's the only thing keeping her from unraveling.

Another knife sinks deep—dead center.

Too much force. *Of course.*

She reaches for the last blade when she hears the sliding door whisper open.

Luna doesn't announce herself. She never does. She just strolls across the patio with that effortless confidence, barefoot, holding a glass of juice like she's hosting a late-night talk show.

"Okay," Luna says, settling onto a lounge chair. "So. Spill it. Why'd you have a breakdown? And don't say 'nothing'— I've never had to hold you in the middle of the street ugly crying before." She gestures wide. "And seriously, bitch, you are *fucking hideous* when you cry."

Jade snorts, even as her chest tightens. "I didn't have a breakdown."

"Incorrect," Luna chirps. "I was there. I saw the breakdown. It was deluxe. It had toppings."

Jade yanks the knife from the target. "You're ridiculous."

"And you're deflecting." Luna sips her juice. "So let me help you not be a disaster, tell me what the hell is going on with you. And no lying—I'll know."

Jade keeps her back turned. "I... messed up."

"Yup, you said that," Luna says, kicking her feet up. "Continue."

Jade drags air into her lungs. Slow. Controlled.

But the words still scrape coming out.

"I fucked Ryder."

Luna freezes mid-sip. Then bursts into applause.

"YES. Thank you, Moon Goddess, for this content. That man has been eye-fucking you since the moment he walked into the mansion."

"Luna." Jade wants to sink into the pool and never resurface. "It was a mistake."

"Was it though?" Luna wiggles her brows. "Because your 'I regret everything' voice is identical to your 'it was so good I'm mad about it' voice."

Jade throws her hands up. "It was stupid. I lost control."

"No," Luna corrects, "you lost denial. Different things."

Jade turns sharply. "Luna, I swear—"

"Okay, okay." Luna softens, which is somehow worse. "Then why the spiral? Why did Ryder showing up feel like... that?"

Jade looks at the knife in her hand.

Focus. Control.

But the lie she wants to give her won't come out.

So she tries the truth.

The safest piece of it.

"It's Senna."

The name cracks something open inside her. Luna sees it immediately.

"Ooookay. What about her? We were talking bout Ryder."

Jade swallows hard. "Senna thought... she thought Ryder was her mate."

Luna's eyes widen. "Wait. Seriously?"

Jade nods once. "She knew when we were still kids. She was so sure. She'd felt something. But Ryder—" Her voice drops to a rasp. "—he rejected her."

Luna's jaw ticks—sympathy flashing before she shoves it back under attitude.

"Yeah... that had to kill her. Rejected mates go through hell. Chemical bonds, wolf instincts, all that crap—it hits like getting your soul drop-kicked."

"It did." Jade presses her knuckles against her thigh. "And then—when I went to kick his ass for hurting her—Ryder told me *I* was his mate."

Luna sits straight up. "I'm sorry—WHAT?"

"No." Jade shakes her head immediately, violently. "Of course he was lying. Teasing. Messing with me. He always messed with me."

Luna's expression turns too sharp, too knowing.

And Jade hates it.

"Are you sure?" Luna asks quietly.

"Yes," Jade snaps.

"Positive?"

"Luna—"

"Because," Luna says, rolling her eyes, "wolves get this worked up about non-mates. The rage, the panic, the obsession, the little snarl you did when Nora put her hand on him

—don't look at me like that, you did. Full teeth. Very Nat Geo."

Jade goes hot. "I did not—Luna, I am not obsessed with him."

"Mm-hmm," Luna hums. "And I'm not planning to commit cyber-arson in the next twenty-four hours."

Jade throws one of the knives at the target—hard—and it buries halfway to the hilt.

Luna whistles. "Yep. Super normal hostility. No mating vibes at all."

Jade turns back toward the pool, gripping the railing until her fingers ache.

"He hurt Senna. She was never the same after that day, so the rejection explains her craziness. That's all there is to it. End of story."

Luna doesn't buy it. Her voice loses some of its bite—just enough to sting.

"Jade... Senna thought he was her mate and she broke when he didn't choose her."

Luna taps her temple.

"Rejection messes with wolves. Chemicals. Instincts. Destiny. All that crap. So if Senna went crazy because he rejected *her*... Jade look at me."

Lifting her chin feels heavy—like even gravity is done with her. The last few days have dragged her to some new bottom she didn't know existed, a place made of tired and over-it.

"Don't you think its possible that Ryder's spiraling because *you rejected him*?"

The words hit harder than the desert wind. Jade's grip falters mid-throw, and the knife drops short—clattering uselessly against the concrete instead of hitting the target.

Before she can snap back—before she can yell or deny

or breathe—movement shifts at the edge of her vision. A shadow. Big. Familiar in the way a wound is familiar.

Luna tracks it too, eyes flicking over Jade's shoulder.

Then she groans dramatically and throws up a hand.

"Well. Well. Timing is everything in this house. Yes, Kai, I'm coming!" she yells to absolutely no one—because of course she knows exactly who's standing behind them.

Jade's stomach drops, cold and fast.

She turns. And there he is.

Ryder.

Ryder watches Luna breeze past him, her annoyance still sparking in the air.

"Ryder," she says with a curt nod.

"Luna." Same nod, same clipped tone. Mutual irritation. Mutual respect.

She disappears back through the sliding door, muttering something sarcastic he doesn't bother to process. His attention is already on Jade—on the way her shoulders tighten, on the way the knife glints at her feet where she dropped it.

The desert air feels... weighted. Not hot. Not cold. Just thick. Waiting.

Jade bends to grab the knife. Ryder sees the subtle tremor in her fingers.

She curses under her breath.

He hates that he notices. Hates that he notices everything about her.

He steps forward, slow and deliberate, making sure she hears him coming. He keeps a few feet of space—enough to keep her from bolting, not enough to stop feeling her wolf pushing against the air.

Her scent is anger and steel and something warm she'll never admit.

"Luna's wrong," he says quietly.

Jade doesn't turn. "About what? You stalking me? You listening to shit that's not your business? Pick one."

Ryder breathes once, slow. He's learned patience when it comes to her. Learned it the hard way.

"I'm not losing my mind," he says. "I'm not some rejected-mate cliché ready to go feral."

Her shoulders lock. "Good for you."

"But," Ryder continues, voice steady, "I heard what she said. And I need you to understand something, Jade... I've never considered you rejecting me."

Her wolf shifts. He feels her—always feels her.

Jade forces a laugh, rough as gravel. "You told me I was your mate when we were kids. I told you to get fucked. That's rejection, Sheridan."

He steps closer. Just a foot. Close enough to let his heat reach her back without touching.

"No," he murmurs. "That was you protecting Senna."

He watches her inhale—sharp. Saw that land exactly where it was supposed to.

"Jade," he says softer, "I didn't know what she told you. Not exactly. But the second you came at me like I was a threat to her, I knew something had been said. Something that made you believe staying away from me was the only choice."

Her grip tightens on the knife. He sees the white of her knuckles.

"Stop," she snaps.

"I'm not blaming her," Ryder says. "I'm saying I understood. You do what you always do—you protect the people you love."

"That's not—"

"But it meant anything I said back then wouldn't matter," he finishes gently. "You weren't ready. You weren't meant to be."

Her throat works, stubborn and tense. Her wolf presses against her like it's trying to push through bone.

Ryder steps to her side now—carefully, slowly. He would never crowd her without warning.

"Senna isn't my mate, Jade."

His voice dips into something that lives deep in his chest. Something he's never said aloud.

"She never was."

She exhales like it hurts.

Ryder feels his own expression pull—not anger, not frustration. Just the truth scraping its way up.

"And you..." he breathes, eyes dropping then lifting to meet hers, "you didn't reject me. You couldn't. Because you never accepted the truth."

Her pulse jumps. He hears it.

Jade is a storm right now—half wanting to run, half wanting to walk straight into him. He feels the war inside her like pressure on his own ribs.

"I can't deal with this tonight," she whispers.

"I'm not asking you to." His voice stays soft, even as everything in him sharpens.

He steps into her space—not touching, not even

brushing her clothes—just *close*. Close enough that she feels him in her breathing pattern.

Her wolf surges. He feels the heat roll off her.

"I'm not here because I've lost control," Ryder says. "I'm not hovering because I'm broken. Or desperate."

He leans just slightly closer, letting his breath blend with hers. No contact. All impact.

"I'm here because we're mates."

Her reaction hits him like a punch—her body tightens, her heartbeat stumbles, her scent shifts hot and furious and terrified.

"I've spent years giving you space," Ryder says, jaw tight. "Years staying out of your way. Years letting you hate me because you thought you had to."

He breathes in slowly, controlled.

"But I'm done acting like I don't feel you every time I close my eyes. I'm done pretending I don't care what happens to you. And I'm done waiting for you to stop lying to yourself."

She grips the railing behind her like it's the only thing keeping her upright. His wolf claws at his insides. He wants to claim them just has bad as the human side does.

"You don't get to say things like that," she snaps, voice thin. "Not after everything. Not after Senna was destroyed by your rejection. And now. Now she's still alive so there is a chance you could find the bond between you."

His chest tightens. Not in anger—at the pain underneath it. The pain she doesn't realize she's misplacing.

"When the truth comes out," Ryder says quietly, "you'll understand why Senna could never keep us apart."

Her pulse slams through the air.

He steps a fraction closer—still not touching. Still giving her every chance to run. She doesn't.

"Not tonight," he murmurs. "Not tomorrow."

His voice softens into something lethal and tender all at once.

"But someday, Jade... you're going to stop fighting your wolf."

He holds her gaze—one suspended, devastating heartbeat.

"And when you do," he whispers, "I'll be here."

Ryder backs away. Slow. Controlled. Every step costing him. His wolf is pissed. *I know what I'm doing. Stop killing me from the inside out.*

He leaves a void behind him—heat fading, tension stretching, her wolf pacing just under her skin.

Jade stays frozen, breath unsteady.

Ryder forces himself to back away from Jade, each step a controlled retreat. His wolf fights him the whole damn time, snarling for him to go back, to fix it, to claim her.

But he doesn't turn around.

He can't.

Not when she's that raw and he's this close to losing his grip.

He heads for the front door, jaw tight, breath low and steady.

When he steps into the foyer, he stops.

The compass inlay gleams under the black chandeliers light—dark stone, gold outlines. He's walked across this thing a few times now, but tonight... it hits different.

Ryder stands on the edge of it, not stepping onto the center. Something inside him pulls tight.

Thirty years of wanting her.

Thirty years of waiting for her.

Thirty years of knowing she deserved better than the hand she was dealt.

Liam appears at the far end of the hall, wiping his hands on a towel, watching Ryder without intruding.

"Red Rock females," Liam says with a low laugh. "They'll knock you on your ass. But worth it."

Ryder doesn't look away from the compass.

He feels its weight, its quiet steadiness. "Yeah," Ryder answers, voice low. "I know."

Liam steps closer, lowering his tone. "You hanging in there?"

Ryder swallows once, slow and controlled.

"I've been waiting thirty years," he says, barely above a breath. "I'll wait an eternity... if it means she finds her way."

Liam's expression shifts—something like respect, something like understanding.

He gives Ryder a single nod and heads down the hall.

He stays a moment longer, standing at the edge of the compass like it's a boundary he isn't allowed to cross. Then he moves forward, skirting its rim on his way to the door, the echo of Jade's wolf still humming under his skin.

IT'S WEDNESDAY... AGAIN?

R yder sits behind the wheel of his most prized possession.

Louise.

She still purrs like she came off the lot yesterday. He rebuilt her twice, restored her once, and loved her like she was the only steady thing he ever had.

When he walked away from C.O.P.S., he needed something to replace the adrenaline he'd been living on. Something loud, fast, and not Jade.

Louise had been the answer. She only stranded him a couple times.

Jade? She stranded him emotionally every damn day.

Very few people know he spent ten years deep undercover.

A decade of crawling through the worst corners of the world, taking missions no sane shifter would touch.

A decade of pretending he had no pack, no name, no future.

A decade of making sure shifters never got tangled in human wars.

Humans wanted soldiers. Shifters wanted peace.

The treaty between them was new, fragile, and ugly—Ryder had been one of the quiet hands keeping it from snapping.

Ten years of that changes a man. He exhales, long and low.

The echo of her wolf still has him buzzing. Being that close to her makes it even harder to stay away.

Without thinking, he picks up his phone.

Ring.

Ring.

Click.

"Oh shit. What trouble did you get yourself into, Ryder Owen?"

A small, reluctant smile pulls at his mouth. "Hi to you too, Ma."

"Hi, baby. You never call just to say hi. So what's wrong? Are you bleeding out? Did someone die? Did *you* kill someone? Blink twice if the FBI is involved."

"Ma..." He scrubs a hand over his face. "No. Nothing like that."

"Well thank God. I don't have bail money this week. Now talk. Your voice sounds all twisted up."

He sinks deeper into the seat, Louise's leather hugging his back like she knows.

Ryder isn't sure why he called her. He just knows he needed her voice. Needed something familiar. Grounding.

He's not prepared to tell her everything—not the part about Jade, not the way his wolf is pacing—but maybe he just needs her to tell him he's not crazy. That he's doing the right thing. That she still loves him even when he feels like he's falling apart in slow motion.

"I'm fine," he says, which is the biggest lie he's told all week.

"Mm-hm," Mama Sheridan answers, unimpressed. "And I'm six feet tall with a drinking problem. Try again."

Ryder closes his eyes. "Ma, you do have a drinking problem."

"Yeah, but I'm not six feet tall." She giggles.

God, he misses her.

"I've been following Jade. She's gotten herself in a bind, so I'm going under."

"Fuuuuuck," Mama Sheridan breathes. "Does Charlotte know? Don't you dare do anything without that Alpha's permission. She'll eat you alive and wait two days before shitting you out."

Ryder huffs a laugh. "She's not my Alpha, Ma. I don't need her permission."

"Ha! But you have it anyway."

Ryder shakes his head. "How do you do that? How do you just know shit?"

"It's a gift," she says proudly. Then, after a beat... "From your sister, dumbass. She calls me every day. Luna keeps *her* updated. See the circle of life, son?"

"Jesus. I should've known." He drags a hand down his face. "So... yeah. You know."

Mama Sheridan's voice softens immediately. "Ryder. Serious for a minute. Are you scared? This one's different. It's not just you and strangers."

Ryder pulls in a huge breath, chest tight. He's never been able to lie to her.

She's his anchor.

The only person who has ever told him the truth without bullshit—and punched him in the face when he needed it.

Literally.

"Yeah," he says quietly. "I'm really scared this time."

There's no judgment on the line. Just breathing. Waiting.

"It's the same but different," Ryder continues. "I know guys like this. I understand organizations like this. But I used to have an entire team feeding me intel. Layers of support. Backup. Eyes in every room."

He swallows.

"It's just me and my instincts now. And the one person I want to protect in this world is walking straight into the thick of it."

His voice cracks—not much, but enough she hears it.

"She's a pawn in a much larger play, Ma. I can see it, but she can't. And it's close for her. Too close."

"Oh please, Ryder. You are the baddest badass wolf shifter walking this earth. You'll keep her safe, you'll drag Senna out of whatever hell she's in, and then maybe you and those two sisters can work this mate thing out."

Ryder hears the deep inhale his mother takes.

Uh-oh.

There it is. That *sound* that means she's shifting from joking to prophecy.

"I know you already feel it, Ryder," she says, voice low and serious now. "If mate bonds are recognized but not connected, it'll start to rot you from the inside out."

He closes his eyes, jaw tight.

Yeah. He knows. He's been feeling the cracks already.

"Yeah, I know, Ma. I'm already dark enough without—"

"Stop." Her voice slices through him with the same authority she used when he was a kid sneaking out past curfew. "You're not dark. You're tired. You're hurting. And you've been carrying things alone that no wolf should ever have carried. That's not darkness, Ryder. That's weight."

Ryder swallows hard.

She continues before he can speak.

"And Jade? That girl has been carrying her own kind of weight since the day she could walk. You two are either going to save each other or destroy each other, but running from it isn't an option anymore."

"Ma..."

"No. Listen to me."

Her voice softens, but it doesn't lose its edge.

"You think you're protecting her by keeping your distance. But you're wrong. The bond won't vanish just because she refuses to accept it. It'll keep pulling you together, and if you don't connect it—really connect it—it'll eat you alive first. And she'll feel every second of your unraveling."

His chest twists, sharp and cold.

Ryder rests his head back against the headrest, eyes burning. The bond. The rot. The danger.

Jade walking straight into the fire.

Senna trapped in the middle of a nightmare.

Everything too close. Too damn close.

Mama Sheridan exhales gently, shifting her tone again.

"You're strong, Ryder. But even the strongest wolves need their mate. And whether Jade likes it or not, she needs you too."

He lets out a long breath.

"Yeah," he says quietly. "I just don't know if she'll ever let me be that."

"Oh honey... she won't." A smile in her voice. "Not at first."

A beat.

"But she will," Mama Sheridan says softly, "when she

finally realizes you've been saving her since she was two years old."

Before Ryder can breathe, loud beeping erupts on her end of the line.

"Oh shit—dammit! I forgot I was cooking." Pots clatter. Something sizzles. "This is exactly why Harper learned to cook. Alright, baby, I gotta go. Make good…"

"Decisions," Ryder mutters.

"Yeah, that."

Click.

The line goes dead.

Ryder sits with the silence for a beat, the words he didn't expect to hear settling into the hollow space behind his ribs. Saving her since she was two years old.

He exhales slowly, the weight of it tightening his chest.

He's parked about a mile from the warehouse. Time to move. He steps out of Louise, the desert air hitting him hard enough to sting.

He starts walking, boots crunching against gravel, and with every step—his memories betray him.

He watches Jade slip away from the group, crossing the wooden floor toward the long tables where the pack had eaten earlier. No one else is over there. No one's paying attention. But Jade moves with purpose, shoulders tight, eyes scanning the mess.

She starts straightening everything—cups, plates, scattered forks.

Lining them up. Fixing angles. Perfecting edges.

Even at twelve, she already unsettled something in him. Ryder frowns. Now he knows why he crossed the room that day—he's never had self control when she was in the same room.

He strides over, hands shoved awkwardly in his pockets.

"Why are you moving stuff around?"

She doesn't look up. "Because it was a mess."

"Yeah, but... everyone's done eating. Who cares?"

"I care." She lowers her voice, just enough that only he hears it.

"It looked like... shit."

Ryder opens his mouth, then closes it. He doesn't understand it exactly, but he doesn't have to. Something in her tone tells him it matters.

So he reaches for the nearest cup and nudges it until it lines perfectly with the next.

Jade freezes.

Slowly, she turns her head to look at him—truly look. Her eyes are wide, surprised, like she's bracing for the joke she's heard a hundred times before.

"You're... not going to make fun of me?"

Ryder shrugs, a little confused, a little shy.

"No. Why would I? You're just making things look nice."

For a heartbeat she just stares at him, like the words don't compute.

Then —the smallest, sweetest smile curls at the corner of her mouth. Soft. Real.

Not the one she uses around adults. Not the one she forces for her father.

A Jade-smile. Ryder feels something warm bloom in his chest, unexpected and almost painful.

That tiny smile was the only reward he needed for the rest of his life.

Jade's smile is still glowing when a shadow stretches across the table.

Her father.

Not an Alpha—but respected, charming, loud enough to fill a room without trying. Everyone likes him. Everyone trusts him.

Except Ryder. He'd known the truth early—that man

was a monster. Senna suffered, but Jade... Jade took the worst of it. She used to come to the Sheridan house for bandages and the kind of love she never got anywhere else.

"Well, look at you two," he says warmly, holding two empty glasses. "Hard workers. Or..." He gives Jade a wink the adults around them find adorable. "...my little perfectionist at it again."

The nearby wolves laugh.

Jade's smile dies instantly.

Her father sets the glasses down—deliberately crooked—then reaches out and ruffles Jade's hair hard enough for the tiny ringlets to pull from their tie.

"You don't have to tidy the whole world, sweetheart," he says in a voice meant for crowds. "Let it be messy sometimes."

The adults laugh again.

Jade's shoulders tighten so subtly but Ryder sees it.

Why didn't they care?

She reaches toward the crooked glasses, instinct taking over.

Before she can touch them, her father catches her wrist.

Not gently.

His fingers wrap around the thin bone, squeezing with a pressure that looks affectionate—but Jade flinches.

A tiny, quick reaction.

So fast no one else would notice. But again, Ryder sees it all.

Feels it like a punch to his own ribs.

"No," her father says lightly, smiling the entire time. "Leave it. It's perfect. Don't fuss."

It's not perfect. Ryder knows that.

Jade knows that.

But her father's grip tightens just enough that she lowers her hand, eyes dropping to the floor.

Something ugly twists in Ryder's gut.

Then Jade's father turns to Ryder with that same charming grin.

"Careful helping her, Ryder. Keep this up and she'll have you lining up the stars in the sky next."

More laughter from the adults.

Ryder doesn't laugh.

Jade forces a small nod, but she won't meet Ryder's eyes.

Her wrist hangs close to her body, hidden. Protected.

Her father walks away, still smiling, still adored.

Ryder stares at the crooked glasses on the table. Then at Jade's slumped posture as she slips back to her chair.

He will never forget how small she went the moment that man touched her.

It was the first time Ryder felt real anger. Real wrongness.

He fixed that glass after she left.

And he didn't know it then, but he'd just made his first promise—to spend his life fixing the things Jade hated because they looked like shit.

Ryder rounds the corner, and there it is—the rusted chain-link fence that stands between him and the shadow-world Jade has been stepping into alone. The metal rattles with every breath of wind, like it's warning him off.

Too late for that.

A single bulb buzzes over the side gate, casting a sickly cone of light onto cracked pavement. Two men sit on mismatched chairs nearby, shoulders broad, eyes narrow, wolves just beneath the surface.

One of them straightens when Ryder approaches.

"What are you doing here?"

Ryder hates how familiar this feels—how similar it is to dozens of off-grid human operations he infiltrated overseas. The same stink of desperation. The same illusion of order. The same kind of men who think they run something important when really they're just guarding rot.

He keeps his voice flat, bored, the tone that makes other men nervous without knowing why.

"Full moon, no mercy."

The guard studies him for a beat too long... then opens the rusted door.

Different password. Same pathetic theater.

Ryder steps inside.

His gut twists hard. Jade walked this path alone. She came here in a dark moment, into a place that stinks of sweat and desperation, surrounded by men who think they can touch her—all because she needed to feel something. Anything.

That truth hits harder than the memory he forced up to weaponize himself.

Ryder moves forward, every sense sharpening. He catalogues exits, shadows, possible weapons, the rhythm of distant voices.

This place thinks it's dangerous.

It has no idea what walked through its gate tonight.

A woman with a clipboard sits under another buzzing light. Same disinterested expression. Same pen tapping. Same too-bright lipstick.

She doesn't look up when she speaks.

"Name?"

"Just call me John."

Her pen pauses. "John? Really?"

With zero expression, she moves on. "Rules."

He interrupts. "I know them."

This time she does look up—studying him like she's trying to place why her heart just skipped.

"Fine," she murmurs. "Don't start shit."

He doesn't respond. He's already moving.

The lights of the fight room loom ahead. Ryder's jaw

ticks.

She came here for control. She came here for pain she could predict and got way more than she bargained for.

Vale.

Miles.

Senna.

She's going to try to save her sister.

Which means his mission is simple and impossible all at once: Save Jade.

Get the Red Rocks out of this world.

Burn down anything that tries to touch them.

Ryder steps inside. The smell hits him first—thick with sweat, blood, cheap beer, and testosterone. The noise rolls over him in a pulsing wave: cheers, groans, fists on metal, the rhythmic thud of someone already losing.

He moves through it like a ghost.

The fighters' section lines the far wall—rows of old bleachers bolted to concrete. He climbs halfway up and drops his duffel onto the bench with a dull thud.

He sits. Unzips the bag. Pulls out the wraps.

His fingers move automatically, muscle memory from a hundred ops and a thousand spars. He winds the fabric tight around his knuckles, watching the room beneath lowered lashes.

A cluster of fighters have claimed the corner near the water station—half posturing, half pretending not to be scared. And there, wedged between two idiots who think they're God's gift to violence...

Nora.

Her arms are crossed. Her expression carved from stone.

She scans the room like she's measuring which man she'd break first.

A younger fighter laughs too loudly near her.

She doesn't even look at him. She just lifts one brow—the kind of slow, unimpressed arch that shuts people up without a word.

Ryder's jaw ticks again. He keeps wrapping, slow and steady.

The air shifts. Not visibly. Not audibly.

Just... in his bones.

A prickle down his spine. A burn behind his ribs. A tightening in his wolf, low and instinctive.

Jade.

He doesn't see her yet. But he feels her. Like a storm rolling in.

He finishes the wrap on his left hand, looping and tucking the edge.

He doesn't look for her. He doesn't have to. She's here.

And she's not okay.

The first fight bell rings, sharp and metallic.

Ryder glances toward the cages—the unofficial rule in these underground rings, you get called when they want you, not when you're ready.

His name is up sooner than he expects.

"Sheridan!"

Ryder stands. Drops down from the bleachers. He doesn't bother stretching; his body is already coiled.

The fight is quick. Too quick.

His opponent comes in wild, sloppy with adrenaline. Ryder sidesteps, pivots, lands a clean shot to the ribs, one to the jaw. The man hits the floor in under thirty seconds.

The crowd roars. Ryder barely hears it.

He wipes blood from his knuckles on a towel and climbs back to the bleachers.

Still no Jade.

Nora's first fight comes next.

The girl moves like she's been fighting men twice her size her whole life—and probably winning. Her strikes are clean, her footwork sharp. She takes the guy down in two minutes flat.

No celebration.

She just walks back to her bench and cracks her neck like she's bored.

Ryder almost smiles. Almost. Another fight. Another round of shouting. Another moment where Jade *should* have appeared by now.

She doesn't.

A ripple of unease slides through Ryder's chest.

Nora's second fight is rougher. The guy is bigger, faster, dirtier. She still handles him—until he catches her with an elbow to the cheek that staggers her. She recovers, but the momentum shifts. She loses by a technical call, shoved against the fence.

She stomps back to her spot, furious rather than defeated.

Ryder respects the hell out of it.

Still... no Jade.

His wolf paces under his skin.

He scans the bodies around him, searching the crowd, the corners, the higher levels, the shadows any wolf could slip through.

Nothing.

Ryder's second fight is longer.

He lets it be.

He needs the distraction, the adrenaline, the violence to sharpen the edge inside him. His opponent lands a few hits—Ryder lets him. Lets the pain anchor him in the moment.

But the end is inevitable.

Ryder drops him with a brutal combination and walks out of the ring without acknowledging the cheers.

His heart is hammering for a different reason.

By now, hours feel like minutes and vice versa.

Still no Jade.

He makes his way toward Nora, sliding onto the bleacher beside her casual enough not to draw attention.

She side-eyes him.

"You seen Jade?" he asks, keeping his tone neutral.

Nora shakes her head once. "No. Not since I've been here and I came early."

A beat.

Ryder's gut goes cold.

Before he can respond, a man approaches—broad shoulders, shaved head, bright *red rope* wrapped around his fists and forearms like some knockoff ceremonial badass.

He jerks his chin at Nora.

"You. Special meeting."

Nora rolls her eyes. "With who?"

Red Rope Dude smirks. "People who matter."

Ryder stands before he means to, towering over the guy.

"Yeah," Ryder says, voice dropping a full octave. "Take me too."

The guy blinks. "Uh... no."

"I'm with her."

Ryder gestures vaguely between himself and Nora, miming some ridiculous "buddy–buddy" motion that looks painfully out of place on him.

"We're a... team."

Nora pinches the bridge of her nose.

"Oh my God, sit down. I don't know this dude. He just wandered over here and started hitting on me."

Ryder blinks. Hitting on—? "What the hell—"

Nora doesn't give him time to protest. She leans back on one elbow and looks him dead in the eyes.

"Like cougars, eh?" she purrs loud enough for Red Rope Dude and half the bleachers to hear.

"I'll find you after the fights. We'll see if you can handle a real one."

Red Rope Dude chokes on a laugh.

Several nearby fighters turn to stare.

Ryder feels heat crawl up the back of his neck—mortification, not embarrassment.

Fantastic.

Now everyone thinks he's trolling the fighters' lounge for dates.

He clears his throat, jaw tight. "That's... not—"

Nora waves him off, already standing. "Relax, sweetheart. You can buy me a drink later."

She saunters toward Red Rope Dude, who looks like he's terrified and impressed all at once.

Ryder sinks back onto the bleacher, muttering under his breath,

"Fucking wonderful."

Ryder doesn't sit until Nora disappears through the door painted almost the same color as the wall.

A trick door. Hidden in plain sight.

Two huge guys shift back into position the second it shuts—shoulders broad, arms folded, eyes blank. Not human. Not wolf. It doesn't matter. They're blockers. Guard dogs. Designed to make people stop asking questions.

Ryder's jaw ticks.

That's the door Jade went behind before.

The one she came out of wrecked—broken, bruised, barely breathing.

His gut tightens.

His instincts start talking to him in that old, familiar way —the one trained in back alleys, warzones, and human conflict zones he wishes he could forget.

That's not a meeting room. That's not administrative bullshit.

That door is where the real danger lives.

And Jade walked through it alone.

Ryder's fingers curl into fists on his thighs.

He needs to get in there. He doesn't care who stands in front of it.

He doesn't care what rules they pretend exist here.

He doesn't care what's waiting behind that painted panel—

His wolf lunges forward inside him, a low growl reverberating through his ribs.

Jade went behind that door.

So Ryder will too.

(UNCONSCIOUS) JADE

Blackness swallows her.

A dragging emptiness that feels like hands gripping her ankles and pulling her under.

Something cold bites into her wrist. Metal. Leather. Pressure.

Jade tries to move—but her body won't answer. Her limbs feel filled with wet sand. Her eyelids flicker open for a single, agonizing second— A ceiling bathed in bright light.

A shadow leans over her blocking the light just enough for her to peek open her eyes. *Blur.* A voice—distant, garbled.

"...dose was too much—"

"...don't break her—"

"...not yet..."

Blackness crashes back over her like a wave.

Somewhere in the void—a scream. Not loud. Not clear. Like it's coming through water.

Jaaaaaade...

Her body tries to react but can't. Her fingers don't move. Her lungs forget how to pull air.

The scream echoes again—closer this time, frayed at the edges.

Jade!

Her vision snaps awake in violent, stuttering frames.

Straps. Across her wrists. Across her ankles. Across her chest.

Her body jerks on instinct—once, twice—but nothing gives.

Her pulse spikes. Her wolf is there but weak—so weak.

And then everything goes dark again.

The house is too quiet. Not the peaceful kind of quiet—the held-breath kind.

The something's-wrong kind.

Jade stands in the narrow sliver of space beside her father's office door, pressed flat against the wall. She's just sixteen. Old enough to understand danger, old enough to know better than to be here, and too desperate for answers to walk away.

Her father's voice hums through the crack in the door— smooth, patient, dipped in that effortless charm he uses on the world. The charm he never bothers wasting on her.

"...we need to remain strategic, Senna. Sheridan blood complicates things."

Jade's breath catches.

Sheridan? Ryder?

Senna's voice answers, soft and composed—too composed.

"I know, Father. Jade told me she has a crush on him."

A beat.

Then a faint smile in Senna's tone, "She trusts them more than she trusts us."

Jade stiffens. Her pulse hammers. She should leave. She can't.

Her father exhales, amused. "Then steer her. That's always been your strength. You've kept her in line since she was small."

He chuckles. "She'd walk off a cliff if you told her you were too scared to do it, just to keep you safe."

Jade can't see her face, only her silhouette—small, slight, the careful, quiet older sister everyone pitied and protected.

Senna has always been gentle. Always afraid of their father's temper. Always whisper-soft and apologetic, like she's trying to take up less space in the world.

But the voice that comes out of her now, doesn't match the girl Jade knows.

It's steady. Unshaken. Sharp as glass. Not trembling. Not hesitant. Not scared as she is talking with their father.

For the first time in her life, Jade hears something in Senna that freezes her in place—confidence.

A tone that doesn't belong to the weak sister she's spent her whole life protecting.

A tone Jade has never heard from her. A tone that feels... dangerous.

Her stomach flips. Her fingers go numb. Part of her wants to step back into the hallway and pretend she never heard this. Pretend Senna is still the fragile girl who hides behind her.

But she can't.

Because this voice—this version of Senna—is a stranger.

"I'll make her stay away from Ryder Sheridan," Senna says.

Her father's voice sharpens with interest. "How?"

Senna doesn't hesitate. "I'll tell her he's my mate."

Jade's stomach drops.

Jade sees the shadow of his chair move. "And she'll believe that?"

"Of course," Senna murmurs, almost fond. "She believes everything I tell her."

They share a soft laugh—two blades sliding past each other.

The sound slices down Jade's spine. The truth hits her so hard *she sways, They aren't protecting her. They aren't guiding her. They're using her.*

Senna continues, voice bright with wicked intelligence, "And once she thinks Ryder is my mate, she'll stay away. She would never hurt me like that."

Her father hums approval. "Good. Very good."

Senna's voice drops to something smooth and controlled—a razor hidden in silk.

"As soon as he rejects me, she'll turn on him. She always defends me."

A pause. A soft, pleased hum.

"So it works out, Father. Jade will do the damage for us."

Jade's breath snags in her throat.

Senna continues, light as a feather and twice as deadly, "And after that... I'll steer her toward a different mate. One that suits our future."

Another pause—sharp, intentional.

"Tell me father, which bloodline would you like her tied to?"

Jade covers her mouth, breath shaking.

She should run. She should scream. She should kill Senna. She does neither only because she hears her father add, quietly, "And if she resists?"

Senna's smile enters her words again—sweet, cold, poisonous. "Then you remind her why obedience is easier."

Air slams back into her lungs like a punch.

Her eyes snap open. Light—too bright. Metal—cold against her spine. Leather straps—biting into her wrists and ankles.

She jerks hard. The restraints hold.

Panic spikes—raw, animal, immediate.

Then she hears it. A soft, shaking inhale beside her.

Jade whips her head to the side.

Senna.

Strapped down just like her. Eyes swollen. Tear-streaked. Weak, trembling Senna.

The version of her sister she's always known.

Jade's whole body jolts like she's been electrocuted.

"You," she chokes out, voice shredded. "You lied to me."

Senna flinches. Hard.

"Jade—what—what are you talking about?"

"You told me Ryder was your mate!" Jade thrashes against the straps, leather cutting into her skin. "You planned it! I heard you—you asked Father what bloodline he wanted—and you—"

Senna's eyes go wide. Terrified. Confused. Small.

"Jade, stop—please—stop. I don't know what you're saying."

"You do!" Jade's voice cracks under the weight of the memory. "I heard you say you'd steer me away from Ryder! You made me hate him! You—"

"No!" Senna sobs now, shaking so violently the table rattles.

"Jade, listen to me—please—it's the powder! They—they make us drink it. It messes with your head. It makes you see things. Hear things. Please—"

Jade's chest heaves. Tears blur her vision. But the memory felt so real. Too real. Senna's voice in that office... the coldness... the calculation...

It felt like truth.

But the girl beside her—this fragile, crying sister—*that* is the Senna she grew up protecting.

Right?

"Jade, I would never betray you," Senna whispers, voice cracking.

"Never. You're all I have. Don't you know that?"

The words slice her open.

Jade shakes her head, shaking with anger, confusion, grief she can't place.

"I heard you," she whispers, a broken sound. "I heard you, Senna."

Senna sobs harder, pulling at her own restraints.

"Please... please don't hate me. I don't know what they did to you. But I swear—I swear—I would never hurt you."

Jade squeezes her eyes shut, forcing herself inward, reaching for the one thing that she needs to live.

Her wolf.

Come on. Please. Say something. Growl. Snap. Breathe. Anything.

But the space inside her chest is... wrong. Not empty. Not silent.

Muted.

Like her wolf is behind a wall thick enough to muffle even instinct.

Jade's breath stutters.

"No," she whispers, panic hooking into her ribs. "No, no, no—not this."

She remembers Lucas—the haunted look in his eyes the way he said the powder smothered his wolf until he felt like he was dying from the inside out.

Senna is still crying beside her, but the world narrows, tightens, tilts.

Jade tries again, pushing deeper into the bond she's always felt like a second heartbeat.

Talk to me, she begs inwardly. Nothing. Not one whisper of the creature that kept her alive when she couldn't.

Her chest locks.

"This feels different," Jade chokes out, voice barely air. "She's gone quiet before but—this—this isn't quiet. This is—"

She can't finish.

Because the truth is crawling up her throat like something feral—this isn't her wolf going dormant. This is someone cutting the connection.

Jade's fingers curl against the restraints, nails digging into her palms so hard she feels skin break. Fear floods her bloodstream. Real fear.

Not the kind she pushes through, not the kind she rationalizes, not the kind she's trained to control.

A primal, suffocating fear she's never felt in her life.

They are killing her.

Senna draws a sharp, shaky breath beside her. "Jade?" she whispers. "Jade, what's wrong?"

But Jade can't answer. Because for the first time—the very first time—she realizes she might not get out of this.

And even worse—her wolf might not either.

Jade swallows hard, her throat raw. She doesn't want to ask. She *shouldn't* ask.

But the terror is climbing, cold and metallic, scraping up her spine.

"Senna?" she whispers, barely breathing. A question she already fears the answer to.

"Do you... still have your wolf?"

Senna's crying cuts off instantly. Not quiets.

Stops.

Like someone hit a switch. Her whole body goes rigid against the restraints. Her eyes go unfocused, staring past Jade at the ceiling—too still, too empty.

Jade's breath falters. "Senna?" Her voice fractures. "Senna—answer me."

A beat of silence. Then another. Then—

Senna exhales, slow and hollow.

"No, Jade," she says, voice flat in a way Jade has never heard before. "She's gone."

The words punch through Jade's chest like claws. Her vision blurs. Her heart stutters.

Her wolf—still won't respond.

"Gone?" Jade's voice shreds apart. "H-how? Senna, what do you mean gone?"

Senna doesn't look at her. Doesn't flinch. Doesn't cry.

She just stares at the ceiling, expression blank—like whatever part of her used to feel anything has already left.

"Just gone," she murmurs. "Like she was never there."

And Jade breaks. Not outwardly—not yet.

Because Jade has lived through beatings, terror, starvation, manipulation, loss, trauma, violence, and wars—she has never imagined a pain like this.

A wolf disappearing? A soul ripped from a body. A piece of identity wiped out like an eraser dragged across a page.

If they can take Senna's wolf—they can take hers too.

Her breathing turns sharp. Fast. Panicked.

"Senna..." Jade whispers, the word breaking apart in the back of her throat. "What if they're—what if they're doing that to me?"

Senna's eyes squeeze shut. For a long, suffocating moment, she doesn't speak. Doesn't even tremble. Still... just... stillness.

The kind that means acceptance, not fear. Finally— slowly—she turns her head toward Jade. Her voice is barely a breath.

"Jade... they don't stop."

Jade's chest tightens.

Senna swallows hard, staring past her restraints like she's trying to disappear inside herself. "They take pieces of you," she says softly. "One at a time. Quietly. So quietly you don't notice until—" Her breath hitches. "Until there's nothing left but obedience."

Jade's pulse claws up her throat. "Senna—don't say that—"

Senna shakes her head, tiny, brittle. Her eyes shimmer with tears she won't let fall. "They took my wolf first," she whispers. "My voice next. And then... then they only had the smallest part of me left."

Jade's stomach caves inward. "No," she breathes. "That's not—that can't—"

Senna inhales, shaky and shallow. "They're going to do the same to you, Jade."

Her voice trembles, cracking like thin ice. "They're going to take your wolf. And when they do... you'll be like me."

Jade shakes violently against her restraints. "Stop. Senna —stop—"

But Senna keeps going, because she's not pleading anymore. She's confessing.

"You'll become what they want. A weapon. A slave. A body they can use."

She looks at Jade with hollow, broken eyes.

"And once they break your wolf, there's no coming back."

The words hit Jade like a blade to the gut. A cold, consuming terror floods her veins. This is worse than death. Worse than abandonment.

Jade can barely hear Senna's voice anymore. She is digging deep hoping to find her wolf and give her the power she needs to fight this.

Senna's breath evens out. Too suddenly. Her tears stop like someone pulled the plug.

"They only put me in here with you to explain," Senna whispers, eyes going distant. "To start the breaking process."

Jade's pulse stutters.

Senna turns her head, slow and deliberate, her expression shifting into something Jade can't process—not fear, not pain... something else. Something practiced.

"This is the playbook, Jade." A faint, eerie calm settles over her voice.

Before Jade can respond, Senna sits up—not struggling, no wincing, just *rising* like her restraints were decorative.

The straps fall away from her arms and chest like they were never buckled tight.

Jade's breath collapses. "Senna..." Her voice warps around panic. "How did you—why are you—"

Senna doesn't move to comfort her. Doesn't look afraid.

She just looks... resigned.

"I'm sorry, Jade," she says softly, the words weighted but empty at the center.

"I tried. I really tried." She leans closer, eyes unreadable. "But once they take her... you're theirs."

Senna doesn't get the chance to say anything else.

Because as if on cue—as if she *knew*—the heavy metal door clanks and swings open.

Jade's head snaps up so fast her vision swims.

Vale stands in the doorway. Perfectly pressed shirt. Perfect posture. Perfect, smug smile carved across his face like he practices it in mirrors.

"Darling Jade," he purrs, stepping inside. "I hate to see you like this."

His voice drips with false sympathy so thick it coats the air.

Two men step out from behind Vale, fanning around him like trained shadows.

But they're not guarding him. They're moving toward her.

Vale's gaze slides to the straps on Jade's wrists, still biting into her blood-slicked skin.

"Oh Jade. I am so sorry for all this. I truly am."

Vale's tone sickly sweet.

"It's just... you came in all huffy and puffy and I thought for sure you were going to go wolfy and mess up my brand new Persian rug. It was a gift you know."

He sighs, brushing invisible dust off his cuff. "This room is so..." He wrinkles his nose delicately. "Yucky." He flashes Jade a smile that feels like a blade. "We should talk somewhere more comfortable."

Jade's pulse detonates. "No—don't fucking touch me—don't—"

But the goons are already on her. Not gentle. Not careful.

Just unbuckling the restraints with bored efficiency, like she's a piece of equipment they're transferring.

Her limbs fold in when they free them. Her wolf is *still* silent.

The men grip her under the arms and haul her upright.

Her feet barely catch the floor. Her legs buckle with every step. She's dead weight, dragged rather than led.

"Please—stop—!" Jade slurs, vision swimming.

Her body is too weak to fight.

Vale walks ahead of them, hands clasped behind his back like he's giving a tour of an art exhibit he's particularly proud of.

Senna follows behind him, eyes down, silent.

They pass through a hallway lit with harsh white bulbs.

Jade's bare feet scrape concrete.

Vale's office door stands open like a gleaming mouth.

He enters with a flourish and settles casually behind his desk—the same desk Jade saw in her memory, the same desk where Senna once stood beside him, the same desk where her father's shadow still clings to the corners of her mind.

"Put her there," Vale says, pointing.

The floor. In front of him. Like an offering.

The men drop her.

Her knees slam into cold tile. Her palms slap down uselessly.

Her head hangs, hair falling forward, breath shuddering in uneven bursts.

Her wolf... still gone. *I'm so sorry.*

Every cell in Jade's body screams danger, but her voice comes out a broken rasp. "Vale... please..."

He leans back in his chair, crossing one leg over the other with a lazy elegance.

"There we go," he murmurs. "Much better. Don't you feel calmer already?"

Senna stands off to the side, hands clasped before her, eyes empty—the perfect, obedient broken thing.

Jade trembles against the floor.

Not because she's weak. Not because she's drugged. Because for the first time in her life—she is completely alone inside her own mind.

Vale steeples his fingers, studying Jade like she's an unruly child who disappointed him.

"Jade," he says softly, as if her name itself is a reprimand.

"Why must everything with you be so... dramatic?" Vale sighs, then tilts his head.

"Senna tells me you don't like messy." His hand sweeps lazily toward her—her blood, her torn skin, her restraint.

"So why all this, Jade? Why make such a mess of yourself?"

Jade raises her head just enough to meet his gaze—a mistake.

His smile widens. "You storm into my establishment snarling like a feral thing," Vale continues, voice warm, patient, almost affectionate.

"You refuse every offer of safety I present you. You insist on bruising yourself—physically, emotionally, spiritually."

He sighs. A father disappointed in a daughter. A teacher scolding a pupil.

"I've done nothing but try to help you. And yet..."

He lifts his hand, palm up, waiting. "Here we are. Again."

Jade trembles, rage boiling under her skin—rage that she can't use because her wolf is still silent.

"I didn't—" she starts, voice breaking.

Vale clicks his tongue.

"No lies, darling. Not today. Especially not after I discovered something quite upsetting."

He leans forward, elbows on the desk, smile sharpening.

"You brought a friend with you."

Jade's heart stops.

"No," she whispers. "No, Vale I..."

He cuts her off with the snaps of his fingers.

"With you sneaking around like a little spy," he says conversationally, "I had hoped you'd at least come alone. But then I found out..."

He lifts two fingers. A signal.

The door to the right swings open. Heavy footsteps. A body dragged. Jade twists just enough to see—Nora.

Nora's head hangs forward, hair veiling her face as the guards drag her in.

Her body is completely limp, feet dragging uselessly behind her.

Dark bruises wrap around her upper arms where their hands clamp down, her limbs swinging with each pull like she's not awake enough to feel it.

The goons drop her beside Jade.

Her body hits the floor with a sickening, wet thud that echoes off the concrete walls.

Jade is already reaching toward her—as far as her weak arms and trembling hands will allow—but the largest of the assholes steps forward. He plants his boot against Nora's shoulder and shoves her over onto her back.

Jade's scream rips from her throat before she even sees it all.

Nora's throat is gone. Not cut. Not slashed. Ripped. Out.

A hollow cavern where her life used to be.

Her eyes, once sharp, stare glassy and empty at the ceiling. A last breath frozen in her open mouth.

Jade's voice cracks apart—"NORA!"

Her scream burns, splitting through the room, shattering whatever numbness she had left.

Jade collapses forward onto her hands, body shaking with grief so violent she can barely keep herself upright.

Her wolf doesn't answer.

"Nora..." Jade whispers, voice raw. "No—no, no, please—"

But her friend is a body now. A shell. A warning.

Vale lets out a thoughtful hum. "As you can see," he says gently, "I don't appreciate dishonesty."

Jade's entire world sharpens into a single point of agony —*I'm sorry Nora. I'm so sorry.*

And then—her grief becomes something else. Something dark. Something violent. Something rising through her veins like poison and fire.

But her wolf remains silent. Leaving Jade with nothing but human helplessness and a rage that's killing her from the inside out.

Vale watches her unravel, amusement twinkling in his eyes.

"That's what disappoints me the most," he murmurs, shaking his head.

"You didn't trust me. You didn't tell me about your little companion. And now..."

He gestures toward Nora with casual disdain. "Now she's hurt because of *your choices.*"

Jade's entire body shakes uncontrollably. "You're a monster," she spits, tears burning her eyes.

Vale's brows lift in surprise. "A monster?"

Then he laughs. Soft. Light. Pitying.

"Oh, Jade. No. No, darling." He places a hand over his heart. "I am the only one here trying to save you."

Jade's voice crumbles. "You're hurting us—"

"I'm preparing you," he snaps. "Giving you purpose. Structure. Direction."

He taps a finger against his desk, slow and deliberate.

"You crave organization. Perfection. And your pack clearly can't give you that."

His tone softens—sweet, almost pitying.

"And if your friend here wound up a little bruised... well... she knew the risks, didn't she?"

He leans back in his chair, utterly at ease.

"Actions have consequences, Jade. And in your case..." He smiles, calm and cruel. "You seem determined to earn every one."

And for the first time, Jade truly believes—she might not survive this.

Jade is curled on the floor, trembling, blood drying on her wrists.

Nora's body lies beside her like a nightmare everyone else seems weirdly calm about.

Senna stands statuesque and hollow, hands folded neatly like a servant waiting for her next command.

Vale inhales deep, satisfied.

"Alright," he says lightly, dusting his palms together. "So now that we've dealt with your little issue of distrust..."

He rises from his chair with deliberate, theatrical grace.

Jade's stomach drops.

"What's next, you ask?"

He begins walking toward her—smooth, unhurried steps echoing off the concrete.

Jade tenses. No wolf. No strength. But maybe—maybe— enough adrenaline to tear at his throat if he gets close enough.

Her fingers twitch. Her nails curl. Her breath stutters into a slow, predatory inhale.

Vale crouches in front of her, smiling like a man greeting a timid child.

"There she is," he murmurs. "The fire. The instinct. You and I are going to make something extraordinary together."

Jade's pulse spikes. Her muscles coil. She waits for the moment he leans in—waits for one opening—waits for a chance to aim every last ounce of human strength at the soft part of his neck—Vale tilts his head, unconcerned. "Do you know what happens next, Jade?"

Barring her teeth, "Yeah," she rasps. "You die."

His smile sharpens—

BOOM

Noise detonates through the building. The walls tremble.

He flicks two fingers toward his men in a lazy, dismissive gesture.

"Go see what the commotion is. And try not to make it worse—you all know how I hate loud guests."

Jade's heart kicks hard once.

Something hits the office door again—hard—wood splintering, the frame cracking top to bottom.

Vale stops mid-step, one brow lifting in mild annoyance, as if someone interrupted a dinner, not a torture session.

"Oh dear," he murmurs. "It seems your shadow followed you."

Another crash.

The impact caves the wood inward, blasting splinters across the room.

Debris smacks the nearest goons in the face. One yelps, clutching his eye, the other staggers back cursing.

A second hit follows—louder, angrier, *inevitable.*

And then the entire door explodes inward, ripped off its hinges and skidding across the floor like it's made of cardboard.

Smoke. Dust. Silence thick enough to stop a heartbeat.

Vale exhales, long and slow. "I suppose," he says, "that would be your rescue party."

Ryder fills the doorway like a storm given a body. Chest heaving. Hands bleeding. Eyes black. No gold. No green. No human.

Jade can see him—the wolf boiling just beneath Ryder's skin.

His eyes snap to her first, a sharp, feral look that steals her breath.

Then his gaze drags across the room—to Nora's body, pale and still on the floor, to Senna standing rigid and ghost-like by the wall.

Every shift of his eyes is a blow.

Jade doesn't need to hear his thoughts to feel the moment he breaks.

Ryder steps farther into the room, shoulders shaking with restraint. "Did you touch her?" Pointing to Jade.

"Oh, goody." Vale claps his hands like he's watching the best show of his life.

"Your hero has arrived. He's ruined my plan and broke my door, but I'll forgive you, Mr. Sheridan—" his smile is infuriatingly calm, "—if you say it. Say you'll burn the earth for her. Come on. Say it." Again clapping softly. "Say it."

Ryder doesn't take the bait.

Jade watches a Ryder she doesn't recognize—calm, terrifying.

"Did. You. Touch. Her?" The growl under the words isn't human at all.

"Control, Mr. Sheridan. Something you've always lacked."

Ryder lunges.

Vale moves faster than he should, palm slapping a switch.

A metal grate slams down between them, rattling the floor.

Ryder hits it with enough force to shake the entire office. The impact rattles Jade's bones.

She tries to push herself upright. "Ryder—"

He drops to his knees on the other side of the grate, gripping the bars like he'll rip them off with his bare hands.

His face—God, his face—wild and devastated and furious.

"Jade," he breathes, voice cracking under the weight of it. "Look at me. I'm here. I've got you."

Her breath breaks apart. "He... he killed her."

Ryder's jaw clenches so hard a muscle jumps violently along his cheek.

Before he can speak, sirens split the air—loud, close, surrounding the whole building.

Vale's expression falters.

Ryder's mouth twists into something feral. Jade doesn't know what he's done, but the satisfaction glints in his eyes.

Jade looks over Ryder's shoulder to see Jase storming through the broken doorway with C.O.P.S. agents, Vegas PD, and her Alpha's behind him.

But Ryder's focus never leaves Jade. "I'm getting to you," he swears, yanking at the grate hard enough the metal whines.

Vale snaps his fingers at Senna. "Come."

Senna flinches—like someone tugged an invisible leash —and takes a step.

"No!" Jade screams, voice tearing painfully. "Senna— don't go with him!"

Senna freezes. Her eyes flick between Vale and Jade. Conflicted. Fractured.

"Senna," Jade begs, tears burning hot down her face as she crawls toward her.

"Stay with me. Please."

A crack forms across Senna's expression—the kind carved from years of damage.

"I... I don't know who I am without him," she whispers.

Jade reaches for her. Her arm shakes. Her fingers barely move. But she reaches anyway.

"Please. I'll show you who you are."

Behind the grate, Ryder roars her name—the sound tearing through the room.

Jade knows he's still trying to break the bars.

"Jase!" he chokes out. "Help!"

Senna flinches at the noise... and takes one step toward Jade.

Vale sees it. His mask snaps. "Senna," he grits out, "choose wisely."

Jade hears none of the chaos behind her. It's as if the whole room holds its breath.

Senna trembles. Looking down, "Jade..." she whispers—

And then she turns, running after Vale. Gone through the door to the left.

The sound that leaves Jade isn't a scream and isn't a sob. It's something older. Something broken.

Metal shrieks.

Ryder tears the grate off its hinges and is at her side in seconds. He gathers her into him, cradling her like her bones might fall apart.

"Jade," he whispers fiercely, "I'm here. I've got you. I swear, I've got you."

Agents flood the room.

Jase kneels beside Nora.

The packs fill the doorway.

But Jade feels only two things—Senna chose Vale.

And her wolf is still silent.

"Charlotte," Liam says tightly. "We need to get her home. We need to heal her."

DO THE FUCKING LIGHT THINGY

Jade slumps against his chest in the back seat, her head tucked under his chin. She passed out again minutes after they left Vale's building, and every second she stays limp, steals another piece of his sanity.

She feels... small.

He didn't notice it before. Jade never seemed small. She was all sharp edges, fire, and fury—impossible to contain. But now her body is feather-light in his arms, nothing but bones and bruises and skin far too cool for his comfort.

Too light. Too fragile. Too wrong.

Ryder adjusts his grip, hating the way her hip fits into one hand. Hating the way her ribs press against him with every shallow breath. Hating himself for not noticing sooner.

What the hell did they do to her?

"Faster," he growls at Jaxson. The man doesn't argue—tires scream around a corner.

Jade doesn't stir.

Ryder presses his cheek to the top of her head, breathing

her in. His wolf paces frantically beneath his skin, claws scraping, demanding he hold her tighter. Keep her close. Never let her out of arm's reach again.

The moment the SUV skids to a stop in the driveway, Ryder is out—carried by instinct alone. He gathers Jade into his arms, her weight barely anything, and storms toward the house.

Charlotte and Liam are waiting in the bedroom, the air already pulsing with some strange energy.

He lowers Jade onto the bed as gently as his shaking hands allow. Her head lolls to the side. Her fingers curl weakly, like her body is still fighting even in unconsciousness.

Ryder sits beside her, refusing to move.

Refusing to let go.

He lays a hand over her heart—because he needs to feel it, needs proof she's still here, still breathing, still his to protect.

"Ryder, move."

Charlotte kneels beside him, voice steady but eyes worried.

"This will help her. Trust me."

He doesn't want to. Every instinct screams *no*.

But he forces himself to stand, backing toward the wall, never taking his eyes off Jade.

Then the light hits.

It erupts so bright it slices straight through his vision. Ryder lunges for Jade on pure instinct—

—but Jaxson and Kai are there, grabbing his arms, dragging him back.

"No, big guy," Jaxson grunts, bracing against Ryder's weight.

"You don't want to get in the middle of that."

Ryder fights them anyway.

Fights until his muscles burn.

Until his wolf claws for control.

Until he's convinced that light is swallowing her whole.

But then—just as suddenly as it flared—the glow dies down, and the arms holding him fall away.

Ryder is at Jade's side before anyone breathes.

"What did you do to her?" His voice is a wrecked rasp.

"Relax, Sheridan," Charlotte says, wiping sweat from her brow.

"She'll be back to her normal bitey self after some rest."

Weakness pulls at both Charlotte and Liam—real, heavy, visible. Ryder has never seen them like this. Whatever they did cost them.

Liam straightens just enough to speak, though his voice lacks its usual weight.

"Let's give her room. Everyone out."

Ryder opens his mouth to argue—but something in Liam's tone stops him.

It reminds him of his own father. Strong as hell, soft in the ways that mattered.

Ryder gives a stiff nod and steps back...but he doesn't leave.

Not yet. Not until someone forces him.

"Not you, dumbass. We get it. You're not leaving until she's okay." Charlotte mutters it over her shoulder as she walks out the door.

Ryder pulls the chair as close to the bed as he can without climbing onto it and collapsing beside her. Jade doesn't move. Her breathing stays shallow but steady, each rise and fall of her chest a tiny mercy he counts like prayer beads.

He sits there for minutes. Then hours.

Time stops meaning anything.

He watches the light of early morning creep through the blinds, striping across the bed. Her skin looks gray at first—too pale, too thin. But slowly, impossibly, color starts bleeding back into her cheeks.

Her face softens.

Her sunken features begin to fill out.

The cuts along her jaw stitch themselves closed, not instantly, but bit by bit, like tiny hands working under her skin.

Ryder keeps staring.

He can't look away.

Every few minutes he glances at the door, half-expecting that strange light to come back. Half-wondering how the hell Charlotte and Liam did that. Half-afraid they're the only reason Jade is still breathing.

He hates not knowing. Hates feeling useless. Hates sitting here while her body fights to come back to him.

Hours slip by. His back aches from the chair, but he doesn't move. Not even when his stomach snarls or his throat burns dry. He watches every breath she takes like it's the only thing keeping him tethered.

At some point his voice slips out—quiet, gruff, barely more than a whisper.

"You know... I've always been drawn to you."

It sounds stupid out loud. Too soft. Too exposed. But the room is empty and she's asleep, so it doesn't matter.

"Before the mate bond. Hell, before my wolf even showed up."

He huffs out something like a laugh.

"You'd come over to play with Harper, and I'd find excuses to be around. Just... orbiting you."

Jade's lashes don't flutter. She's far, far under.

Ryder leans forward, elbows on his knees, hands clasped.

"Senna got that twisted somehow. Thought it meant something else."

His jaw clenches.

"I don't know where she got the idea we were mates. I never paid attention to her. Not like that. She was... background noise. You weren't."

He scrubs a hand over his face. He smells sweat, blood, concrete dust, and fear baked into his skin.

"And I swear to god, when you wake up, you're never walking into something like that without me again. I'll chain myself to your damn ankle if I have to."

"You hate me. I get it. But I can't—" he swallows, jaw tight. "I can't pretend I don't see you. Not anymore."

A light knock on the door barely registers before the handle turns.

Luna slips in, eyes sharp and observant, but softer than they usually arc.

She takes one sniff and wrinkles her whole face.

"Ryder. Holy shit. You smell like you crawled out of a dumpster behind a morgue."

He stares at her. "What do you want."

"To sit with her." She steps inside, gently, respectfully.

"And to tell you that if you don't shower, Jade's going to wake up furious—not because she was kidnapped, not because Senna betrayed her... but because you're stinking up her room. You know how she is."

"Get out," Ryder growls.

Luna crosses her arms. "No. You need ten minutes to scrub whatever that is off your body. I'll sit with her. I won't touch her. I'll scream if something happens. Promise."

"I'm not leaving her."

"You're not helping her by smelling like a dead raccoon stuffed in a gym sock," Luna fires back and pushes a pile of towels and soaps at him.

Ryder narrows his eyes.

Luna narrows hers right back.

It's a silent standoff for a long moment—until Ryder's wolf picks up the faintest flicker from Jade, the tiniest shift of her scent, something alive and trying.

He exhales slowly. Stands. Points a finger at Luna.

"If she wakes up, you come get me. Immediately."

Luna gives him a lazy two-finger salute.

"Third door on the right. Empty room. You can crash there until we figure all this shit out. The guys already grabbed your car—your bag's on the bed."

Ryder freezes. Reaches for his pocket. His keys aren't there.

"The guys did what?" His voice spikes. "Who drove my car?"

"I did, fucker," Luna says cheerfully. "She's faaaaaast."

Ryder's eye twitches. Hard.

Luna rolls hers. "Oh, knock it off. Jaxson drove her. He's the most responsible fuck I've ever met. Your car is fine."

Ryder doesn't dignify that with a response, just grabs the towels.

He just gives Jade one last lingering look—his hand hovering over her shoulder like he's afraid she might disappear the second he takes his eyes off her—then forces himself toward the hallway.

Ryder walks into the guest room, towels and soap still in hand.

He barely has time to breathe before his phone buzzes.

Linus.

Ryder answers.

"Yeah."

"Duuuuude," Linus drawls, voice breezy as beach wind. "Please tell me you didn't get dead last night."

Ryder scrubs a hand down his face. "What did you hear?"

"Oh, you know, little somethin' somethin' about a *mini war* breaking out at the fights? Cops everywhere... both kinds, someone's rug—like, a real fancy one—getting ruined? Ring any bells?"

Ryder's jaw tightens. "I'm fine."

Linus coughs a laugh. "Your definition of fine, bro, is like...medically concerning."

Ryder doesn't have patience for this. "What do you want."

"Right, right, yeah." Linus's tone shifts—still *him*, but serious underneath.

"So there's this weasel—Jim. Total slimeball. My cousin's wife. Dude screwed her over real bad. Left a bad taste in the whole damn family."

Ryder's pulse spikes. "Linus—"

"I'm getting there, man!" Linus snorts. "So anyway, Jim's been struttin' around, braggin' that he's about to get *paid off big time* 'cause he 'delivered a Red Rock bitch.' His words. Not mine. I think your sisters a Red Rock right?"

Everything inside Ryder goes still.

"Where," Ryder growls.

"Oh-ho-ho, there he is," Linus laughs nervously. "Okay, uh—texting it now. But dude? Be cool. Just... maybe don't kill him in front of witnesses. I'm not bailing you out again."

Ryder hangs up without responding. A text pings.

1234 Mushroom Ln

Ryder tosses the towel onto the bed, snatches his keys off the dresser, and moves.

No hesitation. No second thoughts. Just purpose.

That fucker is going to die.

Jim bragged. Jim took credit for Jade's pain. Ryder's vision narrows to a single point.

"Time to end this," he mutters.

And then—he's gone. Keys in hand. Murder in his stride.

WHAT DID I DO TO THE RAVENS

Something drags her upward. Warmth first. Then breath. Then the slow, unwelcome realization that she isn't dying on a concrete floor.

Jade blinks against dim light. For half a second, there's nothing.

Then it hits.

A snarl rips through her chest, violent and sudden, like something slamming against bone from the inside.

Her wolf.

Not quiet. Not distant. Furious. Alive.

The sound that tears out of her isn't a sob. It's rougher than that. More animal. Jade clamps her teeth together too late to stop it.

Her hand shakes as she presses it to her sternum.

"You're here," she breathes. Not loud. Not dramatic. Like saying it too strongly might make it disappear.

A chair creaks.

Luna groans. "Thank god. I was starting to think we were going to have to light more candles or sacrifice something."

Jade huffs a breath that might be a laugh. Her wolf shoves again, a low growl vibrating through her ribs.

"She's pissed," Jade adds.

"Good." Luna leans forward, eyes sharpening. "Angry is back to normal."

Jade swallows. "She was gone."

That lands differently.

Luna doesn't joke. "Gone how."

"She just... wasn't there." Jade exhales slowly.

"That tracks." Luna nods once.

"Tracks how?"

"The bond went dead," Luna says, like she's commenting on the weather. "You know the difference between someone still on the line and that moment where you're just sitting there like, hellooooo—are you hanging up or am I?"

Jade nods. "Yeah."

Luna lifts her phone, gives it a small shake. "This wasn't that. They hung up. Clean. No static. Just—" She flicks her wrist. "Silence."

Jade's throat tightens.

"We couldn't feel you," Luna continues. "None of us. When you go to the game room, you'll see the new wear mark in the floor from Charlotte pacing."

Jade pushes herself upright, testing muscle and bone. Everything responds. Too well. Holy shit—she feels good. Really good.

Oh fuck. Nora.

Her wolf is back. Nora isn't.

Her stomach drops. She swallows bile as dead eyes flare and vanish.

Luna's voice pulls her back.

"Ryder made us pinky promise to wait for his call." Luna

holds up her tiny pinky finger. "For fucking real Jade. He held up his pinky and everything."

Looking ashamed like one of her closest secrets is now out. "Harper must've told him how to get to me."

Standing, Jade stretches. Her wolf settles, just a fraction, but her chest still burns.

"We knew you were alive," Luna adds. "But it was wrong."

"How did I get here?" Jade asks, grabbing onto the question before the other thought can pull her under.

"Are you even listening to me?" Luna snaps.

"Sure." Jade pulls the black hoodie over her head. "I remember Senna..."

The name catches. No tears left for her sister.

"Leaving with Vale. Ryder breaking through the bars." Her jaw tightens. "Nothing after that."

"You were wrecked," Luna says, voice flat now. "Ryder carried you in—again."

She sees flashes of bars bending. Metal screaming. Ryder's voice breaking when he yelled her name.

"Is he still here?"

"No." Luna stretches, bones cracking. "He was here hovering like a gargoyle. I bullied him into showering because he smelled like blood and bad decisions. Next thing I know he's bolting down the stairs like someone lit him on fire."

Jade nods. Files that away.

Silence stretches.

Then, quietly, "Senna and I talked."

Luna stills.

"She didn't feel right," Jade says carefully. "She looked like my sister, but it wasn't... her. She said she doesn't have her wolf anymore."

Luna doesn't interrupt.

Jade just stands there, eyes locked on the floor like it might open and take her with it.

"I had this... dream. Or nightmare. We were teenagers."

A pause. "I overheard Senna and my father making a plan to keep me away from Ryder."

Heat crawls under her skin at the memory.

"Senna told him I had a crush on Ryder and he didn't want 'weak Sheridan blood' in the family."

The words land too easily. Jade exhales through her nose.

"So, she made this plan."

Damnit floor. Why aren't you doing your job?

"She told me Ryder was her mate. To make me back off."

Luna's eyes widen. "What the fuck? That's not the Senna I know."

"It didn't feel right." Jade says. "But when I woke up, she was there. Crying. Sitting right next to me."

"That's... convenient."

Jade hadn't thought it through yet... but, *yeah that was convenient.*

Jade adds quietly. "She swore it never happened."

Luna leans back. "Okay." A beat. "Why do I get the feeling you don't believe her?"

Jade nods. She doesn't say how real it felt.

A knock taps the doorway. *Saved by the knock.*

Charlotte appears, already reading the room. Relief flickers across her face before she reins it in.

"Yeah, I felt a disturbance in the bond." she says, softer than her words suggest. "Don't ever fucking scare us like that again."

"Sorry, Alpha," Jade murmurs.

Charlotte shakes her head once. "I know." A beat.

"Thank the gods Liam and I have that damn light-healing shit."

Jade meets her eyes.

"Pack meeting in ten," Charlotte adds. "Eat something. Shower. Whatever, just don't make me assign Kai to hover. He's been whiny as fuck since he didn't get to kill anyone."

Luna snorts. "It's true."

Charlotte's gaze lingers on Jade a moment longer. "I'm glad you're back."

Then she's gone.

Jade exhales slowly. Her wolf moves again. Not calm. Not settled. But solid.

Luna nudges her shoulder. "Come on. Before Isabell decides to do some witchy shit to get you up."

Jade slides her feet into her favorite pair of slip-ons.

The ground still feels unsteady. But it's there.

Jade makes it halfway down the stairs before the house smells different.

Warm. Toasted. Something trying to be comforting.

Isabell stands at the kitchen island, hair wild, oversized shirt dusted with flour. She looks up and freezes.

Then she moves.

She comes around the island fast, snaps a dish towel against Jade's arm. "¡Carajo!" The word lands sharp and affectionate all at once. She pulls Jade in, crushing her against her, muttering a string of Spanish Jade doesn't bother translating. She knows the tone. Fury. Relief. Love.

Jade exhales into the top of her head and hugs her back. "I missed you too."

Isabell squeezes once more, then lets go like nothing happened, already turning back to the counter. "Look like shit," she adds. "I cook."

Grabbing a blue box from the pantry, popping it open as

she walks. The biscuits inside smell vaguely edible. She bites into one on the way down the hall. It tastes nothing like chicken. Not even a little but they are still fucking heaven right now.

The game room is full.

Charlotte and Liam on the couch. Luna cross-legged on the floor. Kai leaning against the wall by the hot pink pool table. Maddy perched on the armrest of the couch. Jaxson near the window, arms folded. Conversation hums until Jade steps in.

It stops.

Jade freezes mid-chew, blue box still in her hands. "What?"

No one answers.

Charlotte stands first. She crosses the room and places a hand over Jade's heart. "You didn't quit," she says quietly. "Even when it would've been easier."

Liam follows, resting his hand on Jade's shoulder. "You endure."

Luna steps in next, fingers wrapping around Jade's wrist. "You matter. Even when you forget it."

Kai smirks, but his touch is gentle as he presses two fingers to her arm. "You fight like a girl."

Maddy's hand settles on Jade's back. "You're not alone," she says, voice steady.

Jaxson is last. He pauses, then places his hand over Jade's, right on the ridiculous blue box. "I would take you into war with me."

The room stays quiet.

Jade swallows the bite she never finished chewing. Her throat tightens. She doesn't look away.

"Okay," she mutters. "Thanks guys but I'm good."

Luna snorts. Kai grins. Charlotte's mouth curves.

"And you're a terrible liar."

Jade turns—and Ryder is already there, halfway into the room, again, like he belongs in it.

"Oh," she says flatly. "I thought you dropped and ran again."

The bite in her tone surprises even her. Her wolf just might kill her from the inside out.

Ryder's mouth twitches, not quite a smile. "I'm just not in the mood to grant you all your wishes right now, Jade."

His gaze flicks briefly to the others. "I have some information about Isabell's safety."

That gets everyone's attention.

"About Miles," Ryder adds. "And the ravens."

Jade's fingers tighten around the blue box. "Of course you did."

"This isn't just word on the street," Ryder continues. "They want revenge. Miles has been more than happy to help the ravens. Locations. Schedules. The mansion. The businesses." His eyes lock on hers. "You."

The word lands heavy.

"What did I ever do to the ravens," Jade says, not asking.

Ryder nods once. "You're the reason they just lost a main source of income. They were profiting off those warehouse fights."

A bitter laugh slips out of her. "That's rich. I didn't notice any raven's there."

Then a flash. *The raven tie clips.*

"Believe it or don't," Ryder says. "But Jim confirmed it."

The name snaps her head up. "Jim?" Her mouth twists. "You mean *my* buddy Jim from the fights?"

Ryder doesn't flinch. "The Jim that betrayed you. Yeah. He's the one that handed you over to Vale."

Jade exhales sharply. "I'll be killing him after this."

"Too late."

The room goes still.

"What?" Jade says.

Ryder looks to the floor not making eye contact.

Silence, thick and ugly.

Charlotte straightens. "So the ravens are what—going to ambush Isabell on a shopping excursion?"

"Yeah," Ryder says. "Miles is tied to it. I don't have clean proof yet, but his name keeps coming up on the street."

Ryder leans against the edge of the pool table, arms braced, like he's holding the weight of it all in place.

"He wants you dead. All of you. That part hasn't changed." His jaw tightens. "If the ravens do the work, he keeps his hands clean and still gets his shot at Vegas. Vale's in there somewhere. Helping him."

Jade's eyes narrow.

"And we're just supposed to take that at face value?"

She turns fully toward Ryder now, gaze sharp enough to draw blood.

"Jim wasn't exactly a pillar of human virtue. In fact, he was a fucking weasel—but—"

Luna's head tilts.

"I'll get it," she says, already moving.

"What are you—" Jade starts, but Luna is gone.

A beat passes. Then another.

Luna reappears in the doorway just as fast—Jase right on her heels.

"Oh, for fuck's sake. Why Jase? Why?" Charlotte shakes her head.

"Charlotte, I need to take Luna into protective custody."

Silence crashes down.

"Me?" Luna blurts. "Why me?"

"I already have Jon and his family hidden."

"You *what*?" Luna snaps.

Fear spikes through the bond, sharp and feral. Jade feels Luna's beasts stirring, pushing toward fight-before-thought.

Jade steps closer, voice low. "Luna. Breathe."

She presses calm into the bond, steady and deliberate. 'Stay with me.' Jade knows Luna's protective side for her twin brother outweighs logic.

Maddy closes the gap on Luna's other side and takes her hand, grounding her.

Jase doesn't look away from Luna. "I have a lead on the mole. It points somewhere dangerous. For you. For Jon."

"No," Luna says, backing up a step. "No, Jase. I don't want to go back."

"No," Kai repeats, moving between them and Jase. Jade barely sees Jase now. Kai fills the space, broad and immovable—and somehow bigger than he was a second ago.

The room shifts.

"You will not take her," Kai says, stepping in front of Luna. "Not from her pack. And not from me."

Jade has never heard that tone from him. Not playful. Not teasing. Pure steel.

His gaze locks on Jase. "I can protect her better than you ever will."

"No," Jase says, sharp. "Kai, this is bigger than just standing guard."

Kai doesn't move. "Then talk."

Jase exhales through his nose. "This isn't a hit. It isn't an ambush you can muscle through. This is files with no pictures. No faces. Just numbers. Routes. Transfers. Names that don't exist on paper."

The room stills.

"Trafficking," Charlotte says quietly.

Jase nods. "And Luna's name shows up too close to it for my liking."

"That doesn't mean you take her," Kai snaps.

"It means she's already on someone's radar," Jase fires back. "And Luna, you know what that means."

Luna's hands curl into fists. Jade feels the tremor ripple through the bond. Fear, yes. But beneath it, anger. Focus.

"You said Jon's hidden," Luna says slowly. "Safe?"

"For now."

She swallows. "And if I don't go with you?"

Jase meets her eyes. "Then either you or him become leverage if they catch you. That's the last thing I want."

Silence stretches, brittle as glass.

Jase makes one last plead. "Luna, you know I've had your back for years. I've covered your tracks when you couldn't, please don't question my judgement on your safety now."

"No," Kai says again, softer this time. "You don't get to decide this for her."

Luna steps around Kai until she's directly in front of him.

Jade shifts too, angling closer without drawing attention, ready if Luna's control slips.

It doesn't.

Luna lifts a hand and presses it flat to Kai's chest. Her palm barely spans it.

"Hey," she says softly. "Big guy."

Then, firmer. "Kai. Look at me."

Kai's breath stutters. He looks down—and whatever was coiled tight inside him loosens. His shoulders drop. His jaw unclenches.

"Listen," Luna says. "There's a lot about me you don't know."

Kai swallows. "Oh. And he does?"

"He knows about me," Luna says, her gaze cutting to Jase. "That doesn't mean he knows me."

She steps closer, pressing her forehead briefly to his chest. Grounding herself. Grounding him.

"I won't go alone," she says firmly. "I won't disappear."

Jase's eyes narrow. "I'm giving you the illusion of choice," he says. "But the organization wants you brought in."

Luna's smile is thin. Wrong.

"Then you'd better be very clear about what you're asking for."

She steps closer. Not toward Jase—into the space where she can feel her pack behind her.

"And Jase. You and I both know that you better have a truckload of that powder, if my black beast comes out to play. She's a *biiiitch.* So please do not confuse my agreement with subservience."

Luna's eyes change to the red color of her beast.

"Because you don't get me without my pack."

She pulls back just enough to look at Kai. "I'll go," she says. "But only if Kai comes with me."

The room holds its breath.

Charlotte studies Jase like a chessboard. "That's the line," she says. "Cross it or don't."

Jase curses under his breath. A long moment passes.

"Fine," he says at last. "But he follows instructions."

Kai doesn't smile. "As long as you give smart ones."

Luna exhales, relief crashing through the bond so hard Jade almost stumbles.

"This leaves the mansion really vulnerable Charlotte." Luna says. "Miles is still out there. And now the ravens want Isabell."

Her eyes cut to Jase. "What are you going to do about that?"

Jase doesn't answer right away. His gaze drifts around the room, taking inventory. People. Exits. Weak points.

"I'll call in a favor," he says finally. "Eyes on the roads. Eyes in the air."

Charlotte's expression hardens. "You don't control my pack."

"No," Jase agrees. "But I can supplement it."

"With who?" Jade asks. The question slips out before she can stop it.

Jase looks at her. Really looks. "People you won't like."

"That's not comforting," Kai mutters.

"It's honest."

Jaxson, who's been quiet until now, stands up straight. "You're talking about mercenaries."

"Specialists," Jase corrects. "Some shifter. Some not. And this is off the books."

"No," Charlotte says flatly. "I don't need trouble with the C.O.P.S."

Jase meets her head-on. "Then you're betting the lives in this house on the ravens deciding to miss. Which they may, but they do not stop."

Silence stretches.

Jade feels the room tilt, the old familiar tension crawling back under her skin. Everyone is waiting for Charlotte.

Before she can speak, Isabell appears out of nowhere in the only way Isabell can do.

"They come," she says, chin lifting, "I fight."

"No," Jade says instantly. "That's not—"

Isabell glances back at her, eyes soft but unyielding. "Mija. No run."

Jase watches the exchange with something unreadable in his eyes.

"I can move you," he says to Isabell. "Quiet place. Warded. Off the board."

"Alone?" Isabell scoffs. "No. I stay with pack."

Luna shifts closer to Jade, voice low. "He's not wrong about one thing. They won't stop."

Charlotte exhales slowly. "No, they won't."

She straightens. "We lock this place down. No one leaves alone. Isabell stays with the pack."

Jase's jaw tightens. "That's not the safest option."

He exhales, like he's deciding how much to give.

"When we cleared the warehouse, we found more than bodies. Jade didn't just stumble into underground fights and drugs. She tripped a wire."

"Isabell stays with the pack," Charlotte replies.

A beat.

Jase nods once.

"Ryder," Charlotte adds, "can you stay a bit longer?"

"Charlotte!" Jade blurts. She can't believe Charlotte just asked him that.

"Jade, don't be dumb," Charlotte says. "We need help. I'll call Willamena again, but fuck—I'm running out of grace with the vamps."

"Yeah," Ryder says. "I can stay longer." His gaze sweeps the room, already calculating. "I'll call a buddy too. See if he can help us get a meeting with the ravens."

"Fuck this," Jade mutters. Her hands are shaking now. Anger bleeding into fear, impossible to separate.

She turns back to Jase. "So when are you taking Luna and Kai?"

"Now. Go pack," Jase says, already gesturing toward the door.

Luna holds his stare for a second longer, red still ghosting her eyes, then turns and walks out. Slow. Controlled. Like she's choosing every step.

"I have to call Spencer," Kai says, phone already in his hand as he follows her.

The room doesn't relax after they're gone. It tightens.

Jase looks back at Jade, expression unreadable again.

"Before I go," he says, almost casually, "how long had Nora Bennett been with you?"

BREATH

Ryder sits back on the pool lounger, arm firm around Jade where she's tucked against his chest. She fits there like he was created specifically for her.

"Breathe," he murmurs near her ear. Not a command. An invitation.

He slows his own breath on purpose. In through the nose. Out through the mouth. Long. Steady. He feels it when she starts to match him. The hitch easing. The tension bleeding out of her shoulders one exhale at a time.

His wolf settles, satisfied just to have her close. Calm radiates through him, through them. He inhales again, deeper this time. Her scent is familiar and not. Heat and dust and something sharp underneath that's all Jade. He lets himself take it in. Grounds them both.

She doesn't pull away. He's not going to question it.

"I'm a fucking mess Ryder. I don't even have the energy to hate you right now."

"I know. Just stay with me Jade. Breathe with me. There's still plenty of time for you to hate me later."

She takes a deep breath with him and he can't believe he is getting this moment.

He keeps breathing. Keeps holding.

"Why are you so convinced I'm your mate?" she asks. No edge. No challenge. Just honest curiosity.

Ryder doesn't answer right away. He's learned when not to rush her.

"I've always been drawn to you," he says finally. "Before I had words for it. Before it made sense." His thumb traces a slow line against her arm, absent but steady. "It just is."

She tilts her head slightly, enough that he knows she's listening. Really listening.

"For a long time, I thought that meant wanting," he adds. "Turns out it's more like... recognition."

Jade exhales. Long. Even. She doesn't argue. She doesn't pull away.

"Why are you so convinced I'm not?" Ryder asks quietly. He's wanted to ask that question for years.

He feels her tense.

"I don't think..." She hesitates. "I don't think I can answer that the same way anymore."

Ryder shifts, gently guiding her upright so he can see her face. "What do you mean?"

He doesn't let himself hope. Not really.

"I had this nightmare. Or maybe a memory." Her brow furrows. "I don't know. Senna told my father she was going to say you were her mate so I'd stay away from you. She knew I'd take her side." A pause. "Even though I had a crush on you."

Ryder blinks. Then adjusts so they're face to face. "Hang on. You had a crush on me?"

She squints. "I said all that and that's what you heard?"

"Well, I heard the rest," he says, deadpan. "But I'd like to hear that part again."

A smile breaks free before he can stop it. He doesn't smile often. Of course it's for her.

"Fuck you, Ryder."

"And we're back to our regularly scheduled programming." His voice is lighter than it's been in years. He studies her face. No devil in her eyes. Just tired honesty. "I like this version better."

Jade huffs. "Don't get used to it."

"I won't," he says. "But I'm not wasting it either."

His expression sobers.

"Jade... Senna had issues. You didn't see them." His jaw tightens. "I don't know if she hid them from you or if you were just too busy protecting her. But she could be mean as shit."

She looks down.

Ryder reaches out, tilting her chin gently back up. "That doesn't make you stupid. It makes you loyal."

Her throat works. "It makes me feel like I missed something important."

"Maybe," he admits. "Or maybe you weren't meant to see it yet."

Silence stretches between them, warm instead of heavy.

"You still think I'm your mate?" she asks finally.

Ryder doesn't hesitate this time. "Yeah."

"Even now?"

"Especially now." His thumb brushes her jaw, grounding, not claiming. "Because nothing about this feels like fantasy. It feels like truth finally catching up."

She studies him for a long second.

Then, quietly, "That scares me."

He nods. "Good. Means it matters."

He leans his forehead against hers, not rushing, not pushing.

Just there.

"It hit me. If you were her mate, why did she leave with Vale."

She exhales, shoulders loosening.

"If you were her mate, she wouldn't have chosen me anyway. But, she sure as fuck would've chosen you."

The truth of it lands like a blow he never saw coming.

He'd built a thousand explanations over the years. None of them had room for that kind of clarity.

She's right.

"Yeah," he says after a moment. "I suppose."

"I still hate you though."

"Yeah, I get that. Most people do."

Jade's phone vibrates somewhere near the lounger.

She freezes.

When she picks it up, her face goes blank. "It's Senna."

Fuck.

Ryder watches the color drain from her.

"What? She just kept her same number all this time? No... something's off. Don't answer that."

She answers anyway.

"Senna?"

Ryder can hear her voice through the phone. Thin. Fragile. Wrong.

"Jade." Senna sounds breathless. "Jade, I need you."

Jade's jaw tightens. "What—Vale isn't protecting you anymore?"

"I ran," Senna says quickly. "I made the wrong choice. I want to come home. I want to come back to the pack." Her voice cracks. "Jade, I need you."

Silence stretches.

Ryder shakes his head slowly. *No.*

Jade's eyes flick to him. He mouths, *Don't.*

"Where are you?" Jade asks.

A pause. Too long.

Then Senna gives a location.

Ryder shakes his head again, harder this time.

Jade ends the call.

"No," Ryder says immediately. "Absolutely not. That's a trap."

"She sounded scared," Jade replies, even as doubt creeps in.

"She sounded practiced," Ryder fires back. "You don't go alone. Fuck, Jade don't walk into Vale's arms like this again."

She looks at him then. Really looks. And instead of anger, there's something calmer. Colder.

"I have to do this," she says. "I have to see it for myself."

"Jade—"

She smiles. Small. Certain. The kind that never means good things.

"I won't be alone," she says. "My shadow will always be there."

Ryder's wolf stirs uneasily.

And for the first time since she answered the phone, Ryder is afraid—not that Jade won't survive.

But that whatever she's walking toward already knows she's coming.

YOU SAID YOU NEEDED ME

The neon hum of the 7-Eleven buzzes against Jade's skull.

She stands near the edge of the parking lot, hands in her pockets, weight settled on the balls of her feet. Casual to anyone watching. Ready to bolt if needed. The air smells like hot asphalt and burnt coffee.

She doesn't turn her head when she feels him.

Ryder is across the lot, half-swallowed by shadow near the side of the building. Arms crossed. Still. Exactly where she knew he'd be.

She doesn't wave.

He doesn't come closer.

That's the agreement they never said out loud.

Her chest tightens anyway. Old habits. Old feelings. She's not ready to unpack them, let alone let them go. Tonight isn't about Ryder.

It's about Senna.

Headlights cut across the lot. A battered sedan pulls in too fast, jerks into a crooked spot. The driver's door flies open.

The door opens.

Senna steps out.

She looks... smaller. Not dramatic. Not frantic. Just worn thin. Her hair is pulled back badly, like she did it without a mirror. Her clothes hang wrong, borrowed or slept in too many times. She scans the lot once, then twice, before her eyes land on Jade.

She walks over carefully, like the space between them matters.

"Jade." Her voice is hoarse. Not cracked. Used.

Jade doesn't move. "You said you needed me."

Senna nods. "I did." She swallows. "Thank you for coming. I wasn't sure you would."

Jade studies her. "Why?"

The word comes out softer than she expects.

"I always came when you called. I always protected you."

Senna's mouth tightens, then relaxes. She looks down at the pavement. "I left." A pause. "I should've left sooner."

Jade watches her closely. The lack of excuses. The way she doesn't fill the silence.

"And now?" Jade prompts.

Senna lifts her eyes again, cautious. "I didn't know where else to go."

She didn't say *home*. She didn't say *the pack*.

Just... somewhere safe?

That lands.

"I want to come back," Senna says quietly. "If that's even an option." She hesitates. "I'll understand if it's not."

Jade studies her. The tight hands. The way she's bracing for rejection instead of pleading against it.

"You ran," Jade says.

"Yes."

"You chose him."

Senna nods once. "I did."

No justification. No spin.

"I lied," Senna adds after a moment. "About things I shouldn't have."

Jade's gaze sharpens. "Like what?"

Senna opens her mouth, then closes it again. "I'll answer whatever you ask," she says carefully. "If you let me stay."

That silence stretches.

Jade nods once, decision clicking into place. "Get in the car."

Relief flashes across Senna's face, fast and unguarded, before she reins it back in. She nods, hurrying to the passenger side without another word.

Jade glances toward the shadows as she circles the car.

Ryder hasn't moved. His eyes are on Senna now, not her.

The drive back is quiet. Senna keeps her hands folded in her lap, eyes on the road, answering only when asked. Short. Careful. She doesn't ask questions. Doesn't push.

The mansion gates slide open.

Senna exhales softly. "Holy shit, Jade. This place is huge."

Jade pulls in beneath the lights and cuts the engine. "Yeah."

A beat.

"We sold the houses. Wanted everyone in one place."

She opens her door, the night air cool against her skin.

"After we lost so many sisters..." Her voice catches. Just for a second. "We needed space. To rebuild."

She doesn't say *to survive*. She doesn't have to.

As they step out, Jade's phone vibrates once in her pocket.

Charlotte.

They'd agreed. If Senna wanted in, Jade would bring her back. Not for comfort.

For answers.

Jade turns to her sister. "We're going to talk."

Senna nods immediately. "I know."

"You're going to tell us what you saw. What you heard. Everything," Jade says. "Even the parts that make you look bad."

Senna meets her eyes. "Especially those."

Jade turns toward the house.

Behind her, she knows Ryder will follow. Not close. Not obvious.

A shadow doing exactly what shadows do best.

Inside, the house feels quieter than it should. Too many people awake. Too many eyes pretending not to track Senna as she crosses the threshold.

Isabell appears at the base of the stairs. She's been waiting. She takes one look at Senna and doesn't bother softening her expression.

"Come," she says, already turning. "Stink."

Senna flinches but follows.

Jade trails them down the hall, stopping at a closed door near the back. Isabell opens it and flicks on the light, revealing a clean, spare room. Neutral. Nothing personal.

"Bathroom's through there," Jade says, pointing. "Shower. Take as long as you need—but not longer."

She crosses to the dresser and pulls out a stack of clothes. Sweatpants. A soft shirt. Socks. She drops them on the bed.

Jade steps forward. "Get cleaned up."

Senna nods quickly. "Thank you."

Jade doesn't return it.

She points down the hall. "Game room's that way. When you're done, you meet us there."

Senna swallows. "Okay."

Jade's voice doesn't change. "We're not here to judge you. We're here to gather information."

Isabell snorts quietly.

"Everything you saw," Jade continues. "Everything you heard while you were with Vale. Locations. Names. Patterns. Nothing is too small."

Senna nods again, eyes shiny. "I'll tell you everything. I swear."

Jade holds her gaze for a beat longer. Long enough to make it clear this isn't forgiveness.

"Good," she says. "Because we'll know if you don't."

She turns away before Senna can respond.

Isabell pauses in the doorway, glancing back once. "No wander," she adds mildly—then hisses.

A hiss?

Jade blinks. She must've picked that up from Luna.

The door closes.

Jade exhales only once they're out of earshot.

Charlotte stands at the end of the hall. "Kitchen or game room?"

"Game room," Jade replies. "I told her to shower and get her thoughts together." A beat. "We'll let her think the water's washing this away."

Charlotte's mouth curves. "It won't."

"No," Jade agrees. "It won't."

They head down the hall together, the house already shifting—colder, sharper, more focused.

Whatever Senna brought back with her... it's about to be dragged into the light.

The game room is quieter than normal.

Only three men left. That alone puts Jade on edge.

Liam stands at the pool table, lining up a shot he doesn't take. Ryder leans against the wall near the bar, bottle untouched in his hand. Jaxson sits on the edge of the couch, elbows on his knees, eyes tracking the hallway like he expects trouble to come walking back in.

Charlotte steps in beside Jade, conversation dies on contact.

That's how she knows they feel it too. Her wolf hasn't stopped growling since Senna pulled into that parking lot.

Jade lets her gaze sweep the room, cataloging without thinking. Exits. Shadows. Who's standing where. Who's pretending this is normal. Even in her own den, her training is instinct.

She heads for the bar, pouring drinks for herself and Charlotte. The glass shakes just enough that she notices. *Annoying.*

"Ryan and Ivy made it to Humboldt territory," Jaxson says into the quiet, like he's filling space on purpose. "No trouble."

Jade nods once. *Good.* "And Henry?" she asks.

A corner of Jaxson's mouth lifts. "Teaching everyone new dances he learned from Una. Apparently enthusiasm is contagious."

That eases something in her chest. Not much. But enough.

Liam finally straightens. "How's Senna?"

Jade takes a sip before answering. Buys herself the second she needs. "Guarded," she says. "Exhausted. Too composed for someone who just ran for her life."

Ryder's gaze sharpens. He doesn't comment. He doesn't have to.

"I'm hoping she knows something about where Miles

is," Jade adds. "I'd like us to stop living like we're waiting for the other shoe to drop."

Liam nods. "Fair."

Charlotte takes the glass Jade slides toward her. "Jase checked in."

Jade stills. Just a fraction. "And?"

"He says Luna and Kai are secure. Safehouse." Charlotte's voice stays even. "He's going dark."

Of course he is.

"And if something goes wrong?" Jade asks.

"He said he wouldn't stay dark."

That lands heavier than it should.

Ryder finally pushes off the wall. "So silence means nothing's broken. Yet."

"Yet," Jade echoes.

She looks around the room again. Three men. No chaos. No laughter. No pack noise to soften the edges.

If Senna is a lion, they didn't just let her into the den.

They closed the door behind her.

Jade lifts her glass, doesn't toast. Just drinks.

"Alright," she says quietly. "Then we stay sharp. No one wanders. No assumptions."

"And when she talks?" Jaxson asks.

Jade sets the glass down with deliberate care. "We listen."

Her stomach tightens. "Then we verify."

The house creaks softly around them, settling into the night like it knows what's coming.

Liam and Ryder play a game of pool. Jade can't help noticing Ryder's eyes cutting to her between shots. Not lingering. Just checking.

She doesn't feel that sharp flare of anger when she

catches him. The hate is still there, solid and familiar, but it's changed shape. Quieter. Heavier.

"I caught up with Harper and Lucas while you were gone," Liam says. "They're prepared if Miles shows up there."

"So the pack's starting to follow Lucas?" Jaxson asks.

"She said there are still a chunk of resistors, but most have pledged fealty." Liam rolls the cue in his palm.

The room goes still for a breath. Then Ryder reaches for the chalk, already moving on to his next shot.

A loud crash slams into the windows, followed by another. Then another.

Jade spins toward the sound just in time to see black wings blot out the light. Ravens. Dozens of them. Hundreds. Beaks striking glass, claws scraping, the air vibrating with their screams.

The noise is deafening.

"What the fuck—"

"WHERE THE FUCK IS SHE?"

The scream cuts through the chaos like a blade.

Jade's heart drops.

She bolts for the foyer, boots pounding against the floor, everyone right behind her. The sound of wings follows, relentless, as if the house itself is under siege... again.

Senna stands at the top of the stairs.

Calm. Still. Smiling.

"What are you yelling about?" Jade shouts up at her.

Senna tilts her head, eyes gleaming. "Where is she, you stupid bitches?" Her voice echoes, sharp and unhinged. "I only came here to find her."

"Find who?" Charlotte demands, power already rolling off her in waves. "Explain yourself. Now."

Senna laughs. Loud. Bright. Wrong.

"Oh, don't play dumb," she says, spreading her arms as another raven slams into the glass behind her.

"Liam!" Maddy's voice breaks as she comes into view behind Senna. "What's happening?"

Senna moves.

She spins, fingers wrapping around Maddy's throat, slamming her back into the wall with bone-jarring force.

Maddy chokes, feet scrambling, hands clawing at Senna's wrist.

"Senna!" Charlotte roars. "Release her now."

Jade feels the Alpha energy pulse through the room.

Senna doesn't even flinch.

"Oh, I heard this piece-of-shit pack has taken on some new misfits" she says mildly, eyes flicking over Maddy. "From the looks of it they are scraping the bottom of the barrel."

"STAND DOWN," Charlotte commands, power cracking through the air. "You will obey."

Senna throws her head back and laughs.

"No. No, Charlotte." She tightens her grip just enough to make Maddy gasp. "You are no longer my Alpha."

The room goes deadly still.

Jade's wolf surges, fury and horror colliding. Ryder's growl vibrates low and dangerous.

Liam shifts his stance. "Charlotte," he says tightly, "I have to make her stop. Maddy, hang in there."

Charlotte's voice drops, lethal. "Let. Her. Go."

Senna's gaze finally flicks to her. Amused. Mocking. "That only works when someone still believes in your authority."

Her eyes drift past Jade. Past Liam. Past Charlotte.

Then they lock on Ryder, who is now slowly climbing the stairs.

The room seems to shrink.

"Always the hero. I should've killed you," Senna says lightly. "Or fucked you. Either would've been cleaner than tricking my stupid sister."

Jade sucks in a sharp breath.

Senna's smile turns mean. "Thank god you're not my mate." She tilts her head, assessing him like something scraped off her boot. "I would never bind myself to a mangy wolf. Sheridan blood doesn't belong in the Devereaux bloodline."

"You're a psycho bitch. Always have been," Ryder growls.

Senna barely glances at him now. Like he's already boring.

"That's the problem," she says mildly. "You think this is about you."

"No," Jade says, stepping forward before she can stop herself. "I think this is about you, Senna. What are you doing?"

Her voice cracks on the last word. She hates that it does.

For a heartbeat, Senna just watches her. Then her smile softens into something colder.

"You're all staring at the wrong monster," Senna says softly. "The real one's been hiding in plain sight."

Jade's stomach knots. "Who?" Jade snaps. "Who are you talking about?"

Senna looks right at her.

Then she shoves Maddy away.

Maddy crumples to the floor, coughing, dragging in air as Ryder's already there, hauling her back, shielding her with his body.

Chaos erupts. Everyone surges toward the stairs, desperate for answers.

But Senna steps back, untouched, ravens screaming outside like applause.

Before Jade can reach her, Senna shifts. Faster than Jade has ever seen.

A pure black wolf vaults over Charlotte, lands clean on all four paws, and barrels down the stairs. She skids to a stop in the center of the foyer, then turns.

Looks back at all of them.

"Senna?" Jade breathes. "Why?" Confusion knots hard in her chest. *Senna's wolf isn't black.*

She lunges forward, already yanking her shirt over her head.

"NO."

Jade freezes mid-motion.

Charlotte's Alpha energy slams through the room again, harder this time. "There are too many ravens," she snaps. "We can't take them on our own. Not right now."

Jade's fists clench, nails biting into her palms.

"I'll help," Isabell says. She stands in the foyer, eyes locked on the chaos outside.

"No." Charlotte's voice cuts sharp. "Isabell, stay back. I don't want you anywhere near ravens."

Isabell hesitates.

"They already want to kill you," Charlotte adds quietly.

The words settle like ash.

Jade turns back just in time to see Senna's wolf disappear through the front doors, swallowed by wings and night.

And for the first time since she arrived—Jade understands.

Senna didn't come to be saved.

She came hunting.

SO WHAT? WE'RE MATES NOW?

Jade can see his silhouette sitting at the table by the pool. One arm draped over the back of the chair, head tipped forward, attention fixed on nothing. His beer sits half full, condensation bleeding into the glass.

She takes a steadying breath and walks to the fridge, fingers curling around the necks of two brown bottles. The caps pop softly, too loud in the quiet.

Jade hesitates before sliding the glass door open.

The night air rolls in, cool against her skin. Chlorine, desert heat, something metallic she can't place. Ryder doesn't look up when she steps outside.

She sets one bottle on the table in front of him.

He glances at it. Then at her.

"I didn't ask—"

"I know," she says. "I just didn't want to drink alone."

That earns a small huff of breath. Not a laugh. Close enough.

She takes the chair across from him. Doesn't crowd.

Doesn't retreat. The pool light cuts sharp lines across his face, turning his eyes unreadable.

They sit like that for a moment. No rush. No pack. No ravens screaming overhead.

"I heard what she said," Jade finally says. Her voice stays even. "About the mate thing."

Ryder's jaw tightens. "I'm glad it's finally out but, I hate that she hurt you."

"I know." Jade lifts her bottle, takes a sip she doesn't need. "I believed her."

Silence settles again. Heavy, but not hostile.

"That lie cost us years," he says quietly.

"Yes," Jade agrees. Then, just as quietly, "But it ends with her."

His gaze lifts to hers.

"Good," he says.

They don't toast. They don't touch. The distance between them stays exactly where it is.

"This doesn't fix anything," she says.

Ryder nods once. "Didn't think it would."

"I still hate you."

"I figured." He grabs the new beer and takes a long pull, throat working as he swallows. He doesn't look at her when he adds, "Hate doesn't mean you don't feel it."

Jade scoffs. "So what? We're just mates now?"

That finally gets his attention.

Ryder sets the bottle down slowly. "If it were that simple," he says, "we wouldn't be sitting here."

"This doesn't erase anything," she says.

"I know."

"It doesn't erase what I believed."

"I know that too."

Silence stretches, taut as a wire. The pool light throws

moving shadows across his face, across the hard line of his mouth. Jade becomes acutely aware of how close she's sitting.

"You should go inside," Ryder says quietly. Not a challenge. A warning.

Jade doesn't move. "You know, for someone who stalks me and claims I'm their mate, you sure tell me to leave you alone a lot."

His eyes darken. "I'm trying to respect you," he says. "And I'm running out of restraint."

Something snaps. Or maybe it finally lets go.

Jade pushes back from the table, intent on leaving. Her chair scrapes softly as she rises.

She makes it one step.

Stops.

Her wolf is calm. Truly calm. For the first time since she woke up. No noise. No warning. Just certainty. Jade hasn't felt this steady in months. Maybe longer.

She knows she should take this slow with Ryder. Knows there are things she should say. Confessions buried deep. Memories of stolen glances, of quiet rescues, of the way he used to hover nearby while his mother stitched her wounds.

Knows she should tell him she hasn't drawn a full breath since the night in his hotel room.

Instead, she turns back to him.

"Fine," she says, voice steady despite everything in her chest. "I'll be your mate."

Ryder's breath stutters.

He moves so fast she barely registers it. One blink and he's there, close enough that she's breathing him in, heat and tension and restraint snapping all at once. He takes her mouth with his. All restraint gone.

She lets it happen. Wants it.

She doesn't want him to respect her. Not tonight.

"This is a bad idea," she mutters.

"We passed that point a while ago." His breath is uneven, control hanging by a thread.

The kiss isn't soft. It's not tender. It's heat and teeth and years of restraint burned down to ash. Jade shoves him back a step, and he lets her, the table knocking softly behind him. His hands slide to her hips, firm, grounding, like he's making sure she's real.

She breaks the kiss first, breath unsteady. "This doesn't mean I forgive you."

His mouth curves, just slightly. "Good. I don't want easy."

Her hands fist in his shirt. The truth is right there, undeniable now. Whatever else they are, whatever damage sits between them, the pull hasn't weakened. It's sharpened.

Jade exhales. "I will hurt your feelings—"

Ryder kisses the corner of her mouth, slow this time. Intentional. "I know."

She believes him. That scares her more than anything.

She barely registers the shift until her feet leave the ground.

Ryder scoops her up without breaking the kiss, one arm locked beneath her thighs, the other firm at her back like he's afraid she'll disappear if he loosens his grip. The world tilts. Jade's breath breaks as she grips his shoulders, nails digging in hard enough to ground herself.

He doesn't slow. Doesn't hesitate.

The sliding glass door opens behind him, wam night giving way to cool air and shadows as he carries them inside the pool house. Her back brushes the doorframe, then the wall, then nothing at all as he kicks the door shut behind them.

"This is still a bad idea," she murmurs against his mouth.

His answer is a low sound she feels more than hears. "You're still here."

"We will be the worst mates ever."

"Probably."

He sets her down only long enough to crowd her back into the wall, hands braced on either side of her head, heat pressed close, undeniable. Jade tilts her chin up, refusing to give him ground even as her pulse skids.

"Don't be careful," she says softly. Honest. Dangerous.

His forehead drops to hers, breath rough. "I don't think I can tonight."

Whatever restraint they had left doesn't survive the doorway. Clothes come off in a rush—buttons abandoned, fabric dragged and tossed aside, neither of them slowing long enough to care where anything lands.

Jade's breath comes fast as the realization sinks in. There's no guilt chasing this. No second-guessing. Just him, just now, just the pull she's stopped fighting.

Ryder takes them to the floor, and it's like time stutters.

She's suddenly aware of everything. His weight braced above her. The strength in his forearms caging her in without touching her throat. He doesn't move. Just breathes. Deep. Controlled. Like he's holding himself together by force alone.

"Ryder?" she mutters. "What the fuck is wrong with you?"

"Give me a second, Jade." His voice is low, rough. "I've imagined this exact moment for more years than I care to admit." A beat. Honest. "I want to savor it."

She snorts softly before she can stop herself. "Jesus. You're a softy."

His mouth twitches. Dark. Dangerous. "Careful."

She lifts her chin, defiant even now. "Out of all the mates I could've ended up with, I get the one who wants to talk about feelings."

Ryder's smile fades completely.

"Nothing about me is soft right now," he says quietly.

He drives into her and the world fractures.

The impact steals her breath, fast and overwhelming, like something long-starved finally snapping into place. Jade's back arches instinctively, a broken sound tearing from her throat before she can stop it.

This is exactly what she needed from him tonight.

Their bodies find a rhythm without effort, movement answering movement, their breathing syncs like it always knew how. Heat. Pressure. Release building and breaking in waves she doesn't fight.

Inside her, her wolf surges—awake, alive, *whole*—finally claiming what it's craved for years. The bond locks in with a force that feels ancient and inevitable, threading them together until she can't tell where she ends and he begins.

No guilt. No doubt.

Just right.

The bond settles into place with a quiet finality that steals Jade's breath.

Not fireworks. Not chaos.

Just certainty.

Ryder stills above her, forehead dropping to hers, his breath rough against her mouth. For a moment neither of them speaks. Neither of them needs to. Whatever they were fighting before tonight has gone quiet, replaced by something heavier. Truer.

"You okay?" he asks softly, like the question matters more than anything else in the world.

Jade nods, fingers curling into his shoulders. "Yeah." A beat. Honest. "I am."

His mouth brushes her temple, reverent without being gentle. "Good."

He holds her there for another second, weight warm and solid, then shifts. Not away from her. With her.

Ryder rolls onto his side, guiding her with him, one arm sliding beneath her shoulders, the other settling firm around her waist. He tucks her in close, chest to her back, like he's decided this is where she belongs for the night. Safe. Contained. Chosen.

Jade exhales as her spine fits against him, her head finding the hollow beneath his chin without effort.

And maybe that's why it slips out.

"Tonight," she murmurs, voice low, steady against the quiet, "that wasn't my sister."

Ryder's arm tightens just a fraction, his thumb brushing once over her ribs. He doesn't interrupt. He waits.

"I spent my whole life protecting her," Jade says. "Standing in front of her. Taking the hits. Making excuses." Her fingers curl into his forearm. "Turns out I was guarding the wrong thing."

He presses his mouth briefly to her hair. Not soothing. Anchoring.

"She wasn't weak," Jade continues. "She was quiet. And I mistook that for needing me." A breath. Controlled. "She's more like him."

Ryder's chin settles more firmly against her head.

"My father," she says. "Cold. Calculated. Always moving people instead of caring about them." Her jaw tightens. "I hate that it took this long to see it."

The silence stretches. She feels his breath steady behind her and decides to go on.

"When Charlotte and I went back to check on the pack," Jade says, softer now, "I found my mother." Her voice roughens. "She was alive. But empty. Like whatever made her was... gone."

Jade tucks herself a bit tighter.

"And that fucker—*my father*— was no where to be found," she continues. "No one would tell me where. Just silence." A pause. "Part of me thought he ran."

"That's because he was dead,"

Ryder was so matter of fact it was jarring. Jade shifts just enough to look back at him over her shoulder, eyes sharp.

"Good," she says. Then quieter, unfiltered, "I hope it was long. And brutal."

Ryder meets her gaze without blinking.

"It was."

Something inside her finally lets go. Not relief. Not forgiveness. Just an ending.

She settles back into him, heavier now, like she's done holding herself upright.

"Ok," she murmurs. "Then he doesn't get to follow me anymore."

Ryder's arm tightens, deliberate.

"No," he says. "He doesn't."

Silence takes the space. Ryder's arm is heavy, anchoring. Jade is already fading when the phone shatters the silence.

Not a normal tone. A sharp, synthetic trill that slices through the room like an alarm.

Jade freezes.

Ryder lifts his head immediately. "What is that?"

Her stomach drops. "That's Luna. It's a number that only I have."

She reaches blindly for the phone on the floor, heart

already racing as she unlocks it. One line flashes across the screen. No emojis. No preamble.

> Don't trust the vamps

The air shifts.

Ryder's body goes tense, all warmth gone in an instant. "What?" he asks, already pulling back enough to look at her. "Jade, what is it?"

She turns the phone so he can see the screen.

Jade swallows, dread curling low in her gut. Luna doesn't send emergency messages unless it's already bad. Unless she's certain.

And Luna is always certain.

She locks the screen and meets Ryder's eyes. "Looks like we have bigger problems than Miles or ravens," she says quietly.

His jaw tightens, expression hardening into something lethal and resolved. "Good thing I'm staying in Vegas."

Outside, somewhere far beyond the walls of the mansion, the night goes unnervingly still.

Jade doesn't look away. Luna never warns without reason.

If the vamps are in play, then everything she thought was contained isn't.

And whatever comes next won't stay in the shadows.

RAGE
OF THE DESERT WOLF

Red Rock Series
Book 4

JD WOLFE

RAGE OF THE DESERT WOLF

Book 4 in the Red Rock series.

The war isn't over.

Secrets are unraveling, alliances are shifting, and Luna's past is no longer willing to stay buried. Some threats don't announce themselves until it's already too late.